Krista Davis is the author of:

The Domestic Diva Mysteries

The Diva Cooks Up a Storm
The Diva Sweetens the Pie
The Diva Spices It Up
The Diva Serves Forbidden Fruit
The Diva Says Cheesecake!

The Pen & Ink Mysteries:

Color Me Murder
The Coloring Crook
Murder Outside the Lines
A Colorful Scheme

The DIVA Serves Forbidden Fruit

KRISTA DAVIS

Kensington Publishing Corp.
www.kensingtonbooks.com

KENSINGTON BOOKS are published by

Kensington Publishing Corp.
119 West 40th Street
New York, NY 10018

All Kensington titles, imprints, and distributed lines are available at special quantity discounts for bulk purchases for sales promotion, premiums, fund-raising, educational, or institutional use.

Special book excerpts or customized printings can also be created to fit specific needs. For details, write or phone the office of the Kensington Sales Manager: Kensington Publishing Corp., 119 West 40th Street, New York, NY 10018. Attn. Sales Department. Phone: 1-800-221-2647.

The K and Teapot logo is a trademark of Kensington Publishing Corp.

ISBN: 978-1-4967-3275-0 (ebook)

ISBN: 978-1-4967-3274-3

First Kensington Trade Paperback Printing: May 2022

10 9 8 7 6 5 4 3 2 1

Printed in the United States of America

For Amy and Betsy

Acknowledgments

This book is dedicated to my friends, Amy and Betsy, because they went on a fabulous trip to Portugal that inspired the book. Happily, no one was murdered on their tour, but some of the events are based on things that happened to them. Bare feet in the airport? I couldn't make that up!

Alas, I did not go with them, so I had to do a fair amount of research. Any mistakes are my own. Special thanks to Susan, who listened so patiently and joined in the fun.

Thanks to my terrific editor Wendy McCurdy and her wonderful assistant, Elizabeth Trout, who have been so patient with me and are always there to take care of problems that crop up.

As always, I must thank my agent, Jessica Faust. Not only is she a fabulous agent, but she is a kind and caring friend as well.

Cast of Characters

Sophie Winston
    Daisy, her hound mix
    Mochie, her Ocicat

Nina Reid Norwood
    Muppet, her foster terrier-mix

Lark Bickford
    Bennett Bickford, Lark's son
    Paisley Bickford Eames, Lark's daughter
    Frank Eames, Paisley's husband
    Carmela Eames, Frank's mother (Avó)
    Thomas Eames, one of Paisley and Frank's six sons
    Oscar Eames, one of Paisley and Frank's six sons

Cal Bickford
    Lark's brother-in-law

Dulci Chapman
    Emery Chapman, Dulci's husband

Mars Winston

Bernie Frei

Natasha
    Wanda Smith, her mother
    Griselda Smith, her father's second wife
    Charlene Smith, her half-sister

Chapter 1

Dear Sophie,
My wife's uncle brought an antique lamp back from Europe and gave it to us as a gift. My wife thinks it's beautiful and expensive. But when I plugged it in, it sparked and shocked me. Do you think my in-laws did that on purpose?
Wary Husband in Shockeysville, Virginia

Dear Wary Husband,
European lights have long had a different voltage from US lamps. Your lamp probably also has a different size bulb fitting. You should rewire the lamp and change the bulb sockets before using it.
Sophie

Nina Reid Norwood shuffled out of Dulles International Airport barefooted. It was night, but the bright airport lights shone on her hobbling toward me. I was waiting for her in the passenger pickup lane and jumped out of my car at the sight of her. She dragged a suitcase and a carry-on as if she no longer had the strength or will to set them straight so they would roll. Her mascara and eyeliner had smeared under her eyes, giving my pretty friend a hollow, sickly appearance.

"What happened to you?" I picked up her suitcase and slung her carry-on bag over my shoulder.

She gave me a pathetic sideways look. "Not the best trip."

I opened the car door for her, something I wouldn't normally have done. But she looked so downtrodden! I closed the door and opened the back hatch to stash her bags.

A few of our friends had been on the same trip. I spied some of them coming out of the building. They all looked tired, but they were all wearing their shoes.

Everything safely closed, I pulled the car into the slow parade leaving the airport.

Nina leaned her head back and closed her eyes. "If I don't get a divorce now, I never will."

Her husband, a forensic pathologist, had suggested she accompany him to a medical convention in Portugal. She had blathered about it enthusiastically before the trip, eager to vacation with him in the sun. "Did you have a spat?"

"I didn't see him long enough to argue! I'm not sure I can ever forgive him for dragging me to Portugal."

"Not your favorite place?"

Her eyes still closed, she said, "Lovely people. Beautiful country. Delicious food. Honestly, Sophie, he abandoned me. If I had known I would ride endlessly on a bus with Dulci Chapman and Lark Bickford, I would have planned a vacation with you instead."

"I'm flattered. But Dulci and Lark are nice."

"Not exactly the life of the party. The last couple of days I wandered around by myself. I don't think I'm the type for guided bus tours. I find them . . . tiresome and monotonous. I don't like being shuffled about like a steer to market. On the bus. Off the bus. You have twenty minutes to eat. Please use the restroom now because we will be riding in the bus for the next fifty-three hours without stopping."

I giggled a little. "It's supposed to make sightseeing easier for us."

"I think I'm more the Audrey Hepburn–on-a-red-scooter type. You know, like in *Roman Holiday*."

"What happened to your shoes?" I turned the car onto our street.

"The customs people were awful. Just awful! But wait! They didn't snag your present." She took two green mugs out of her carry-on baggage.

"Majolica!" I exclaimed. "I love them."

We stepped out of the car. I carried her bags up the stairs to her house while she unlocked the door and turned on the lights. When I walked into her foyer, she was actually hugging the newel post on her stairs. "I've missed you, home. Tomorrow, I will pick up a sweet dog or cat to foster and return to my regular existence, which, while somewhat boring, won't be nearly as awful as my trip."

Nina gazed at me. "What did I miss?"

"Not a thing."

"In three weeks? Nothing happened?"

"The Do-It-Yourself Festival starts tomorrow morning."

Nina lifted her upper lip in a sneer. "Not my thing."

"Aw, come on. You love decorating your house."

"Correction. I love paying people to decorate my house."

That was definitely true. "Wash your feet and get some sleep. I'll see you in the morning."

"Good night, Soph. Thanks for picking me up." I heard her lock the bolt behind me.

Frankly, I was glad my best friend and across-the-street neighbor was back. Life wasn't nearly as much fun without her. I moved the car to my garage, placed the mugs on a shelf in the kitchen, put a halter on my hound mix, Daisy, and took her for a walk.

Old Town Alexandria, Virginia, dated back to the 1700s. Once a busy port on the Potomac River across from Washington, DC, Old Town had become an elegant and cozy neighborhood. Historic Federal-style houses lined the streets, and some still had flickering gas lanterns by their front doors.

Daisy and I strolled along the brick sidewalk, heading for a street that would be closed off at midnight for the next week so the vendors would have plenty of room to set up booths and demonstrate how to do-it-yourself.

I had my own event planning company and usually worked for large organizations, but I had taken on the Old Town DIY Festival for fun and a change of pace. So far everything had fallen in place. The NO PARKING signs had gone up and I trusted the few remaining cars would be moved by midnight. Barriers had been erected to keep traffic out, but there was still room for the stragglers to move their vehicles elsewhere.

Lights twinkled in the buildings and houses as we walked. If the weather held up, the weeklong event should be a success. It was that transitional time between late spring and early summer. People opened their windows to let in the fresh air and cleaned the winter grime off their porches to enjoy them before the humidity set in. Flowers bloomed profusely. Lavish purple wisteria blossoms hung on porches and fences, and outdoor dining had recommenced.

We turned back and approached Lark Bickford's house. I assumed she had been on the same flight as Nina. Until the death of her husband a few years ago, Lark had been one of Old Town's busiest socialites. Invitations to her dinner parties were coveted, even sought after. In true Southern style, Lark pulled out all the sterling hollowware, fine china, and sparkling cut crystal. She entertained effortlessly and elegantly.

As I watched, a light went out upstairs. She was probably exhausted and dealing with jet lag. It would take a day or two for Nina and Lark to get back on schedule.

The sun had just begun to show its rays at five forty-five on Monday morning, and I dressed in jeans that stretched in every direction. They were soft but not clingy. I would be perfectly comfortable but no one else would realize they were fake jeans with the give of spandex. A crisp white blouse with the collar turned up just a little bit added the professional look I wanted. I added a string of pearls because they went with everything, gold earrings, and a light blazer that I could discard if the weather turned hot. If I had worn heels, the outfit might have even been chic. But I knew better than that. I needed sneakers for all the walking I would do.

My Ocicat, Mochie, watched me from the bed. Purebred, he was supposed to have spots like an ocelot but instead had fur that looked like bull's-eyes on his sides, necklaces around his throat, and bracelets on his front legs. His buddy Daisy sat on the floor nearby.

"What do you think?" I asked.

Daisy wagged her tail but Mochie said, "Mrrr," and jumped off the bed. I suspected that translated into, "Where's my breakfast?"

After spooning tuna into his bowl, I suited up Daisy in

her halter and crossbody leash, jammed my wallet and phone into a small crossbody bag so my hands would be free, and collected my clipboard with all the relevant information for the festival. The two of us set off toward the center of town as the sun rose.

People were already unloading their goods and setting up tables. The day before we had arranged a large tent on Market Square for demonstrations of everything from refinishing furniture to quilting and wreath-making. There would be a new demonstration every hour starting at nine. Not only did it give people the opportunity to learn, but each of the vendors had a chance to show off the clever things they had available for sale.

I stopped at the sidewalk window of Bean Time for a tall mocha latte, a croissant, and a Puppucini for Daisy. We sat at an outdoor table and took a few minutes to enjoy the peaceful morning while we had breakfast. The sky was a bold blue without a cloud in sight. The air was crisp, and people went about their business refreshed after the weekend break.

I tossed our trash and we ambled down the street that had been closed.

In front of Lark's house, Frank and Paisley Eames were setting up a canopy tent with walls that could be rolled up and down. Six little boys ran around them in circles, dodging back and forth, and tormenting one another. Their parents didn't appear to hear their screams.

Lark's daughter, Paisley, looked much like her mother. She had the same short, naturally curly peanut-brown hair and the same square face. Lark smiled more than her daughter, but then, she wasn't usually surrounded by six boys.

I glanced over at Lark's house, expecting to see her at the door watching her grandchildren. The front steps led directly from the sidewalk to the door. With no porch or yard, Lark had made the best of it, with a rectangular window box that overflowed with pink and white petunias, ivy, and yellow dahlias. An urn on the other side of the front door featured the same greenery and happy seasonal color.

An ear-splitting wail from one of the Eames boys drew everyone's attention. He sat on the street and blood leached from his skinned knees. A bigger brother stood over him with a guilty and horrified look on his face.

Paisley dropped her side of the tent, which drew a moan from Frank. Slim and dark-haired, he was only a few inches taller than my five feet.

"Thomas Eames, that's enough," Paisley said, pointing to her mother's house. "You go inside the gate and stay in Grandma's side yard where I can see you until your dad comes to get you."

"Pais!" Frank shouted. "If we don't get this done in five minutes you won't have a tent today."

"What am I supposed to do?" she snarled.

"Oscar will be fine. Do you think your mom has some rope or bungee cords or something?"

"Oh sure," she grumbled as she grabbed one of the tent poles so the whole thing wouldn't collapse, "there's no such thing as germs and bacteria." In a louder voice she said, "If Oscar has to go to the hospital because of an infection, then you're taking him."

"Fine!" he yelled back.

Two boys who couldn't have been older than five wrapped their arms around Paisley's legs. She must have been used to it because I would have fallen for sure.

"Where is your mother?" she shouted to Frank.

He shrugged. "She'll get here. It wouldn't hurt your mother to come out here and help us, you know."

"Sophie?" Paisley called. "Would you mind knocking on my mom's door for me? I can't let go of this pole. I didn't want to wake her this early, but now I guess I have to."

"No problem." I walked to the front door of Lark's house and raised a doorknocker in the shape of a sweet bird. I rapped it three times, but no one answered the door.

Chapter 2

Dear Sophie,
I love the way beds look in magazines but no mat-
ter how hard I try, I can't quite manage to get that
fluffy, elegant look. What am I doing wrong?
                    Tired in Sleepy Eye, Minnesota

Dear Tired,
The look requires European shams against the
headboard. Then regular pillows, then throw pil-
lows. Only a duvet will give you that truly fluffy
look. Place a sheet underneath in a coordinating
color and turn it back. Fold a blanket across the
foot of the bed and display a casually placed throw
on it.
                                          Sophie

"Are you sure she's home?" I asked.

"Aargh," Paisley groaned. "She probably went out to get breakfast or groceries. If I had been a good daughter, I would have thought ahead and filled her fridge yesterday before she came home from her trip. Her keys are in my purse, on top of that pile of boxes. Check the drawers in the laundry room."

I retrieved Paisley's Kate Spade handbag and found keys with a tag on them that said *Mom* in tiny rhinestones. I unlocked the door and called, "Lark? Lark, it's Sophie Winston. Are you home?"

There was no response. Daisy and I walked through the house to the kitchen where I thought I had caught a glimpse of a laundry room once. The kitchen had been beautifully updated with cabinets that looked like furniture. It was all white with touches of rustic bronze on the light fixtures and the cabinet grips. It smelled like coffee and there were two mugs in the sink. Lark was already up. "Lark!" I shouted. I didn't want to scare her. I felt the coffee maker. It was completely cool to the touch. It had been a while since she had brewed the coffee.

Sure enough, a doorway led into a laundry room with a washer and dryer. On the opposite wall was a counter with a laundry sink. I envied the built-in storage station for coats and shoes that also provided a bench near the back door. A grocery tote leaned against it and canvas bags hung from hooks. The laundry hamper appeared to be full and several piles of laundry lay on the floor. I thought how nice it would be to come home from a long trip and empty out all the dirty clothes before lugging the suitcases upstairs.

I found twine and bungee cords in a drawer and returned to the street. I handed them to Paisley. "No sign of your mom."

"What? Would you mind going upstairs and peeking into her bedroom? I bet she's fast asleep." Little boys still clung to each of her legs and Frank started to yell instructions to her again.

"I don't mind at all. But I did see coffee mugs in her

sink. She's probably out." One of the boys howled when his brother hit him with a plastic shovel. It was a wonder Paisley got anything done.

To help Paisley out and calm her worries about her mom, I returned to the house with Daisy and walked up the stairs.

It was an elegant home. The staircase and foyer were papered with a soft turquoise paper peppered with brown branches and white blooms. It wasn't in style anymore, but it was beautiful and made a statement that plain walls couldn't achieve.

The door to the master bedroom stood open. Lark's four-poster bed looked like an advertisement, beautifully made with blue and white linens. Everything in the room seemed to be in perfect order. I spied a walk-in closet, also perfectly neat and organized, except for a bench where a suitcase lay open. Beneath it, on the floor, lay a second open suitcase and a blue bag with the tour company's insignia on it. It appeared Lark had dug through them in a hurry, leaving a mess of clothes and souvenirs on the carpet.

"Lark?" I called, peering into the bathroom. There was no sign of her.

I peeked into the other bedrooms before heading downstairs and out of the house.

"She must have gone out," I said to Paisley. "I don't see her anywhere."

"Pais! Did you fasten your end?" yelled Frank.

Little Oscar had already forgotten about his scraped knees. The tears on his face dried fast when he spied Daisy. He ran to us and hugged her.

"This is Daisy," I said, glad she was wagging her tail and seemed to be okay with his attention.

He stroked her lush fur. "I want a dog like Daisy."

Thomas reappeared at the gate. "Mom!"

Paisley looked over at him, clearly annoyed. "Thomas, I said stay in the backyard."

"But Mom!"

"No. I do not want to see your face until it's time for school, which will be in about five minutes. Honey," she called to Frank, "are we done yet?"

Thomas's face was pale, with two round blazing spots on his cheeks like a painted doll. Even I could see fear in his eyes.

"We'll see you a little later, Oscar." I walked Daisy over to the gate. "Are you okay?" I asked Thomas.

He shook his head fast. "Something's wrong with Grandma."

Chapter 3

Dear Natasha,
Your show on decorating porches was fantastic. I
was so involved that I missed the trick you shared!
Would you please tell me what it was? My front
porch is a nightmare.
Embarrassed by My Veranda in Porchtown,
New Jersey

Dear Embarrassed by My Veranda,
Pick three colors. The first must be the color of
your front door. The second should be the color of
your house, shutters, or your porch. The third can
be anything you like. Use those colors to decorate
with planters, urns, wreaths, chairs, pillows, house
numbers, etc. Sticking to those colors will bring
everything together.
Natasha

Daisy and I entered the yard and I closed the gate behind us. We followed Thomas to the back. I could
make out a turquoise blue sneaker in the grass.

Daisy and I ran toward the blue shoe, which was still on Lark's foot.

She lay near the back porch on her stomach, her right arm bent, and the fingers of her right hand outstretched to a flower garden. Next to her was a ladder. The kind that extended as far as a person needed.

"Lark!" I exclaimed. I reached for my cell phone and called 911. I punched *speaker* on the phone and knelt beside her.

"Lark?" I said her name softly and gently patted her cheek, but she didn't respond.

The 911 operator came on the phone. "Where is your emergency?"

Lark felt cold. Dead cold.

I gasped and drew back, my hands shaking. With the other hand, I reached for Lark's neck. Deep inside, I knew she was dead, but I sought a pulse anyway.

I told the dispatcher the address and in the vain hope that Thomas wouldn't hear me and be scarred for life, I whispered, "I think Lark Bickford is dead."

Every fiber in my body wanted to stay with Lark, but I had to get Thomas out of the yard first.

I scrambled to my feet. It was then that I realized she had drawn something in the mulch. Dried up chunks of wood aren't the best medium for drawing. Why couldn't it have been sand? I stared at it, realizing with a chill that Lark had left a message. At the risk of completely grossing out Thomas, I whipped out my phone and took three quick photos of it.

I took Thomas's hand. "Let's go get your mom."

"Is Grandma alive?" he asked, looking up at me with scared eyes.

I dodged the question. "We'll know more when the rescue squad gets here."

Still holding Thomas's hand, I opened the gate and

marched him toward his mother, who was speaking with a chubby woman about my height. Short dark hair fluffed in large curls around her face. One of the Eames boys had attached himself to her leg. The others ran among the canopy tents across the way.

"Excuse me. Paisley," I said softly, "there's something wrong with Lark. It's probably best if Thomas waits out here."

Paisley looked at her son. "What did you do?"

"No, no," I said. "It's not him. He's a hero because he found her."

At the word *hero*, Thomas's little chest swelled with pride.

"Frank! Help your mom watch the boys. Thomas, stay here with Dad." Paisley followed me through the yard and screamed when she saw her mother on the ground.

Fortunately, the gate swung open again with a creak and Officer Wong strode toward us. She had let her hair grow out into a sleek bob that framed her face. One of those modern cuts, high in the back and longer in the front. She walked with calm reassuring confidence, as if there wasn't anything she couldn't handle. From what I had seen of her in terrible situations, I thought that was probably true. The African American Wong had had a terrible marriage and been glad to divorce her husband, but she'd kept his last name anyway.

Like me, Wong had never met a cupcake she didn't like. Her uniform strained against a generous bosom. I had never understood why women's police uniforms fit them so poorly. Women had been on police forces for ages. Surely someone in charge had noticed that problem by now.

She nodded at me briefly while assessing the situation.

Paisley kneeled beside her mother, tapping her cheek and talking to her.

"Ma'am? Could you please step aside for me?" she asked Paisley.

Paisley reluctantly got to her feet. In a flash, Wong was on her knees beside Lark. I could hear her talking into her radio to make sure an ambulance was on the way.

"Is she . . . ?" asked Paisley.

Wong stood up and turned to Paisley. She pulled out a pad and a pen. "Are you related to her?"

"I'm her daughter, Paisley Eames. Will she be okay?"

"Can you tell me what happened?" asked Wong.

"No." Paisley squeaked, tears rolling down her cheeks. "I guess my son found her. Sophie came to get me. Is she conscious?" Paisley started toward her mother.

"Hey, Sophie," said Wong. "How about you and Paisley go to the gate and make sure the EMTs know where to find us?"

Wong was a master of finagling a difficult situation. She wanted Paisley to stop tampering with the crime scene. But it would sound so terribly cold to actually say that.

"Absolutely." I wrapped an arm around Paisley and walked her to the gate where Frank waited anxiously.

"What's going on?" He tapped his watch. "Should I start school?"

Paisley wiped tears from under her eyes with her fingers and sniffled. With a bright smile, she said, "They wouldn't want to miss school."

Five little boys protested simultaneously. Only Thomas remained silent. He watched his mom carefully. When she walked outside the gate, he wrapped his arms around her and clung to her.

Frank frowned at her. "Are you okay?"

She shook her head from side to side. "We . . . we might need to call Mrs. Gurtz to help us out with the kids for a few days."

She whispered something to him that I couldn't hear.

"Nooo," he said sadly. He gently brushed her hair back off her face and kissed her cheek before hugging her. "What happened?"

"It looks like she fell off a ladder," choked Paisley with tears streaming down her face.

When Frank let her go, he clapped his hands and acted happy. "Okay, gang. Let's go."

Thomas didn't move. "Me too?"

Frank ran a fond hand over his hair. "Yeah, you too. Avo will take you. You're going to learn about the planets today."

After a glance at his mom, Thomas hurried off with his brothers and the dark-haired woman.

Their timing couldn't have been better. The emergency medical technicians walked up and in through the gate. Paisley and I followed them.

While they worked, they asked her questions about her mother's health. One of them came over to Wong, who stood beside me. "I think you'd better call the medical examiner."

Wong nodded and asked for a medical examiner on her radio.

Seeing Lark's lifeless body pained me to the core. She had been such a lovely person, kind to others, and generous with her time. The scene was oddly incongruous with Lark sprawled on the grass, her colorful garden blooming all around.

As I looked at her, I became curious about Lark's position. She lay with her head close to the house. The ladder had landed beside her. I walked closer for a look at the ladder. I didn't see any broken rungs.

Wong whispered to me. "If she fell off that ladder, wouldn't she be lying in the opposite position?"

"That's what I was thinking. And wouldn't the ladder be on top of her, or askew?"

"Mmm," she murmured. "Too perfect. Somebody placed it there."

"She just got back from a trip last night," I whispered. "It was dark when their plane arrived. It doesn't make sense for her to be out here cleaning gutters or washing windows at six in the morning."

"You wouldn't catch me doing it that early. Must have been dark then. Have you been in the house?"

"Yes."

"Did she make coffee?"

"There are two mugs in the sink," I said.

"And just how would you happen to know that?" asked a nicely masculine voice that I knew very well. I turned to find Wolf Fleishman of the Violent Crimes Unit of the Alexandria Police. Wolf and I had dated for a while. We parted under unusual circumstances, but I was happy to say that we remained friends. He had a wife and took care not to be alone with me so as not to upset her. I respected that even if it was sometimes inconvenient. Wolf fought a battle with his weight, too, but he looked quite handsome, if not exactly the image of fitness. He had dark brown hair that had gone silver around his temples, and the most aggravating poker face that I have ever encountered. It was next to impossible to determine what he might be thinking.

"Her daughter, Paisley, asked me to get some bungee cords for their tent."

A man with a terrific tan and beautifully trimmed hair arrived. He wore gold wire-rimmed glasses and a white lab coat. The EMTs and Wolf appeared to know him well.

A police photographer and a couple of crime scene investigators followed him in.

He walked toward Lark but stopped to introduce himself to Paisley. He murmured condolences with the ease of someone used to death and the attending pain of their loved ones. I had a bad feeling that Daisy and I were about to be kicked out of a crime scene.

He kneeled and uttered, "Oh no. Not Lark!"

Wong whispered, "The most sought-after man in Old Town. Kind of a young Richard Gere."

Why didn't I know this good-looking guy? "More like Hugh Grant. Where did he come from?"

"Dr. Peter Chryssos," she whispered. "Joined the medical examiner's staff about a year ago. Newly divorced and available." She gave me a sharp glance and grinned. "Try to restrain yourself."

"No problem."

Dr. Chryssos stood up and stepped back. Much as Wong and I had done, he gazed up at the porch roof and down at the ground where the ladder lay. "What's your assessment?" he asked Wolf.

"I think her killer staged this scene. He must have been in a hurry because he didn't think it through."

"I'm inclined to agree," said Dr. Chryssos. "I'll know more about the time of death from the autopsy, but I'd guess no more than two or three hours ago."

Paisley gasped and cried, "No! Not an autopsy. She would hate that."

Dr. Chryssos gazed at her in surprise. "I'm sorry, Paisley, but autopsies are required by the state when there is an unexplained death."

Paisley looked pained. "Unexplained? She fell!" Paisley covered her face with both of her palms. "I knew she was too old to live alone. I should have done something. Made her move in with us." She dropped her hands, weeping. Wiping them like a child, she looked my way. "She would have hated that, but she would still be alive."

"I need to get her out of here," whispered Wong. "No

one should have to see this part." Wong wrapped an arm around Paisley. "Let's see if we can find your husband." They walked toward the street.

"I gather you noticed that her body is the wrong way around. If she had fallen off the ladder, her head would be away from the house," said Dr. Chryssos to Wolf.

"Unless she's got a missing cat who was on the porch roof, I can't think of any reason for her to be climbing a ladder in the dark of night. Cause of death?" Wolf asked.

"Not sure. Right now, I'd guess blunt force trauma resulting in traumatic brain injury."

"I thought you agreed that she didn't fall," said Wolf.

"Not from a fall. From a blow to the head." Dr. Chryssos kneeled beside Lark as Wolf looked on. "There's definitely blood on the back of her head. It's largely hidden by her hair, but someone whacked her from behind." He squatted and studied the mulch. "Looks like she left us a message."

Wolf peered at it. "A circle with a dot in the center?"

"Or possibly a G," opined Dr. Chryssos. "Does that mean anything to you?"

"Can't say that it does. But mulch isn't the best medium for writing." Wolf glanced at the photographer, "Make sure you get some good shots of this before someone accidentally steps on it."

When Dr. Chryssos stood up, he turned and spied Daisy and me. Daisy readily introduced herself, wagging her tail and kissing up to him. He peeled off his gloves and squatted to pet her. "Lark didn't mention that she had a dog."

He rose and I held my right hand out to him. "Sophie Winston. Daisy is my dog."

His eyebrows actually jumped. I could hear Wolf stifling a laugh.

"I've heard about you," said Dr. Chryssos.

"Don't believe half of it," I responded.

He smiled at me. "Has anyone been inside? I'd like to have a look."

I volunteered to fetch the keys. Maybe if I made myself useful, they wouldn't be so quick to throw me out. I found Paisley and Wong in front of the house with Frank. A crowd had gathered. It was awful. Half of them were whispering and watching, the other half were clustered around Paisley, crying and asking what had happened.

I pried Paisley away and asked for the house keys.

She extracted them from her purse. Her face wrinkled with grief and tears stained her cheeks. Holding a tissue to her nose with one hand, she handed them to me with the other. I was glad to leave the scene in the front and return to Wolf. Wong came with me.

Chryssos, Wolf, and Wong pulled on gloves. It was already apparent that someone had murdered poor Lark. As much as I wanted to go inside with them, I knew I couldn't take a chance that I would further contaminate the crime scene with Daisy's fur. And they would only kick me out anyway. Besides, I had been in the house earlier and Lark had probably already been dead by then. The only things I had touched were the coffee machine and the drawers in the laundry room, so I didn't think I had ruined any evidence, unless something had been contaminated by a loose bit of Daisy's fur that had wafted off inside the house.

The photographer got to work right away. Lark was fully dressed in blue pedal pushers, a blue and white tunic top with three-quarter-length sleeves, a chunky white necklace, two bangle bracelets, one blue, one white, and lapis earrings. Not the attire for sleeping or cleaning gutters. She must have been up early, otherwise she would have been wearing bedclothes. And she must have been killed before her family arrived to set up the tent. Otherwise, she would have gone outside and said hello to her family or invited the children in for cinnamon toast and juice. Not to mention that she would have been wearing a sweater or jacket at that hour if she had planned to be outside for any length of time.

I approached Wolf. "Just so you know, Daisy and I were in Lark's house this morning."

Wolf looked chagrined. "Of course you were."

"You don't have to be sarcastic. It's not like I knew she had been murdered. You can ask Paisley about it. She requested that I go in the house and she gave me her keys. I'm just telling you in case you find Daisy's fur or my fingerprints."

He tried to suppress a grin. "Yeah, okay. Thanks for letting me know."

It would take a while for them to go through the house. They were still suiting up in protective gear to avoid contamination when Daisy and I left.

Frank must have unloaded a van while I was in the back. A beautifully renovated sideboard was under the tent, along with two sets of nightstands, a vanity, headboards, and assorted tables and chairs. A couple was admiring them and asked me the price of a set of nightstands. I couldn't exactly say someone had been murdered and ask if they could come back later. I was stammering a bit when a man with cinnamon brown hair and a high forehead stepped up and stated a price.

I had never met him before. He was confident and surprisingly knowledgeable about Paisley's pieces. He chatted up the couple with ease, brushing his hair out of his eyes a few times. I assumed it was supposed to stay up but insisted on falling flat. I put him in his late twenties, short in stature with well-muscled arms that strained the sleeves of his t-shirt. He had a stubble beard that was quite short, except for an odd fluff under his bottom lip.

The couple wrote a check for the furniture, which he promptly tucked into his jeans pocket. He loaded the nightstands on a dolly and offered to wheel them to their car. The three of them chatted merrily as they walked away. Clearly, he had to be a friend of Paisley and Frank. I couldn't imagine a stranger having the moxie to accept money and sell their goods.

I waited for him to return, not completely sure that he would.

Chapter 4

Dear Natasha,
I'm trying to put up a gallery wall with words for
my daughter's bedroom. Should the words all be
the same size and font? How big should it be?
                    Loving Mom in Font Hill, Maryland

Dear Loving Mom,
Don't bother. Wall words are out. Everyone knows
it's the laundry. You don't have to put up a sign
saying so. Instead, hang a bookshelf. Use it to
show off the things that are important to your
daughter.

                    Natasha

The man whistled as he strolled back. It sounded like
Pharrell Williams's "Happy." He *looked* happy as he
walked along with almost a bounce to his stride.

"Hi," I said. "Sophie Winston. I'm in charge of the festival."

"Toby Wallace," he said. "Terrible what happened to
Paisley's mom. I had offered to help Frank unload the van

this morning, but I was running a little late. And then I had to call my girlfriend. She's Paisley's cousin, Maddy. Do you know her?"

"I don't think so."

"It's awful having to tell someone that her aunt died. I never had to do that before. Hope I don't have to do it again! Lark seemed like a nice lady."

At that moment, a slender woman with long strawberry blond hair ran toward us and flung herself into Toby's arms. She sobbed on his shoulder. I presumed she was Maddy. A couple in their fifties trundled along behind her. I might have thought they were here for the festival, but their expressions were anything but festive. The woman sniffled and dabbed at her eyes with a tissue. Her auburn hair was cut short and styled well. She wore a long gauzy skirt with a matching blouse and a diamond on a short chain that lay in the hollow of her neck.

The man with her had lost most of his hair. He was stout and walked with a slightly stiff penguin wobble, as though he might suffer from arthritis. His face was red as a Christmas candle.

"Where is Paisley?" asked Maddy.

"Dunno," said Toby.

The older couple had reached us.

"Paisley and Frank are in the crowd just outside Lark's front door."

"What happened?" asked the man. "I was told she fell. Why are the police here?"

"Who are you?" the woman asked.

I introduced myself and explained my presence.

"Frank thought he should stay here with Paisley, but I refused to take those kids of his back to their house and babysit," said Toby. "I helped him unload the van and I've been watching the stuff in their tent."

"Why Toby!" The woman sounded shocked. "I had no

idea that you don't like children. You mean I'll never have grandchildren?"

"Not six of them. I can promise you that. I would have wrecked the van with all of them crying at the same time."

"I understand you're related to Lark?" I asked politely.

The woman gave me a harsh look. "We are her in-laws, Cal and Doralee Bickford. My husband is . . . was her husband's brother. He passed a few years ago. Poor Paisley was so close to her mother. I don't know how she'll manage without her."

"We should go check on her," said Cal.

"I'll make some coffee," said Doralee. "What's Paisley doing outside anyway? We should move her into the house where she can sit down and be with family."

"They may not let you in the house," I pointed out. "The police are all suited up so they won't contaminate the crime scene."

"Crime scene?" shrieked Doralee.

It was like a cue for Maddy to start crying again.

Throwing me a smug glance, Cal said, "Oh, they'll let *me* inside the house." He stalked through the gate and disappeared.

"Is he with the police?" I asked.

His wife seemed surprised by my question. "No, he's just Cal."

It wasn't much of an explanation. But since they were Lark's family and there wasn't anything I could do, I said goodbye and got back to work.

I tried to focus on the DIY Festival but found it to be a struggle. I had dealt with several murders in my life, but this one felt oddly personal. She lived only a few blocks away and someone had killed her in her own home. She was sweet and kind. And she'd been away! Surely her absence had been long enough for any hot tempers to cool off. Was that why she had gone on the three-week trip?

Had someone been waiting eagerly for her return to murder her? It all seemed so cold and horrible.

Nina ran down the middle of the street toward me. "Is it true?" she gasped.

"I'm afraid so. How did you hear about it?"

"One of my friends lives on this block. I knew something awful had happened when she said she saw Wolf going into Lark's yard."

I told her what little I knew.

"I can't believe this. She was on my flight yesterday." Nina's eyes narrowed. "Of all the people in the world who could be murdered, Lark would be way down at the bottom of the list. What could she possibly have done to tick someone off like this?"

"I don't know. Poor Paisley is in shock." I checked the time. "I'm running late. I need to walk over to Market Square to be sure the do-it-yourself demonstrations are in progress."

Nina fell in step with me. "I should call Dulci. The three of us spent a lot of time together in Portugal. She'll be as devastated as we are."

I was pleased to see Ari Hoffmann under the demonstration tent, showing people how to reupholster a chair. I had tried it myself once and given up. In fact, the poor chair was naked down to the frame and still in my basement. He asked people from the audience to come up and try stapling materials on the dining chair he had brought with him. He had wisely provided a matching chair that was mostly stripped and another that was finished. I was inspired to try reupholstering my chair again.

I saw the woman who was next preparing her material for a gallery wall with words. We had arranged for folding chairs to be available, which turned out to be a good move. They were packed. I was pleased to see people drinking lattes and watching the live DIY demonstration.

"Good turnout," said Nina. "There's Dulci!" Nina waved her over to us.

Dulci Chapman had retired early from her career as an art therapist for troubled children to become a food blogger. No one could figure out how she remained slim while her husband's girth expanded.

She had sharp brown eyes that seemed to catch everything. Maybe that was because her eyebrows dipped down toward her eyes near her nose, which always made me think of an owl. Her hair, the color of dark chocolate, hung just past her shoulders in the latest simple style. She had always been lovely to me, but she often wore an expression that said don't-mess-with-me. As far as I could tell, she usually got what she wanted.

She clasped Nina's arm. "Did you hear? I'm just sick about it. We haven't even been home for twenty-four hours. How was there even enough time for someone to murder Lark?"

"Did she seem worried about anything on your trip?" I asked.

"Not anything unusual. She's concerned about Paisley, but what mother doesn't worry about her kids? Six boys under the age of ten! I would be out of my mind." Dulci widened her eyes.

"Two children were a lot for me to keep up with and mine were actually very good. The stories I've heard from other moms are enough to make me grateful for the two I raised."

"Was she seeing anyone?"

Nina and Dulci exchanged a look.

"What?" I asked.

"She was evasive," said Dulci. "To the extent that I became suspicious. I remember telling my husband that something was up with Lark."

"Dulci's right, Soph. That adorable Dr. Chryssos teamed up with her a few times—"

"Of course, they were the only two single people on the tour," Dulci interjected. "It only made sense for them to couple up. I don't think it meant anything."

"But if Lark wasn't seeing someone, wouldn't she have snapped him up?" asked Nina. She eyed me with a mischievous glint. "You really need to meet him."

"I have. Just this morning. He's the medical examiner on Lark's case."

They shot me inquisitive looks.

"He's very attractive. But I'm not so desperate that I have to jump a guy when poor Lark is sprawled on the ground dead."

"Ugh." Nina grimaced. "Nothing like bringing us back to reality."

"Three weeks is a long trip. Think back. Was Lark relieved to be away? Did she seem hesitant about returning?"

"Lark acted perfectly normal. She talked a little bit about her son-in-law being of Portuguese heritage and how she hoped he and Paisley could go on a tour like ours one day," said Dulci.

"She bought endless toys and trinkets for the boys," said Nina. "She seemed perfectly happy."

"It has to have been a random attack," said Dulci with conviction. "It won't make me sleep any better to think that, but maybe she was an easy target because she lives alone."

That didn't make *me* feel better.

Dulci realized her mistake. "But you have Daisy. Or maybe a burglar had been watching her house and didn't know she had returned."

Nina groaned. "I'm on my way to the rescue to pick up a foster dog right now. The biggest one I can find. Growly with giant jowls."

Dulci laughed at her. "Want to borrow my husband?"

Dr. Chapman did sort of fit that description. Nina and I chuckled.

"I'm going to watch this next lady with the photo gallery and inspirational words. I want to make a wall like that for my grandchildren." Dulci took a seat in the front row and Nina hurried off to the animal shelter.

Satisfied that things were going well, I headed home to drop Daisy off. She needed a decent breakfast and a nap. I hurried through the street where Lark lived so I wouldn't be detained by anyone. But that didn't work out quite as well as I had hoped.

I had almost left the area of the tents when I heard my name being called. I knew that voice and the irritated tone she used. It could only be Natasha—friend, neighbor, and nemesis. Natasha thought she knew best and that it was her obligation to inform everyone of their shortcomings so they could better themselves. She could be highly annoying. And then, when I least expected it, she would do something so thoughtful and kind that I thought I had been wrong about her.

We had known each other since we were children in the same little town of Berrysville, Virginia. We had grown up competing at everything except for the beauty pageants she loved. I don't find competition particularly entertaining. I'm quite happy to do my thing without having to battle with anyone. But Natasha thrived on it and continually sought to challenge me. Sadly, we now wrote competing advice columns on all things domestic, which had only fueled her determination to best me.

She caught up to me. I had no choice.

Natasha was as tall as I was short. My clothes might be snug, but she was beginning to look too thin. Her collarbones jutted out above the neckline of her soft white top. Naturally, her exquisite slim white trousers hung on her like on a mannikin. A jacket in Burberry plaid hung over her shoulders, and large golden chain bracelets circled her bony wrists.

"I've been waiting for you," she said huffily, impatiently tapping her forefinger against her arm.

Chapter 5

Dear Sophie,
I see all the beautiful things people have done by painting furniture. I would love to try, but I don't want to sand or strip it first. Is there a way to get around stripping and sanding?
Not a Stripper in Strip Crossing, Texas

Dear Not a Stripper,
Use chalk paint! No stripping required. You can paint to your heart's desire. When you're finished painting, top it with a wax for a matte or shiny patina.

Sophie

"Were we supposed to meet?" I asked, thinking I might have forgotten.

"No. But I have a problem and it's all your fault. You're the only one who can fix this."

That something was my fault didn't particularly surprise me. Natasha rarely accepted blame for anything, even though she often managed to be at the root of the problem. That I could fix it was a change. I unlocked my kitchen door and slid Daisy's halter off.

I opened a can of dog food and scooped it into Daisy's bowl, then added leftover hamburger and pinto beans from my fridge and set it on the floor for her. "I don't have much time. I'm working today."

"Mars says if I can't afford to buy his share of the house, then we have to sell it."

Mars, short for Marshall, was my ex-husband. After our divorce, or perhaps before, I wasn't really sure, Natasha had set her sights on him and they proceeded to cohabit. That would have been unpleasant but tolerable, except, much to my dismay, they chose to buy a house on my block, so they were very much a part of my life. A couple of years back, Mars had had enough of Natasha but very kindly allowed her to continue living in their huge house while they sorted things out. No progress had been made. Whatever happened, clearly none of it was even remotely my fault. In fact, I had made a point of staying out of their issues because they weren't any of my business, and what they did with their house wasn't my problem.

"If you hadn't paid him for his half of this house, he wouldn't expect *me* to pay him," she huffed.

Aha. Had I set a precedent for all of Mars's future paramours? "It was only fair." We had inherited the house from Mars's aunt Faye. He didn't particularly care about keeping it, but I loved the historic home, creaking stairs, slanting floors and all.

"You have to talk to him. Reason with him."

I had to do no such thing. As the saying went and so very aptly applied here, she had made her bed and now had to lie in it.

"He doesn't care about the house," she whined.

"That's undoubtedly true. But he cares about the money he invested in it, which was surely no small amount. As I recall, you sold your country house. You must have gotten a pretty penny out of that."

"It was ages ago. And I've had a few expenses since then. We had to rip out the horrible old kitchen and redecorate several times, and then there was the chocolate business I started, and the gardening clothes business, and the chicken business, and—"

I interrupted her litany of failed businesses. "You have your own TV show and an income. You'll just have to apply for a mortgage like the rest of us peons. Pay Mars off and be done with it."

She gazed at me and licked her lips. "I don't want to be done with Mars."

"Good grief, Natasha. I have to go. And you have to let go of Mars."

I hustled her out the door and locked it behind me, leaving Daisy at home to snooze with Mochie. I had hoped Natasha would head home, but she walked beside me, blathering about money.

"You have two tenants now," I reminded her. "Surely your half-sister and her mother can pay rent. That should help a little bit."

Natasha inhaled sharply. "I can't do that. Charge my own sister? You wouldn't expect Hannah to pay rent."

She was right about that. I wouldn't have expected Hannah to pay rent. She was family. But Hannah would have insisted if I needed help. The sisterhood worked both ways.

We had reached the closed street. Natasha slowed down and gazed at the tents with interest.

"Who's manning your tent?" I asked.

"My sister and her mother."

She was actually a half-sister. They shared a father but had different mothers. I was pleased to hear Natasha claiming her as a sister, without the *half* in front of it. They'd only learned about their familial relationship recently. They must be getting along, which made me very happy.

"No wonder I can't make any money. I didn't realize all these people were competing with me. Do you know one man came up to me and had the gall to tell me his wife learned how to make wreaths from *my* show and now they're making a living selling their wreaths!"

She stopped in front of a wreath-making tent. Wreaths for all seasons hung on a back wall, ready to purchase. Natasha darted inside and hurried back out to me. "I *must* have that peony basket to hang on my door. Have you seen the price? It's outrageous."

We stopped in front of Paisley's tent. A painted armoire stood where no one could miss it. The background was a neutral cream, but lush roses in shades of pink and red, brown branches, and shiny green leaves cascaded from the top about halfway down. At the very bottom Paisley had painted three petals of spent blooms. That tiny detail made me love it all the more.

"Paisley paints flowers on furniture?"

"Where have you been? People have been doing that for a long time."

"You know how I loathe stuffy old furniture. That armoire was probably ancient."

She was the only person I knew who didn't appreciate beautiful antiques.

Happily, Jim Hill approached the two of us. A man of large stature, retired military I thought, he was an old-school type, and even doffed his baseball cap to us, revealing a shiny bald pate. Holding the hat over his heart, he said, "I don't like to ask for favors, but I'm going to today." He motioned for us to follow him to his tent. Even though he had a large selection of items, the handmade bar stood out. At least eight feet long, the top was covered with shiny copper pennies. He smacked a meaty hand on the top of it. "This is worth a whole lot more than pennies. I can't load it up and cart it away every night because of the weight. But a couple or four drunk guys could easily make off with it when no one is out here. I know you've got security wandering through here after hours, but I'd be mighty appreciative if you could ask them to pay particular attention to my tent. I'm going to tie it down with locks that will go off if anyone messes with it. All the same, even though it's just pennies, you'd be surprised how many people are willing to steal my stuff."

"I never thought about pennies this way before," said Natasha. "It's quite impressive."

Jim grinned. "I put a penny backsplash in a man cave last month. It's a beauty when the overhead lights gleam on it."

"I'll be sure to talk to security about it," I promised.

Happily, Natasha was so taken that she stayed and examined some of the vases and mirror frames that he had transformed with pennies.

I scurried away and noticed Paisley sitting in her tent alone, slumped and drained.

"Are you all right?" I asked softly.

"I never expected anything like this. Mom was a source of strength for me. She was always there for me. I don't know how I can manage without her." She swallowed hard. "I can't believe that some idiot killed her. For what? She probably had some cash in her wallet, but she was worth so much more than that as a person. And she would gladly have given him that cash. Don't these people have families? How would they feel if someone knocked off their moms?"

"The police think it was an intruder? A burglar?"

"They're saying she let him in."

"What?" I couldn't even imagine her horror.

"As near as they can tell, she must have heard him outside and opened the door. He hit her over the head with something, and probably threw her off the porch"—her voice leaped to a shrill pitch—"to be really and truly sure that she was dead. Can you even imagine? Her final moments must have been sheer terror. It's just the most horrible and barbaric thing that could have happened to her. And she was so kind and good to everyone."

I sat down in a chair beside her and placed my hand over hers. "What happened to your cousin and her parents?"

She buried her face in her hands. "I don't know. They came, and argued, and left. That's what they do. Mom always said she couldn't believe dad and Cal were brothers. They were so different." She gazed around. "I'm at such a loss. I don't know what to do."

"No one would fault you for closing up your tent and skipping the festival this year. You don't have to sit out here today. Go home. I'll take care of the things in your tent."

"I can't." She glanced at me sideways. "The truth is that we need the money. I've been working on these pieces like a madwoman. Maybe it's better for me to be here. To keep busy."

I understood that. If I were in her shoes, I might prefer a distraction, too. "I think I can find a couple of responsible people who would be happy to help you out for no charge."

A soft-faced man in a nice business suit strode up. When Paisley saw him, her tears started anew, and she eagerly ran to his arms. They hugged for a few minutes. If I'd had to guess, I would have put him just at thirty. He wore no wedding band.

Paisley separated from him. "Sophie, this is my baby brother, Bennett."

Bennett smiled at me. "No matter how old I get to be, Paisley will always see me as the baby."

"You're not alone. I think that's how it generally works. It's lovely to meet you. I believe I'll take off. You two have a lot to talk about. But before I go, should I try to wrangle up a couple of reliable salespeople to man your tent at no charge?"

"Really?" asked Paisley. "That would be fantastic. Just for a couple of days, maybe? Thank you, Sophie."

"One quick question." It may not matter if Lark's killer had chosen her randomly, but I thought I'd ask anyway. "Was your mother seeing someone?"

Paisley snorted. "Mom was in her fifties!"

I was completely taken aback at her insinuation that a woman in her fifties was too old for romance.

Bennett shook his head. "No. Not a chance. Mom would never have considered dating anyone. She was totally devoted to our dad."

I had a feeling that Lark had allowed her children to think that. Maybe they didn't know their mother quite as well as they thought. I simply nodded and said, "Thanks." But I walked away wondering if there might be more to Lark's death than Paisley thought.

I pulled my cell phone out of my pocket and called Nina. "Any chance that you and Francie would be willing to sit in Paisley's tent and sell her stuff? She's worn to a frazzle."

"No problem. I'll call Francie. Don't give it another thought. It's the least we can do for Lark."

I continued through the tents, resolving minor problems and making sure people remembered what time and day they were supposed to demonstrate their crafts at Market Square.

At four o'clock the vendors were still going strong. But

I was parched. I headed to The Laughing Hound, a restaurant run by my friend, Bernie Frei.

Bernie had been the best man at my wedding. Born and raised in England, he had traveled the world after graduating from an American university with Mars. Bernie's mother had married a succession of wealthy men around the world and had recently moved from Shanghai to New Delhi. No one ever expected footloose Bernie to manage a wildly popular restaurant as an absentee owner, nor did we think he would settle down in Old Town. He surprised us all, but he still looked like the Bernie we knew and loved, no pretenses there. His sandy hair was always tousled like he'd just rolled out of bed and he had a kink in his nose where it had been broken once, if not twice. For years I had thought that his hair looked wild because he really had just gotten out of bed, but now I was beginning to think that maybe he needed a good hairdresser.

Just outside of the restaurant, I spied Wolf and hurried to catch up to him. "Hi. Paisley says Lark was murdered by an intruder, a thief whom she let into her home."

"You know I can't talk to you about that."

He was so infuriating. "As a citizen of Old Town, who lives only a couple of blocks away from Lark, I believe I have the right to know if there's a person roaming the streets at night and knocking on doors with the intention of murdering women."

Wolf's emotionless face worked well for him as a cop, but I had always found it extremely frustrating because he didn't show how he felt about anything.

After a painful few seconds that seemed far longer, he said, "It's too early to draw any conclusions. We don't even have an autopsy yet. Lock your doors and you should be fine."

"I heard she opened the door to him."

He sighed gently. "We don't know that, either. Only that he managed to gain access to the house without leaving any signs of damage."

Oh no. I knew what that meant. "Lark knew him!"

"It's a possibility."

"As awful as that is, I'll sleep better tonight. Thanks, Wolf."

When I turned away, he said, "Keep your ear to the ground for me. I'd like to know who she associated with. And whether she was dating anyone."

"Do you feel people are being coy about that?" I asked.

Wolf eyed me. "You've noticed that, have you?"

I smiled at him. So Lark had a secret. Maybe more than one secret. She seemed like such an open book. The proper widow who threw tasteful dinner parties and volunteered in the community. Could it be that she wasn't what she seemed?

I walked away and into The Laughing Hound where I spied my ex-husband, Mars, outside on the terrace with Bernie.

In spite of our divorce, Mars and I remained friends and even shared Daisy. Neither of us could bear to give her up and frankly, it was wonderful for her and the two of us to have a reliable and loving dog sitter who was crazy about her on the odd occasion when one of us left town. Mars had been blessed with a boyish look. He had dark hair, and blue eyes that twinkled with mischief and humor. A political consultant, he had the charisma and looks to be a politician himself. Thankfully, that wasn't the life he sought. He was content to remain in the background.

"May I join you, or am I interrupting something?" I asked.

"You're always welcome here, Soph. What can I get for you?" asked Bernie.

"Just a plain iced tea would hit the spot. No sugar, please."

He rose and walked inside the restaurant for two seconds. A minute later, a waiter brought us an iced tea and a platter of spiced shrimp.

"*I* was not worthy of shrimp," Mars teased.

But that didn't stop him from digging in and eating his fair share.

"I suppose you heard about Lark Bickford?" asked Bernie.

"Heard? I was there when her body was discovered!"

They stopped eating. Mars raised his eyebrows. "So what's the story?"

I told them what little I knew. "Was Lark seeing anyone?" I asked.

"If she was, I never saw her come in here with him," said Bernie.

Mars shrugged. "I never gave it any thought. Are you suggesting that someone she was dating knocked her off?"

"It's a possibility. One that I like a whole lot better than some burglar doing her in. Nina and Dulci were on the trip with her and they thought she was oddly evasive when the subject of a beau came up."

"I'll ask around discreetly," offered Bernie. "If they stayed local, someone surely knows about it."

"Thanks, Bernie. Her son Bennett is here. I feel terrible for him and Paisley. What an awful way to lose your mom. And she was still so young! Although her kids seem to think she was ready to be put out to pasture."

"Bennett . . . kind of flaccid-looking guy?" asked Mars.

"Yes. Paisley is obviously very fond of him. Do you know him?"

Bernie's expression grew grim. "Believe the opposite of whatever he says."

"Ouch! You have clearly run into him before." I peeled a shrimp.

"Lark loved him," said Bernie, "but I wouldn't trust him."

"He seems nice enough," I said.

"So does Mars," Bernie teased. "It's an interesting notion. What if we all looked like our inner thoughts? Sneaky or devious, boneheaded or clever? I'm not sure I know what those people would look like. At any rate, I've heard things about Bennett Bickford. I can't swear that any of them are true, but I'd be on my guard around him."

Chapter 6

Dear Sophie,
I've heard there's a way to clean silver without having to polish it. Is that just wishful thinking or is it possible?

Tired Arms in Silver, Texas

Dear Tired Arms,
You can clean silver with very hot water, aluminum foil, and baking soda. However, you cannot do this in a metal sink or basin, or one with a metal drain because it will discolor the metal. Lay a piece of aluminum foil on the bottom of a plastic basin that is large enough to accommodate your silver item. Pour a generous amount of baking soda on top of the aluminum foil and place the silver piece on top of it. Pour in just boiling water and watch the tarnish disappear. Repeat as necessary to get all the tarnish off.

Sophie

That night, I checked all the doors twice to be sure they were locked. I wasn't actually afraid, but why take chances?

At four thirty in the morning, I woke to Daisy howling along with an annoyingly shrill siren.

Daisy wasn't the best guard dog. She barked sometimes and had been known to growl if she didn't trust someone, but generally she was more of a kisser than a snarler. She happily plodded down the stairs along with Mochie, who was far wiser and more cautious. He jumped up on the bay window in the kitchen, ready to flee if necessary.

The siren grew louder.

I opened the kitchen door and looked outside. Only then did I realize that the wailing siren emanated from Nina. She was running across the street to my house holding up a little personal safety siren. A small white dog followed her, yelping the whole way.

"Sophie! Sophie!" she screamed.

I flicked on the outdoor light.

"Turn that off! He'll see us and know where I am!"

The noisy siren took care of that. Nevertheless, I switched off the light and Nina raced into my kitchen faster than I had ever seen her move. The little white dog sped in on her heels.

She closed the door and locked it. "Don't turn on any lights." She gasped for breath and lurched over to the bay window to gaze out at her house. "I don't see him."

I joined her at the window. The street was quite calm. "You might turn off your siren."

She switched it off. But Nina was clearly terrified. Still wearing sky blue pajamas, she trembled from head to foot. Nina ran to my landline and dialed three digits, which I presumed to be 911. She gave the dispatcher her address and said she had an intruder but was safely inside a neighbor's home. She hung up the phone.

Oblivious to Nina's panic, Mochie perched on a chair watching the new dog, ready to flee if necessary, but Daisy wagged her tail and proceeded with the traditional dog welcome ritual of polite sniffing.

I wrapped my arm around Nina and spoke softly. "You're okay now. Tell me what happened."

"This is Muppet, my foster dog. I was sound asleep when she barked at me. I tried to shush her, but she just wouldn't stop barking. I didn't see anything amiss in the bedroom, so I followed her downstairs, thinking there might be a mouse in the house or something else that would excite a dog, like a cat peering in the back door. That was when I saw a shady figure trying to get in my back door! All I could think of was what had happened to Lark. I ran through the house to the front door and over here."

Lights flashed out on the street as a police car arrived.

"I'd better get out there," said Nina.

I suited Daisy up in her halter and nabbed an extra leash for Muppet. Nina and the dogs waited patiently while I turned on all my outdoor lights and locked the kitchen door behind us. We crossed the street to Nina's house. Bernie and Mars ran toward us wielding baseball bats.

Two uniformed officers stood on Nina's front porch, no doubt ringing the doorbell.

"Hello!" Nina shouted from the street. "I'm the owner of this house."

The two officers were in their twenties. A thin man with a sweet young face had a frightened look in his eyes. Fresh out of the police academy I guessed. His name tag identified him as Officer Farber. The woman with him, Officer Seapiza, wore her hair super short and if she hadn't been in uniform, I would have thought she might be an elementary school teacher from her no-nonsense expression.

Nina told them what had happened.

Officer Seapiza sent Farber around the side of the house to check out the backyard.

I saw him take a deep breath. He was clearly afraid.

Mars must have noticed, too. He volunteered to go with him.

Meanwhile, Nina opened the front door for Seapiza, who told us to wait outside on the porch while she determined that no one was lurking in the house. After what seemed like hours, she reappeared. "I don't see anyone inside the house. Show me where you saw this person."

Nina led her to the back door. They flicked on outdoor lights, which surely startled Farber but probably gave him courage as well.

With the two leashed dogs, Bernie and I trailed into the house behind Nina and Seapiza.

We followed them into Nina's kitchen. The door in question was glass and stood open about three inches.

"Your dog probably scared him away," opined Officer Seapiza. "I can get someone over here to dust for prints, but thanks to TV, everyone knows about wearing gloves, so it's highly unlikely that we'll get any." She nudged the door open and walked outside for a look. "Farber! You back here?"

"Yes, ma'am." His voice was eerie because we couldn't see him. In spite of the spotlights, he and Mars somehow managed to be in the shadows.

"Find anything?" she asked.

"No, ma'am. No footprints or anything that appears out of place."

"I'd appreciate it if you would check for fingerprints," said Nina. "Doesn't this point to a professional thief? He picked the lock *and* the deadbolt."

"Not really. Anyone can Google it." Seapiza walked away and spoke into her radio.

We could hear voices outside.

Two hours later, half the neighbors had gathered in Nina's beautiful professionally decorated living room. I had darted home for tea and frozen chocolate chip cookies and returned to Nina's kitchen to brew coffee and Irish breakfast tea while the cookies thawed. Bernie and Mars had dressed in jeans and T-shirts hastily pulled on without regard for the night air and were probably chilled. Francie, my elderly next-door neighbor, had ambled across the street with her golden retriever, Duke, to make sure Nina was okay. A handful of other neighbors had come outside in an assortment of bathrobes that ran from shabby and embarrassingly well-worn to elegant. They clustered in the living room munching on cookies and drinking tea, while expressing concern that a ruthless burglar had targeted the neighborhood.

Officer Seapiza had gone off to take another call, leaving Officer Farber in charge. He stood in the doorway, drinking tea and eating cookies. Every minute or so, he glanced nervously at the back door, which was in the process of being fingerprinted.

Naturally, more than one person suggested there could be a connection between Lark's killer and Nina's intruder.

"It has to be more than a coincidence that you're both just back from Europe," said Bernie.

"Could the burglar have gotten the dates wrong?" asked Mars. "Maybe he thought you hadn't returned yet and your homes were empty."

I scanned the collected neighbors. How many people knew that both Lark and Nina were away? Nina had talked nonstop about her trip before she left. Lark probably had, too.

Nina must have been thinking along the same lines because she whined loudly, "Is this what we have evolved to? A society where you can't even let anyone know that you're going on a trip?"

Several neighbors assured her they thought it must have been a coincidence.

Mars, Bernie, and I exchanged glances. We weren't so sure.

But at that moment, Officer Farber announced that the fingerprinting had been concluded and everyone was free to go home. "I'll be patrolling periodically through the night and we'll make a point of having a squad car cruise through occasionally after dark."

There was a good bit of grumbling as the neighbors departed. Bernie, Mars, and I cleaned up Nina's kitchen.

"Would you like me to stay over tonight?" asked Mars. "I can stretch out on a sofa down here. All I need are a pillow and a blanket."

Nina glanced at me. "I thought I might sleep over at Sophie's house. If I stayed here, I would be awake all night, afraid that he might return."

"Great," said Mars. "I'll bunk in the den."

It was already past six in the morning, but I nodded my head, thinking Mars and Nina might manage to sleep in but I had to be up and at the Do-It-Yourself Festival.

When we returned to my house, Mars went straight to bed.

Nina sat down in a chair by the fireplace and I filled the kettle for tea.

I poured tea for both of us, and gave Muppet, Mochie, and Daisy treats. "And Muppet gets extra love for being such a super watchdog!"

Her little tail wagged happily, and she helped herself to the water in the bowl on the floor.

"Do you think there's a connection to Lark's intruder?" Nina asked in a high-pitched and slightly hysterical voice.

I wanted to be honest with her. "It's hard to tell. For all we know, it could have been someone who was casing your house while you were away and didn't realize you had come home."

She nodded her head.

"Are you going to ask your husband to return?" I asked.

She shrugged. "I don't know. I'm going to tell him what happened but I'm not sure I want to drag him home. Do you mind me staying with you for a few days?"

"Of course not! I love having you here." I looked down at Muppet. "And you, too!"

Nina went upstairs to the guest room for a nap.

I showered fast and pulled on a bright pink sweater set with khaki pants that instantly made me regret the cookies I had eaten only hours ago. There was no time for changing, but I did anyway. A pair of dark gray elastic-in-every-way jeans fit far better. I slid on sneakers, added simple gold hoops, a little makeup, and ran a brush through my hair. I hurried down the stairs and straight to the back door to let out Daisy and her new friend, Muppet. I fed Mochie in the kitchen and rounded the corner to peek in at Mars. He was fast asleep.

I dashed to the back door to let the dogs in on the assumption that they would probably prefer to lounge at home than hang around the DIY Festival with me. I would have loved to go back to bed if I could. Instead I let myself out the kitchen door, taking care to lock it behind me.

In daylight, Nina's house looked perfectly normal and it was almost hard to believe that someone had broken in the night before. The entire street slumbered peacefully. Only birds and the distant rumble of traffic were evident.

I was dying for a mug of strong coffee but went straight to the street of DIY tents. No one there had overslept. Not even Paisley, who had more right than anyone to stay home.

To my surprise, she was in her tent with a fresh supply

of refurbished furniture, including a collection of whimsi-
cal rocking chairs for children's rooms in the MacKenzie-
Childs style. They had black-and-white checkered seats,
blue and purple arms, polka-dotted legs, and pink, blue, or
yellow backs that she could personalize with a child's name.
The colors, dots, stripes, and diamonds were riotous and
absolutely darling. They could have come from the Mad
Hatter's tea party.

I walked over to her. "These are incredible. Have you
considered making them for wider distribution?"

"They're my best sellers." She pointed at a child's dresser
painted in the same adorable patterns and bright colors. "I
even make matching dressers and changing tables. But I
can only do so many. Painting details takes time. And
Frank is completely incapable when it comes to manual
labor. He can't stay inside the lines," she said with a sad
smile.

"There has to be a way," I said. "Maybe you could hire
some people to paint them."

Paisley laughed aloud. "With what?"

"I know, it's hard to get a new business off the ground.
Still, I think you have something very special here."

The gate to Lark's house creaked open and Frank staggered out, carrying a box which tinkled when he plopped
it down on a painted sideboard. "Morning, Sophie."

Yellow police tape lay in a heap on the ground next to
the gate. Was he allowed to go inside?

"What have you got there, Frank?" asked Paisley. She
walked over and peered in the boxes. Her face went white
and I could hear her gasping for breath. She looked at him
with horror.

Feeling an argument was coming on, I waved, though I
doubted that they noticed, and walked away, stopping to
say hello to each of the merchants and ask how things
were going.

Most of them had a theme. One fellow painted everything in red, white, and blue with stars and stripes, while the one next to him only made garden items, like signs and birdhouses. There were wreath specialists and polka-dot painters. Lantern decorators, lamp and chandelier creators, Christmas ornament makers, and tiling experts. So many niches and talented people!

They had me thinking about changing up some things in my own house. Why not paint that dreary side table I had bought on a whim because the price was so low?

I swung by Market Square, where a woman demonstrated how to clean silver without silver cleaner.

But I needed my coffee. Desperately! I popped in at a café and ordered coffee and an everything bagel to go.

"Heard someone broke in at Nina's last night."

I recognized Wolf's voice and turned. "He picked two locks on her back door."

"Is she okay?"

"She wasn't physically hurt, but she spent the rest of the night at my house. She's very upset. If she hadn't been fostering a barky little dog, she could have awakened to find someone in her bedroom!"

"I can't blame her. That's a very scary thing, especially on the heels of Lark's murder," said Wolf.

Chapter 7

Dear Natasha,
I saw the most fabulous clock mounted in a friend's house. It was giant, probably four or five feet in diameter. It wasn't in a case, it was mounted directly on the wall. How do I make one in my house?

Always on Time in Clockville, New York

Dear Always on Time,
You can buy a kit or separate parts from online clock part companies. Don't forget that you can be creative with the numbers. Use family photos or start a theme (seashore, forest, soccer) that is meaningful to your family.

Natasha

"Any leads on that yet?" I asked, collecting my coffee and bagel.

He stared at me without speaking for a moment. I guessed he was trying to figure out what he should and should not divulge.

"No one should die the way Lark did. But it's still early in the investigation."

In other words, there wasn't anything he was willing to share about Lark's murder. Not yet anyway. A wise friend had recently pointed out to me that Wolf didn't share information about murder because he liked or trusted me. He carefully chose what information he parceled out to me. He never divulged police information unless there was a good reason to do so. As frustrating as that was for me, I couldn't fault him for his silence. It was his job and I had to respect that.

"Any chance it was the same person who hit Nina's house last night?" I asked.

Wolf took a deep breath. "I've thought about that. There isn't anything that connects the two events."

"Really?" I sipped my coffee and played innocent. "You don't think it's peculiar that both of them just returned home from the same trip abroad?"

"I'm aware of that detail. But at this point, it appears to be coincidental."

"Is it also coincidental that the intruder picked the locks on their doors?"

"It's interesting," he said, "but the prevailing thought is that Lark let her killer into her house."

I pushed him a little. "Is the autopsy report back yet?"

Wolf smiled and looked into his coffee cup. "I expect it any time now."

At that moment, Greer Shacklesworth, one of the DIY exhibitors, approached me. "Sophie, could I have a word, please?"

Wolf waved at me and walked away. Greer and I stepped outside. She was in her late forties I thought, though almost no wrinkles marred her long aristocratic face. She knew how to apply makeup well, but it was scant on her deep brown eyes, giving her a fresh and barefaced appearance. She had nailed the blond hair color preferred by women in the Deep South, very light with no roots showing even though she had twisted it up, leaving errant strands that looked like they had come loose when everyone knew they'd been artfully pulled out. Greer wore significant gold earrings that I bet were the real thing, a light blue blouse that fell like it was silk, and café au lait–colored trousers. The sleeves on her blouse were rolled back exposing a bracelet of gold coins adorning her wrist. The kind of casual look that screamed money and lots of it.

"What can I do for you?"

"I'm not one to complain," she said in a cultured voice with a heavy Southern accent. "But Paisley and Frank have turned their tent into a yard sale. I know that DIY isn't for everyone, but some of us are high-quality dealers and we would never have signed on if the DIY Festival was a shabby place to pick up, well, *junk*. I admit I'm not a yard sale fan, but there is a difference between emptying out a house and being creative. It's just that I don't want others to get that idea and start hauling all their trash out here to sell. It would diminish the value of the festival."

"I'll take a look," I assured her. "I happen to like yard sales, but I do get your point. There is a distinction."

Greer's shoulders sagged with relief. "I'm so glad you understand my concern! I really hate to make a fuss."

"No problem. I'll go straight there now." I walked toward Lark's house and could see the trouble before I was at Paisley's tent. They had lined up tables outside the tent and covered them with every conceivable household item, from half-empty bottles of dish soap to partly burned candles and dishes piled on top of each other.

Paisley, her husband, Frank, and brother, Bennett, were in the tent.

Waving my hand at the tables, I asked as sweetly as I could, "What's this?"

Paisley's face flushed red. Her eyes were rimmed pink from crying. She glared at her husband.

Frank said angrily, "Bennett found Lark's will. She has cheated her children out of their rightful inheritance."

I was confused. That didn't sound right, but even if it was true, what did that have to do with bottles of shampoo and kitchen equipment?

Paisley's voice sounded like she was holding back tears. "Mom left her money in a spendthrift trust. We can't have any of it unless it's approved by some stranger. Bennett looked it up on his phone. Apparently, this man gets to dole it out to us as *he* sees fit."

"We're contesting the will and taking him to court," said Frank. "It's absolutely outrageous. I'm filing the papers this afternoon. We cannot have this."

"I would understand it," said Paisley, "if Bennett and I were children who couldn't handle our own money, but that's not the case. I cannot imagine what Mother was thinking."

"What does that have to do with lamps and boxes of Christmas ornaments?" I asked.

Paisley gulped and appeared pained. She flicked a look at her brother but quickly averted her eyes.

"We're selling Lark's junk. People are coming by to gawk anyway. Why not?" asked Frank.

I didn't feel I should mention how unseemly it was to clear out Lark's possessions when she had been dead for less than forty-eight hours. Paisley seemed uncomfortable with it, but I had to wonder what kind of cold and contriving man Bennett was to allow the sale of his mother's belongings so soon after her death.

Everyone grieved differently. I could understand throwing oneself into work as a diversion from the harsh reality of loss. I could understand packing it all in and going home to be with family or even to be alone. But I could not grasp how anyone could sell the possessions of a newly deceased loved one when the body was barely cold. In fact, it forced me to question their involvement in Lark's death.

Not to mention that there was crime scene tape crumpled by the gate. I knew how to stop this instantly. One call to Wolf and they would be in major trouble.

I said as kindly as I could, "I'm so sorry, but the contract you signed to participate in the DIY Festival specifically limits what you are allowed to sell and demonstrate. Yard sale items are not permitted."

"That's baloney," cried Frank. "What about the lady with the action figures and mirrors across the way? Or the man who makes birdhouse lamps?"

His tone drew attention to us. I tried to keep my voice even and calm. "*Makes* may be the operative word here. Didn't you notice that she creates lamps out of action figures? And those beautiful mirrors look like the ones in a trendy upscale store, but she creates them out of inexpensive mirrors and garlands. The birdhouse lamps are completely handmade, too."

Frank changed his tune like a chameleon changes colors. His entire demeanor was suddenly different. Quietly, he said, "Maybe you could give us a break. After all, Paisley and Bennett just lost their mom."

"I'm so sorry, but other vendors are complaining."

The anger returned in a flash. Frank shouted, "Then we'll move the tables into the side yard. That's private property and you can't tell us what to do there!"

Everyone was watching now.

Frank marched over to the gate and swung it open with such force that the discarded police tape intended to keep everyone out flapped up into the air.

That was a huge mistake. I didn't have the power to do much about their display of yard sale items, but the police would not be happy about them trampling on a crime scene, which they must have done all morning to carry the items out of the house.

I walked to the end of the street and around the corner so they wouldn't notice me calling Wolf.

He answered his phone, "Sophie? Didn't I just see you?"

"I'm afraid Frank Eames has removed your police tape and is trying sell Lark's possessions."

"I'll be right there." The phone clicked off.

I dallied a bit at the other end of the street, hoping it wouldn't look as though I was waiting for Wolf or had called him.

I watched as a woman demonstrated how to make a clock directly on a wall. It was very clever and easier than I ever would have expected. She sold the various components to excited buyers.

When I looked down the street, I could see an elderly lady embracing Paisley. She was thin, but not frail, with short hair so white that it almost glowed.

As I watched, Wolf arrived at Lark's house and I wondered what had happened to Nina and Francie, who were supposed to be manning the tent so Paisley and Bennett could grieve.

I wandered in that direction to see if I could hear what he was saying. I paused near the tables loaded with Lark's possessions. As I gazed at the tables, my own thoughts crowded out the voices around me. I had known Lark socially, seen her at fundraisers for worthy local charities, chatted with her at the best grocery store in town. She hadn't been in my close circle of friends. But looking at her possessions on the table was like looking at my own things after my death. I knew this woman better than I thought because she was just like me.

Her fine china was Waterford Lismore Lace Gold. Even stacked in unceremonious heaps, it was stunning. A lacy, but not fussy, golden pattern surrounded the edge of the perfect white background on each plate. She had the entire complement of Waterford Lismore stemware. Old-fashioned tumblers and their elegant stemmed iced tea glasses, and white wine, claret wine, and water goblets filled the table. A shimmering array of cut to clear wine hocks in ruby, sapphire, emerald, and amethyst stood next to a small collection of Hummel figures. On the next table over was the Villeroy & Boch French Garden Collection of dishes in cheerful greens and yellows, along with select pieces of Portmeirion, and a Baccarat crystal elephant and bear cub. Four Lladró pieces, still in the boxes, lay on top of duty-free bags. She must have bought them on her last trip. They were even selling her silver. Twelve place settings of repoussé from Kirk Stieff. The ornate floral pattern was classic.

Lark had been known for her formal dinner parties. And now all of her cherished belongings were out on display like worthless trash.

Frank interrupted my thoughts. "This is your fault," he hissed at me.

"I beg your pardon?"

"Frank, you've made enough of a scene," whispered Paisley. "Mother would be mortified. Leave Sophie alone. She has nothing to do with our problems."

"Paisley, have you lost your mind? What are we going to do for money?"

She turned lobster red. "I'm so sorry, Sophie. Please forgive us. It's a very trying time."

The elderly woman wrapped a reassuring arm around her.

"Um, this is Mrs. Gurtz," said Paisley. "She cleaned for my mom and took care of Bennett and me when my mom needed a sitter."

A child screamed a few booths down. "Mommy! Mommy!"

Paisley screamed, "Oscar!"

Oscar lay underneath a tall chest of drawers that appeared to have toppled over on him.

Frank and Paisley ran to him immediately, with Mrs. Gurtz wisely looking after the other boys.

The chest in question had been on display with the drawers open to show off the clever paintings of mermaids on the sides of the beach-themed drawers.

The vendor in that tent, Beall Hattaway, was saying, "He climbed up the drawers! Is he okay?"

Frank and Beall picked the piece of furniture up and off the little boy. Frank yelled at Beall, "How could you be so irresponsible? What were you thinking setting up a piece of furniture that way? It was a clear invitation to a kid to climb it."

Beall snapped back, "Maybe you ought to watch your kids instead of letting them run wild through everyone's tents."

Paisley cuddled her son, examining him for injuries. "Frank, I think Oscar needs to go to the emergency room."

"Don't be silly. I fell a hundred times when I was a kid."

"Honey, I'm serious. He could have a head injury. What if he cracked his skull?"

That suggestion brought on a torrent of tears from Oscar.

All five of his siblings stood in a huddle staring at their brother, the smallest ones clinging to Mrs. Gurtz. "Is he going to die?" one of them asked.

As if Oscar wasn't sobbing hard enough already, that question brought on panicked screams. Oscar's face was now redder than his mother's.

"Do you know what that will cost?" hissed Frank.

"I. Don't. Care. Oscar is my baby and we are taking him to the emergency room right now. Do you understand?"

"Don't make a scene, Paisley. There's no need for that. I'll take him." He lifted the child out of his mother's lap and said, "Come on, kids."

"You're taking all of them with you?" Paisley asked.

"Sure. It will be fine. You go sell your furniture."

He walked off with Oscar in his arms and five little boys trailed along behind him, subdued by one of their own being injured.

I reached a hand to Paisley and helped her up off the pavement.

"Thank you, Sophie." She brushed off her clothes and glanced sideways like she was looking for her brother.

"Could I buy you a cup of coffee?" I asked.

She chewed her lower lip. "Not now. I have to get back to the tent." She scurried off like she was afraid of something, or someone.

Chapter 8

Dear Sophie,
I am home schooling my kids, as are other parents
in our neighborhood. Apparently, our school day
runs later than theirs, and we're constantly inter-
rupted by neighborhood children knocking on the
door. Of course, once they knock, school is over!
How do I politely deter them from this behavior?
Desperate Mom in College Ward, Utah

Dear Desperate Mom,
Make a sign to place by the front door. It could be
chalkboard or corkboard. Write two lines on it: We
cannot come out to play. Do not knock; and We're
ready to play. Please knock! Make boxes that can
be checked, or arrows that can be pinned, and
change them as the situation warrants.
Sophie

I was beat that evening. Loads of the vendors had told me
how delighted they were with the turnout. I wasn't surprised. I had enjoyed walking through the tents and had

several DIY projects in mind for my home. But at the moment, all I wanted was to put my feet up and eat something that I didn't have to cook.

Fortunately, Nina and Mars picked up Chinese takeout and brought it home for dinner. Nina had called a locksmith, who was coming to install something called half-bolts on Friday so no one could enter the house by picking a lock. It wouldn't stop someone from breaking a window, but it would give her some peace of mind and that meant a lot. Until then, she could stay with me.

I set the table with Cottage dinner plates from Villeroy & Boch. They were white with a blue border and a few sprigs of berries. Nina poured herself a glass of chardonnay and Mars found a Heineken in the back of my refrigerator. I knew I would fall asleep if I had any alcohol, so I opted for rose hip tea, which might not be a chef's choice as a match for Chinese food, but it worked for me.

While we ate spring rolls, Szechwan eggplant, General Tso's Chicken, Shrimp with Lobster Sauce, and Moo Shu Pork, I asked Nina about her trip.

"It was very nice. I expected to be able to spend more time with my husband, but he was in great demand and even when we went out to dinner with people from his conference, it was . . . boring. If I hadn't had different expectations, it would have been very enjoyable."

"Did you pout the whole time?" I asked.

"Not the *whole* time. The most fun I had was when I got lost. It was so interesting. I found my way into a part of Lisbon where no one spoke English. I found a wonderful bead store, and a tile store, and had a lunch where I ordered the food by guessing and pointing. It was delightful. I had the best time! Well, until I wanted to go home and then I had no idea where I was or how to find my way back."

Mars laughed. "I'm not much of a get-on-the-bus kind

of tourist, either. That sounds like fun. How did you go back to the hotel?"

"I thought I would walk back, so I asked a policeman, who showed me the way on a map. But that didn't work out at all. I went into a small hotel. You should have been there! It was like an episode from *I Love Lucy* with me not knowing any Portuguese and them not understanding English. We were all laughing. They called me a cab and I gave the driver a card that I had in my purse from the hotel. He knew exactly where it was."

"At the risk of bringing up sore subjects, exactly why were you barefoot when I picked you up?" I asked.

"Barefoot? In the airport?" Mars nearly choked on his dinner.

Nina gulped her wine. "Let me just say that the people in customs were not nice to me. I bought some special Iberian ham to bring home to you, Sophie. It was wonderful! You know how they give you a customs form to fill out? They ask you to declare the things you bought, so I listed the ham. I won't ever do *that* again! Dulci and Lark bought tons of gifts including the very same ham. Emery Chapman told me he had to go out and buy an extra suitcase at the last minute because Dulci had bought so much. But did they declare anything? Nooo. The Chapmans and Lark just waltzed through customs looking completely innocent while I was detained!"

"Detained?" I was horrified. I hoped that wasn't as bad as it sounded.

"They put me in a room all by myself. Meanwhile, I had a connecting flight to catch. I have no idea whatsoever why I had to take off my shoes and socks. Well, maybe I can understand the shoes, but socks? Who could hide anything in socks that are on their feet? Your Iberian ham, I am sorry to say, landed in the trash. They quite unceremoniously pulled it out and flung it into a big trash bin. They actually rifled through my luggage! There I was with a plane to catch and all my carefully packed things falling out of the suitcases. You know how you jam souvenirs in just so to get everything to fit. I crammed it all in and ran out of that horrible little room to catch my flight. It wasn't until I got to the gate that I realized I had left my socks and shoes in customs. Heaven knows what else I left there."

Mars had stopped eating. "Are you telling us that you ran through the airport barefoot and then flew here without any shoes?"

"What else could I do? It was that or miss my flight."

"You must have taken more than one pair of shoes," said Mars. "Sophie always takes a pair for every outfit."

"That's not exactly true," I protested, but I did tend to pack a few pairs of shoes when I traveled.

"They were holding the plane for me and grabbed my bags when I ran up to the gate. I didn't have any shoes in my carry-on bag. What was I supposed to do?"

Mars and I burst out laughing. It could only happen to Nina. She joined in the laughter. I had a feeling it was a story she would be telling for the rest of her life.

I fell asleep during the movie they had selected and dragged myself up to bed when it was over. I pulled up the blanket and quickly looked up how to call 911 on an iPhone if you can't dial. The recommendation was to press the volume button and the side button simultaneously. If you don't choose something on the screen, the phone automatically dials 911. I hoped I wouldn't need that nifty tip.

At five in the morning, little Muppet began to bark. Daisy backed her up with a few deep barks of her own and Mochie joined the two dogs in running down the stairs. I hadn't planned on getting up quite that early, but they were going to wake up everyone if they didn't stop barking.

I threw on a bathrobe and walked downstairs. They weren't at the front door or the kitchen door. I found the dogs looking out the French doors in the living room wagging their tails. Mochie sat regally on an end table and watched them.

I couldn't believe my eyes when I saw someone in the still darkness before dawn trying to get into my house. Was this Nina's burglar? Lark's murderer? But surely a burglar wouldn't rap on the glass door like that.

Emboldened by the knowledge that Mars and Nina were in the house, I flicked on the outdoor lights and the person waved at me. It was Paisley.

I opened the door and let her in. "Oh gosh, did I wake you? I was afraid of that. Hi puppies!" She bent to pet Daisy and Muppet.

What do you say to someone who is cheery and has appeared at your door at an hour when most people still slept? *What are you doing here? What can I do for you? What would you like for breakfast? Why aren't you home asleep?*

I decided to go with something simpler. "How is Oscar?"

Her cheerful expression changed dramatically. "Frank didn't take him to the emergency room as he promised. He took the kids home."

"Oh!" I would have been furious! "How's he doing? Oscar, not Frank."

"I think he's okay, but you can't tell with head injuries, you know? I'm going to take him myself today. I just have to figure out how to sneak him away from Frank. Maybe if I give him some money, he'll do the grocery shopping or something."

"You have to trick him?" That didn't sound like a healthy marriage. Then again, my ex-husband was sleeping on the pullout sofa in the den, so what did I know about marriage?

"It's awful, isn't it?" Paisley asked. She winced and rubbed her forehead. "I never thought I would have to lie to him about something like taking a child to the doctor."

"Would you care for some coffee or tea?"

"I'd love a cup of coffee. If it's not too much trouble?"

"Come into the kitchen. Mars is sleeping in the den, so we'll talk softly if you don't mind."

She followed me into my kitchen and turned around slowly in wonder. "This is lovely. So cozy."

I put on the kettle and poured coffee grinds into the coffee press. "Thanks. I wanted modern appliances and an island, but I couldn't give up the beautiful old parts. We kept the beamed ceiling and, of course, the stone fireplace wall. We think it's original to the house, but even if it isn't, it's still very old. They tell me the stones were ballast on boats and unloaded down at the river. When Mars and I inherited the house, the kitchen still had *mod* 1960s-style orange countertops, if you can imagine that!"

I poured coffee into the Pinheiro Majolica mugs Nina had brought back from Portugal. They were the traditional green color with raised bunnies around the base of the mugs and raised leaves emerging from behind them. "Would you like some breakfast?"

"No, no, no. I'm fine. I'll have to cook breakfast anyway when I go home. Coffee is great. I remember Mom telling me about your kitchen." She sighed. "I miss Mom. She was my best friend. I could talk to her about anything." Paisley took a deep breath. "She loved to travel. Even when Bennett and I were little kids, she'd have Mrs. Gurtz come over to stay with us while she flew off somewhere exotic for a few days."

Paisley looked at me and bit her upper lip before saying, "Sometimes I find myself thinking that Mom's just away having an adventure somewhere and she'll be back the next day."

She scratched Daisy and Muppet behind their ears. "She didn't like Frank though. Don't look so surprised. It was difficult for me because I adore him. I have to admit that she was very nice to him and welcomed him into our family. But I knew. She thought I could have done better. Pretty ironic considering that he's Portuguese royalty."

I led her back to the living room so we wouldn't wake Mars. His aunt Faye had entertained a great deal and had extended the dining and living rooms to accommodate crowds of people. We settled on the yellow sofa that faced the fireplace. The room was decorated in soft shades of yellow with red accents. It wasn't so posh that people felt they had to sit up straight. Rather than painfully formal, I thought it comfortably elegant.

I wasn't particularly knowledgeable about Portuguese history. "I didn't know that Portugal had a royal family."

"It's a republic today, not a monarchy, but the lineage still exists and those people are regarded as royals. It's in Frank's blood. His family was royalty once. You'd think my mom would have loved that!"

I didn't like to be critical, but I figured being royal didn't necessarily mean you had to be a nice person. I smiled at her. "It must be fun to know you're from a royal lineage. Too bad you didn't have girls. They would have loved being princesses."

"It wasn't for lack of trying. We had Tommy first. He was such an easy kid. He slept through the night and was just a little angel. When he was three years old, I got pregnant again, this time with the twins. Let me tell you, twins are tough. But we got through that and wanted a little girl. And that was going to be all. I thought three boys and a baby sister would be the perfect family. And then I had triplets, all boys. I love them more than anything on this earth. But you cannot imagine how tired I am all the time. My mom paid for a nanny to help us when the twins and triplets were infants. I don't know what we would have done without the nanny and my mom. It's a family joke now that I don't dare get pregnant again for fear of having quadruplets—all boys! My little rascals are not at all impressed by the notion that they might be royalty. They'd much rather be Spider-Man or Superman than a prince."

Paisley took a deep breath. "I hope you don't mind my coming over unannounced like this. I needed to talk with you when Frank and Bennett weren't around. I often go running early in the morning. It's the only time I can sneak out and have a few minutes alone. If Frank wakes, he won't suspect anything."

It worried me that she felt the need to keep things from her husband. And why hadn't Lark liked her son-in-law? I wondered if Lark had confided in Nina or Dulci on their trip.

I watched Paisley as she spoke. She clutched her mug so tightly that the knuckles on her hands shone white. She turned her head, as though she couldn't bear to look me in the eyes.

"You can't imagine how expensive six children are. We're homeschooling them, which is working out fine, but I feel like they need to go to school if only for the socialization. I don't want my kids growing up without friends and fun and prom and sports, other than the ones Frank happens to like. Frank refuses unless they go to private school, which simply isn't feasible. It's not that I don't want them to have a good education, but there's just no money for that. Frank is totally unrealistic about our finances."

"Have you tried applying for scholarships?" I asked.

"Frank won't hear of it." She stared into the coffee mug that she held on her lap. "It makes no sense to me. I guess it's a matter of pride. Sometimes I wonder if he married me for my parents' money. When we met, I was a research scientist for a pharmaceutical company and made a decent income. But it's not exactly the kind of job you can do from home while teaching six kids."

"What did you say Frank does for a living?" I asked, knowing full well she hadn't told me.

"He's an advice guru."

I'd never heard of that title before. "What is that exactly?"

"People come to him with their problems and he helps them," Paisley explained. "I don't particularly care for the word *guru*. I think it's misleading and suggests some kind of mystical connection. *Counselor* sounds more appropriate to me but apparently that requires certification and implies certain education."

"Sort of like a life coach?" I asked.

"I guess it can be. But it's more than that. The problem is getting his name out there and building a reputation. Most of his business is from word of mouth. Frankly, I think Frank wastes far too much time on an organization he started. If he spent that much time at a regular nine-to-five job, we wouldn't find ourselves scraping by so often."

"An organization?" I asked cheerily.

Paisley huffed. "He likes to boast that he's a CEO, but he barely makes any money at all. It might as well be a Facebook group of like-minded people."

"What kind of company is it?" I asked.

"He advises other people who believe they are of royal lineage on how to get their status back," she said feebly.

"I'm not knowledgeable about this kind of thing at all, but wouldn't countries have to, I don't know, pass some kind of legislation reinstating a monarchy?"

She looked at me with tired eyes. "You wouldn't believe the arguments they come up with. Most of the stories are the same. Their ancestors sold their grand homes and anything valuable, including their titles, generations ago. The people with whom he's in communication are struggling along, just like us. They talk a big game, but the truth is that's all they do. And probably all they will ever be able to do in that regard. It's not like you can demand the return of the family castle and land that your great-great-granduncle sold over a century ago."

I saw the problem. Frank lived in a dream that would most likely never come to be.

"Frank is very smart. Make no mistake about that. He has a high IQ, and likes to remind me when I question his bogus organization. But it's not a business! It's just a bunch of people complaining about their status quo. Half of them probably aren't royalty at all."

"Sounds more like a hobby than a job," I said.

"Exactly. He has an online site where he orders mugs, and T-shirts, and even stationery for people with their family names or crests on them. I guess it's fun for them, but I worry that it makes them feel legitimate when they might not be."

"I guess they don't submit to DNA tests? Wouldn't there be some way of determining who was related to royalty?" I asked.

Paisley grinned. "I have suggested that. There's some guy who did a lot of research and says virtually everyone with European roots has a direct lineage to Charlemagne. I suppose almost anyone could claim to be related to a royal if you go back far enough."

She gulped her coffee. "As soon as the triplets are in first grade, I hope to go back to my regular job full time. I have a work-from-home job right now teaching chemistry online, but I don't make as much as we need. I supplement it with the furniture that I paint. Things like the festival are so helpful. They take a lot of time, loading and unloading, and getting everything ready, but without them, it's really just word of mouth. I'm sorry, Sophie. I didn't mean to go on about our lack of money." She closed her eyes for a long moment as if she was gathering courage. "You must be wondering why I came here."

Actually, I wasn't. I had a fairly good idea. It wouldn't be the first time someone had murdered for money. "You're afraid Frank killed Lark so you would inherit her money."

Chapter 9

Dear Sophie,
Our deck is way too close to our neighbors. We'd
like a little privacy, but we're not allowed to put up
a fence screen. My husband says he's not sitting on
a fussy deck with curtains. Any suggestions?
                In Broad Sight in Deckerville, Michigan

Dear In Broad Sight,
Buy three tall wooden shutters and paint them a
color that you like. Attach them securely to the
railing. They can be right next to one another or a
few inches apart. Hang a lantern or a wreath from
each one. Voilà. A screen but not a screen.
                                        Sophie

Paisley gasped. Her eyes large, she asked, "How could you know? Is that what the police think? Are they arresting him as we speak? I have to go home to the children!"

"Relax. It was simple deduction on my part."

"You're sure? I couldn't bear for them to take my children."

"I don't think that would happen." Unless, of course, both parents were involved.

I noticed that she didn't have a problem with the police arresting her husband. "I honestly don't have a clue what information the police might have. Would you like me to let Wolf know?"

"No! No, please don't do that. It's why I came to you. I need to know. It, um, could also have been my brother, Bennett. He was always hitting up Mom for money. And he flipped when he found out about the spendthrift trust. She wasn't super wealthy, but she was comfortable, and the house is worth quite a bit. When Frank and Bennett began to bring out her belongings yesterday, I tried to stop them. I spent the better part of the day crying. I can't tell you what a relief it was when Wolf came and told them to take everything back inside. He even called a young cop to make sure they didn't touch anything and that the house was locked up and the crime scene tape was replaced."

She stared into her coffee cup. "I don't understand. How could they do that to Mom? How could they take her life, the things she loved, and just sell them to strangers? They had no consideration for me at all. I would love to have her china and crystal. The boys don't appreciate them now, of course. I consider it a good day if no one spills milk or spits up on the table. But one day, when they bring their girlfriends home, they'll be proud of their mom for having lovely table settings at the holidays, just like my mom did. I don't want to sell her things. I want to keep them to remember her by. Her house isn't huge, only three bedrooms, but I've figured out how we could make that work. It's paid off, so if we moved in, we could save a ton of money by not having to pay rent or a mortgage. But

Frank and Bennett want to empty the house and sell it. It breaks my heart. There's no reasoning with them."

"Perhaps your mother anticipated that," I suggested gently.

She looked at me blankly at first. "Oh! I see what you mean. She expected them to run roughshod over me? We had no idea that she put everything in trust, which has angered both of them no end."

"That could be why she didn't mention it. And it sounds as if she might have done it as a favor to you."

"So there wouldn't be a squabble, you mean?"

"I think the trust probably prevents your husband and Bennett from frittering away her estate. Someone else is managing it, so the two of them won't benefit from arguing with you about money. Maybe she saw what was happening in your marriage."

"Or it could have been because of Bennett."

"Oh? Why is that?"

"He calls himself a professional gambler. He even has business cards with pictures of chips on them. But professional *loser* would be more accurate. He travels to casinos all over the country. He tells me he checks to see where big conventions are being held, then he poses as an attendee so as not to draw the attention of the casino when he's card counting. My mother hoped he would mature out of it. She thought he was a mathematical genius to figure out all those formulas and remember which cards had been played. She was always after him to use those skills in a better way. Sadly, *I* think he's addicted and can't give it up."

I hadn't realized that Lark had these kinds of problems in her family, though I suspected most of us didn't really know what went on behind closed doors, even in the lives of people we saw every day. My heart went out to Paisley. She hadn't inherited immediate money but when her mother died, she had inherited all the family problems. And now she worried that one of the men in her family, her husband or her brother, had murdered her mother in the belief that his money troubles would be solved.

"I . . . I can't pay you," said Paisley.

"I'm not a professional investigator. I've just been lucky a few times," I said.

"Sophie, I'm terrified."

"For your own safety?" I asked.

"A little bit, although I have no power over Mom's money, so even if one of them knocked me off, it wouldn't do him any good."

Wouldn't it? I wondered. If Paisley died, what would happen to her half of the estate? Would it go to her husband? Skip him and go to the children? Or did the trust provide for it to go to her brother? "Who gets your share if you die?" I asked.

"Frank, I would think." She buried her face in her hands and her breath came hard. "I don't know. I can't stand to even imagine what might happen to my children if I were to . . . not be there for them."

"Maybe you should ask your lawyer who inherits if you should die. What is it you want me to do?"

"Find out who murdered Mom. I have to know if it was one of them. I have to protect my boys."

"Paisley, if you truly believe that Frank might harm you or the children, then you need to tell the police and move out." I tried not to sound harsh, but she had to face that fact.

"I hope it doesn't come to that. I feel so guilty. How can I think for even a minute that my husband, the man I love, could have killed my mom? I'm so conflicted!"

There might be an easy way to know. She was probably his alibi. "Lark was murdered early in the morning. Where was Frank?"

Paisley gazed at me in horror. "He should have been asleep next to me, but I couldn't swear to that. I was asleep!"

"Are you a light sleeper? Would you have noticed if he slipped out and wasn't there?" I asked.

"I'm so tired every night. I make dinner, clean up, give all the kids their baths. Read them books, tuck them in, and then, even though I'm exhausted, I lie there awake unable to drift off, so I've been taking sleeping pills. I figure Frank would hear if one of the kids needed something."

"So you can't actually give him an alibi?"

"No. I honestly can't."

"Does Wolf know that?"

She froze. "No. And I don't want him to know."

"Paisley, you have to be honest with Wolf," I cautioned.

"But I don't know anything. I know it sounds like I hate Frank, but I don't. Quite the contrary. I love the guy! I've never met anyone like him. He's knowledgeable about so many things. He's brilliant and fascinating and he loves me more than I deserve."

And yet, she thought he could have murdered her mom. I supposed that being brilliant and fascinating didn't exclude also being ruthless, cruel, and immoral. Jails were probably full of brilliant and fascinating criminals. But I didn't see the point in mentioning that to her. She already knew it, or she wouldn't have paid me this visit.

"I'll see what I can find out. But you must promise me that you will take the boys and leave at the first sign of danger." It fell on deaf ears and it was too late anyway. I feared that the first signs had already played out.

Paisley thanked me profusely and left through my living room door. I watched as she walked through the backyard to the gate and closed it carefully behind her.

At times like these, it would have been nice to pick up the phone and call Alex German for legal information.

Since I had broken off our relationship, that wasn't an option. I went into my little home office and did some research online.

Much as I had thought, a spendthrift trust was to prevent someone from squandering an inheritance. Lark would have chosen a person or a bank to be the trustee, who would have the power to decide when and how much money would be parceled out to the beneficiaries.

Muppet and Daisy approached my desk, tails wagging. "*You* are a very good watchdog," I said to Muppet.

She wasn't much bigger than a cat. A white floof-ball with bright eyes that didn't miss a thing.

"I assume all this attention means it's time for a walk?" I raced upstairs and pulled on comfortable jeans and an oversized sweater. I flicked my hair back into a ponytail.

As far as I could tell, Nina and Mars still slept. I helped the dogs into harnesses, locked the front door behind us, and we strolled along the sidewalk. Daisy and Muppet wagged their tails and sniffed as though wonderful scents had been left there for them to find.

People in business attire hustled on their way to work. The sun was just coming up and I caught a few people stepping out of their front doors in bathrobes to pick up the morning papers that had been delivered.

No one lingered around the DIY tents. We had hired security guards to keep an eye on them, but I didn't see anyone, which troubled me.

Daisy, however, saw Mrs. McElhaney watering the flowers in a planter in front of her house, and pulled me in that direction.

"Good morning!" she sang. Curly white hair fluffed on her head. She had to be eighty or very close to it. She stuck her hand into a deep pocket on her gray sweater. "Who is your friend, Daisy?" She produced two treats and handed them to the dogs. No wonder Daisy had pulled me over to her.

"That's Muppet. She's up for adoption."

"Oh my," she cooed to Muppet. "If I were five years younger, I'd have snapped you up!"

"She's a great watchdog," I said, hoping she might change her mind.

Mrs. McElhaney scowled. "My children have called repeatedly to inform me that assisted living is like living on a cruise ship. Do you believe that?" Her violet eyes watched me carefully.

"Maybe a little bit," I said.

"Bah! You must think me as stupid as they do. I'm fine here in my home and that's where I intend to stay. Though I must say that Lark didn't help matters by going and getting herself killed. It was all over the newspaper and my children soon found out that Lark lived right across the street from me. I haven't heard the end of that yet."

"Why do you say she 'got herself killed?'" I asked.

"She had a gentleman friend. I saw him leaving the house that morning."

My breath caught in my throat. She was an eyewitness! "Did you tell the police?"

"I phoned them immediately. They had me come down to the station and look through photographs." She shook her head. "He wasn't in any of them. It was as though they didn't listen to me. He wasn't any ordinary thief or burglar. He was always well dressed and very polite."

"You spoke to him?" I gaped at her.

"On a regular basis. He always said, *Good morning*. He had exquisite manners. I never imagined that he would murder Lark."

"Who is he?"

"I never asked his name. He left her home most discreetly. I don't suppose many other people noticed him. But I did. I might be an old gal, but I see things and have my wits about me."

"What did he look like?" I asked.

"Very distinctive. I can show you a sketch if you'd like."

Chapter 10

Dear Natasha,
On our honeymoon, my husband and I went to
Paris. I took so many great photographs and I'd
love to put up a photo display over our sofa. How
do I go about doing that?
Parisian Memories in London, Kentucky

Dear Parisian Memories,
Select the photos you want to use. Matt and frame
them all exactly the same way. It's easiest if they
are all the same size. If they're not, lay them out on
the floor and rearrange them until you are happy
with the way they look. Then hang them.
Natasha

I had little hope that Mrs. McElhaney's sketch would re-
semble a living person. Still, it wouldn't hurt to look. "I
would love to see it."

She clapped her hands together, then picked up her watering can. "Do come in."

"May the dogs go inside?" I asked.

"Of course. My cat, Murphy, may not approve, but he'll get over it."

She led me into a narrow hallway, where she had wisely hung an oversized mirror to make it feel larger. We walked through a sweet living room, tidy, but with all the comforts of life. Magazines, remote control, books, a bottle of lotion. I could imagine her lounging on the chintz sofa in the evening. It matched the fabric of the curtains with large roses in various shades of red and pink. It felt like an English garden room.

A stunning still life painting of lush peonies in a blue and white vase hung over the fireplace. Other paintings adorned the walls, but the one that caught my eye was of a young bride. The top of her dress had a round neckline and short sleeves made of lace. At the waist, the lace gave way to satin and billowed out behind her. She wore short white gloves and a short veil attached to a floral tiara. The girl wore her hair up in a French twist and had a stunningly beautiful face.

"Is that you?" I asked.

"Hard to believe, isn't it? My husband insisted we hang it there. For many years I thought we should replace it with something else. It seemed sort of pompous to have a painting of myself hanging in the living room like I thought I was some kind of princess. But I don't get much company these days and I don't mind looking at my past anymore. It reminds me what a wonderful life I've had."

She continued to the kitchen, where all the cabinets were painted a soft green. Through French doors, I could see her garden and immediately knew where she spent her days. Unlike most people, she hadn't bothered to separate flowers from vegetables. It was a curious mix of blooms and vines, but it worked. Not a single weed dared invade.

"You have a lovely house and your garden is amazing!"

She was thanking me when we heard a yowl and a flash of fur shot to the top of a kitchen cabinet. Murphy the cat looked to be larger than Muppet. Long-haired and clearly annoyed, his tail hung over the cabinet swishing and twitching.

"Murphy! You be nice to our guests."

From deep inside his throat, he issued an angry murmur.

"May I offer you a cup of coffee?" she asked. "I had just put on a pot when I went out to water the plants. I'm afraid I haven't any croissants, though."

"Coffee would be nice, thank you," I said, taking a seat at a small table covered by a cloth in a purple and blue wisteria pattern.

Mrs. McElhaney brought sugar and a small pitcher of cream to the table. I looked around while she poured the coffee into Roy Kirkham fine china mugs with roses on them. I recognized his style immediately.

On the wall behind the kitchen table was a collection of framed pen-and-ink sketches of Old Town. They were incredibly precise and captured the quaint beauty. I squinted at the signature in the corner of one, *A. McElhaney*.

Mrs. McElhaney set the mugs on the table, along with spoons and crisp white napkins. "It's such fun to have a visitor," she said. She stirred the sugar in her tea. "Especially one who isn't extolling the virtues of assisted living." She winked at me.

"Who is the artist in your family?" I asked, gesturing at the sketches.

"I'm afraid it's me, dear. My children make fun of *mom's drawings*," she said snarkily with a smile. "I never appreciated my father's hobby of carving wood until I was an adult. One day, I hope they'll look at my drawings and be glad to have them. How we change as we go through life!" She sipped her tea and said, "I almost forgot the reason you came." She stood up and retrieved a sketchpad. "This is the man I saw coming out of Lark's house the morning she died." Mrs. McElhaney handed it to me.

I very nearly spilled my coffee.

Chapter 11

I knew that face.

Mrs. McElhaney had drawn a very becoming sketch. One nice enough to give to him as a gift. It couldn't be him. It just couldn't. I cleared my throat and asked her a question that would confirm or alleviate my fears. "What color is his hair?"

"Very faint blond, almost verging on white. You look shocked. Do you recognize him?" she asked.

Why couldn't she have said he had black hair? Or red, or brown? There was simply no mistaking him. It was my old friend Humphrey Brown.

Old friend didn't describe our relationship properly. He had gone to grade school and high school with Natasha and me. All that time, Humphrey had a childhood crush on me. Absorbed in my own childhood angst, I barely even noticed him. A few years ago, after my divorce, my mom took it upon herself to see that I remarried. To that end, she invited Humphrey to my house for Thanksgiving dinner. That celebration had been a nightmare from beginning to end with Wolf present and Mars carted off to the hospital after being poisoned.

In the beginning, Humphrey hoped to rekindle something that never existed. When he persisted, I tried to let him down gently and we eventually became friends.

Humphrey's most distinctive features were his pale hair and gaunt physique. Totally inept with women in a helpless sort of way, it didn't help that he was a mortician. His lack of confidence sometimes resulted in humorous behavior, but he certainly wasn't a killer.

I forced myself to admit that I knew him. "Your sketch is perfect," I said. "You must have seen him often."

"I don't like to gossip but I did see him on occasion. He slipped away early in the morning, mostly before dawn. If I hadn't been an early riser, I wouldn't have known that he visited Lark. What's his name?" she asked.

"Humphrey Brown," I replied.

"Humphrey. People don't name children Humphrey anymore, do they? I like that name. It conjures up a figure of authority for me. A distinguished, confident gentleman. Is he nice?"

"Very. I have trouble imagining that he killed her. To tell the truth, it's equally difficult to think that Lark and Humphrey were an item!"

"Lark was always very discreet. Her children are as bossy as mine. I don't know why they think they have to run our lives when we lose our husbands."

"Maybe they're being protective. They probably mean well."

"We don't lose our sensibility or judgment." A wan smile appeared on her face. "If I were engaged in a relationship with a gentleman, I don't believe I would tell my children, either. They'd probably try to run him off. Oh!" Her cheeks blazed. "What a fuss they would make!"

I tried to bring her back to Humphrey. "When you saw him on Monday morning, did he look upset or rushed?"

Mrs. McElhaney tilted her head and thought about it. "No. Not at all. If anything, he appeared shocked."

Was that worse than nervous or hurried? Would the police think he was regretful now that Lark was dead? Or had he seen her dead body after someone else killed her? "What time was it when you saw him?"

"Quite early. Five thirty, maybe. I had left my favorite trowel in the front planter and was retrieving it when I saw him."

"Did he leave through the side yard and the gate or by the front door?"

"I really don't know. I wasn't spying on them! And a lot of the tents were up, blocking my view."

"You're certain it was him?"

"Yes. He walked quite close to me."

"But he wasn't running?" I asked hopefully.

"Not at all. He was dressed quite nicely as though he was off to work. What does he do?"

"He works for a local mortuary."

She started in surprise. "I wouldn't have imagined that. An accountant or bookkeeper, I thought."

I finished my coffee. "I think I'd better go have a talk with Humphrey."

"I hope I didn't get him in trouble. Unless he killed Lark, of course."

In trouble? "Have you shared this sketch with the police?" I asked.

"Yes. That nice Detective Fleishman was very impressed and said they ought to hire me as a police artist to draw sketches for people who can remember the face of a criminal but can't draw."

She was as sweet and hospitable as a person could be and yet my blood ran cold. Wolf knew Humphrey. He would have recognized him immediately.

I thanked her again and tried not to appear to be running out the door. But when we were outside, the dogs and I walked home as fast as we could.

I barged into the kitchen and found Mars, Bernie, and Nina at the banquette. The aromas of bacon and coffee hung in the air. A platter of breakfast breads sat on the table. I said *good morning* and headed straight for the telephone.

"Where have you been?" asked Mars. "We were worried about you."

"I'll explain." I dialed Humphrey's number. "Please be there, please be there," I muttered.

Nina got up and darted toward me.

When Humphrey's answering machine came on, I panicked. He could be at work, I reasoned. I hoped the police hadn't taken him in for questioning. I dialed Wolf's cell phone, but Nina flicked her finger out and hit the plunger switch, disconnecting the call.

"Who are you calling?" she asked, a deep furrow in her brow.

"Wolf."

Behind her, at the island, Bernie said calmly in his British accent that made him sound very clever, "I don't think you want to do that."

I hung up the phone. "What's going on?"

Mars handed me a mug of English breakfast tea and a slice of bacon.

"Is this supposed to make me feel better? Because it didn't work. Now I'm highly suspicious."

Nina gasped and stared out the bay window. "Wolf just pulled up outside!"

"Oh good. I wanted to talk with him," I said. "But you so rudely disconnected my call."

At that exact moment, something crashed in the living room. I quickly inventoried the animals. Two dogs, one cat. "What was that?" I asked them.

I set down my mug and dashed into the living room, still clutching the slice of bacon. Nina was on my heels.

Chapter 12

Dear Natasha,
My evil mother-in-law gave me a set of plain white dishes. Apparently, she couldn't be bothered to read my gift registry. My husband refuses to let me throw them out. I'm very tempted to break a few so I won't have a full set and can ditch them. What do you think?

Miffed in Breakman, Ohio

Dear Miffed,
It was inconsiderate of her not to check your gift registry. Sell them on eBay and get something that you like.

Natasha

I stopped short when I saw Humphrey. Nina nearly ran into the back of me.

"Humphrey! What are you doing here?" I asked.

"There's no time for this," said Nina. "Wolf is already at the door. Humphrey, hide in Sophie's office. No one ever goes in there. Hurry!"

She hustled me back through the dining room, hissing, "Just go along with us and we'll explain everything later."

Wolf already stood in the kitchen when we returned.

We both said hello.

"Everything okay here, Sophie?" he asked. "I was in the neighborhood when my phone rang. Looked like the call came from your phone."

"Oh, sorry!" I mumbled, frantically trying to come up with an excuse. "I didn't realize it had gone through. Nina was telling us this hilarious story about why she was barefoot in the airport."

Wolf was no fool. He knew something was up. I tried to be calm. "I just came in from walking the dogs. Would you like to have breakfast? Nina and Mars made bacon and scrambled eggs."

Mars coughed. "Correction. Nina made the coffee. I did the cooking and Bernie contributed the breakfast breads."

I picked up a plate and filled it with bacon and eggs. I held it out to Wolf.

"I'll pass. Maybe some coffee."

Nina poured him a mug and we all sat down at the table.

"What were you calling about, Sophie?" asked Wolf.

Yikes! Now I was stuck. I scrambled for something that would sound vaguely plausible. "Bennett Bickford. Is it possible that he killed his mother for money?"

Wolf's shoulders relaxed. "I guess you heard that he's a gambler."

"Precisely," said Bernie. "Any chance he took a loan from an unsavory type and is under pressure to pay it back?"

"That's always a possibility but we don't have any evidence of that."

"Do you know where he was the morning Lark was murdered?" I asked.

Wolf gazed at me. I munched on a piece of bacon and tried my best to look unconcerned.

"He doesn't have an alibi if that's what you're getting at."

"Really? He's a suspect then?" That was the best news ever. If they focused on Bennett, it would let Humphrey off the hook.

"Do you know something about Bennett that you'd like to tell me?" Wolf asked.

I hadn't handled this conversation well. "You saw how eager he and Frank were to sell off poor Lark's belongings. I just found that oddly suspicious. Who does that? Only someone in dire need of money!"

"He's on our radar." Wolf rose, took a plate, and helped himself to the food on the stove after all.

Nina's eyebrows rose and her eyes grew large. Clearly, she wanted him to leave. But she managed to put on a fake happy face when he returned to the table.

Wolf sat down and sipped his coffee. "Nina, Lark was on the same tour as you, right?"

"Yes. Three weeks in Portugal."

"I imagine you had many opportunities to speak with Lark?"

"Heaven knows my husband wasn't available," she said in a snarky tone. "Lark, Dulci, and I spent a lot of time together," she said.

"Did Lark say anything to you that caused you concern?" asked Wolf.

"There were a few critical comments about her son-in-law, Frank. He thinks he's descended from a Portuguese king or something like that."

"That bothered her?" asked Wolf.

"No. She didn't believe it. She was worried about Paisley because she's under so much stress and Frank doesn't do his share. Apparently, he spends a lot of time and money on his claim to royalty and Lark thought he ought to concentrate more on providing for his family. Paisley works an online job, and renovates furniture, while doing the lion's share of the childcare. Lark wanted Frank to spend more time working to support his family, royalty or not."

"Was she afraid of Frank?" he asked.

"If she was, she didn't tell me. After that guy tried to break into my house, I thought back about our trip. I hoped Lark had said something that I would understand differently in retrospect. But she seemed very content."

Wolf finished his eggs. "You said you thought about it after the guy tried to break into your house. Do you think he is the same person who murdered Lark?"

"Well, sure! Statistically speaking, the odds of my intruder being someone else are rather low. Why wouldn't he break into Bernie's mansion or Natasha's fancy house? Why choose mine?" Nina sounded angry.

"Did Lark visit any of Frank's relatives in Portugal?" asked Wolf.

"Not that I'm aware of. What an odd question. Do you think one of them followed us back to Old Town and murdered her? That seems unlikely. Even if that had happened, what would he want from me?"

Wolf shrugged and wiped his mouth with a napkin. "Did Lark take a day off from sightseeing when you were in Portugal?"

"We had some free days to do what we wanted. I know Lark went to the beach and did some shopping. I was the one who ran out of patience with those bus tours and bailed on them."

"Thanks for breakfast. Nina, if you think of anything, even if it's insignificant, please let me know." Wolf rose and walked to the door.

When it shut behind him, Nina jumped up and pretended to be pouring coffee, but it didn't take a genius to realize that she was actually looking out the window watching for his car to leave. "Thank heaven he's gone. Humphrey! You can come out now!"

Humphrey emerged from the foyer, glancing around to be sure Wolf was gone. He had filled out a little and it suited him. His face was slightly less angular, his chin rounder. He was still on the slender side, but the extra pounds looked good on him.

I stood and gave him a hug.

"Thanks for hiding me."

"Is Wolf looking for you?" I asked.

"Apparently." Humphrey sank into one of the chairs by the fireplace. "He went to the funeral home and asked for me. It's only a matter of time."

Nina and I exchanged glances. I suspected I knew more than they did. I tried to make him comfortable. "You're safe here with us. Have you had breakfast?"

He shook his head. "I can't eat."

"Oh, Humphrey," I said softly. At Mrs. McElhaney's I had been convinced there must be some mistake, but now I was beginning to wonder.

He burst into tears and buried his face in his hands.

Fear clutched at me. He'd killed her. Humphrey had murdered Lark. Instead of comforting him, I found myself taking a step back. This was a Humphrey that I didn't know.

Nina handed him tissues and said, "You have to eat. You'll only feel worse if you don't. Sophie could make you a three-minute egg. And some toast. Will you try to eat it?"

He sobbed louder. I forced myself to pat him on the back but that didn't seem to comfort him. I put on the kettle and prepared a cup of hot tea with lots of sugar and milk.

"Drink this," I said.

The milk had cooled the tea enough to drink it. And he did. Hungrily, he downed the entire mug.

I boiled a couple of eggs for him and Mars took care of the toast.

Humphrey came to the table and ate while we watched. His pale eyes were rimmed in red. Wine-colored blotches blazed on his cheeks. I couldn't imagine how such a gentle and relatively weak guy could have killed anyone.

When he finished eating, I asked, "Were you seeing Lark?"

He nodded, his Adam's apple jerking up and down.

Bernie's mouth dropped open and Nina huffed, "And you didn't tell us?"

"Lark insisted we keep it quiet. She didn't want her children to know. Have you met them? They expected her to be chaste and devote herself to their father's memory." His mouth twisted to the side. "At first, I was uncomfortable about it, but as time went on, it became sort of fun. We were living this wonderful secret life, and no one knew about it."

"How could you possibly have kept it a secret?" shrieked Nina.

"Mostly we stayed home at her place. I would go over after dark and leave in the morning before people were up and about. It wasn't as hard as you'd think. No one knew."

"Mrs. McElhaney knew," I said softly.

Humphrey scowled. "So that's how Wolf found out. And I thought she was such a nice lady."

I tried to find a way to ask if he had been involved in Lark's death. I finally settled on a simple, "What happened?"

"I don't know."

"You blacked out?" asked Mars. "That might be a defense."

"No! When I left Lark's house that morning, she was fine. We got up and dressed like usual. She was planning to give some gifts to her daughter and grandsons. She had lots of laundry to do, that sort of thing. It was a perfectly ordinary day."

"Then why are you hiding from Wolf? asked Nina.

Chapter 13

Dear Sophie,
My life is chaos. Between the kids and my hus-
band, I can't keep track of anything. Bills to pay,
permission slips that need signing, not to mention
my car keys! They're always lost, and I waste
hours looking for them.
                    Need Help in Messmore, Pennsylvania

Dear Need Help,
You need a home command center! They're so easy
to make. With a blank wall and a few inexpensive
items, you'll be more organized. Start with a calen-
dar that is large enough to write on so you won't
miss appointments. Add a clock, a grocery shop-
ping pad, a key hanging strip, a basket for permis-
sion slips and another for bills. A chalkboard is
helpful, too. Mount everything on the wall and put
a frame around it. Now it's all at your fingertips.
                                        Sophie

"Because I knew it wouldn't look good. They're going to arrest me." Humphrey reached into his pocket and pulled out a tiny velvet box. He flipped the top open to reveal an engagement ring. A stunning square diamond sat in platinum prongs. On each side, three smaller square diamonds were embedded in the band, decreasing in size.

For a long moment, no one said a word.

Mars finally asked, "You chickened out and didn't propose?"

"Worse than that," Humphrey moaned. "She turned me down."

"Humphrey," I said gently, "I'm so sorry."

"I missed her so much while she was away. For three weeks I thought of little else. I bought the ring and planned how I would propose. Romantic, but not corny. She was exhausted from her trip. It was a mistake, but I was so excited. She fell asleep while I was pouring champagne, so I waited until morning. She woke early because of jet lag and the time difference, I guess. While she showered and dressed, I made coffee and brought it upstairs to her. It was wrong. I shouldn't have done it that way. She said, 'Oh Humphrey, I'm so *flattered.*'"

Mars winced.

"Flattered! As though I had told her she was wearing a pretty dress, or her hair looked great. She closed the box and handed it back to me, saying, 'I can't.' I felt like I was twelve years old and had misread the intentions of a girl who had been sending me notes in class."

Nina patted his hand. "What did you do?"

I got to my feet and stumbled down the stairs and out the door. I didn't even say goodbye. I couldn't bring myself to speak. It was all I could do to put one foot in front of the other and keep going like I was in a daze. That was the last time I saw her. Now I'll never be able to . . ."

Nina withdrew her hand and said, "To what?"

"To ask her why she declined. To tell her that I love her. To change and be whatever she wanted me to be. But now I'll never get a second chance." He bit his upper lip and avoided our eyes. "Maybe I never would have seen her again anyway. Maybe she would have dodged me."

I felt terrible for Humphrey and barely knew what to say. He had looked for a girlfriend for so very long. If Mrs. McElhaney could be believed, Humphrey and Lark had been seeing each other for months. Of course, marriage was a different matter entirely. Who knew why she turned him down? And now that someone had killed Lark, Humphrey would go through the rest of his life wondering what went wrong.

"You see the problem, don't you?" asked Humphrey. "Besides her killer, I was probably the last one to see Lark alive. My fingerprints are all over the house. I can't prove my relationship with Lark because we kept it secret. Either the police will think I didn't have a relationship with Lark and that I killed her or that I murdered her because she turned me down when I proposed. Either way, they're going to think I killed her."

We sat silently. He was right.

I reached for a pad of paper and a pen. Drawing a circle with a dot in it, I asked Humphrey, "Does this mean anything to you?"

They all stretched and craned their necks to see it.

Nina said, "It looks like the Target logo. The circle and dot in theirs are thicker, though."

Mars laughed. "It's just like you to see a symbol for shopping! What is it supposed to be, Sophie?"

I didn't want to say yet. Maybe it would mean something to Humphrey, and I didn't want to throw him off. I watched his expression, but it didn't change. I had hoped that it was some sort of signal between Humphrey and Lark.

Maybe I had gotten it wrong. I took out my phone and found the photo I had taken. I showed it to Humphrey, and everyone else leaned in for a look.

"Lark drew this in the mulch," I explained. And that was all I said, though I was wondering if perhaps it was actually a G or something else that I hadn't seen in it yet.

Humphrey shook his head and buried his face in his hands.

Nina snatched the phone. "Are you sure it's a complete circle?"

"It represents the sun," said Bernie.

Mars raised an eyebrow and looked at him doubtfully. "Right."

"Seriously. It means *sun* in hieroglyphics," protested Bernie.

Nina glared at the two of them. "Really? Like Lark happened to know hieroglyphics and her last word was a symbol that only an Egyptologist would recognize? Target was a better guess than that."

Mars gently touched Humphrey's arm. "Any chance that Lark might know something about hieroglyphics?"

"Not that she ever told me," said Humphrey.

Mars sucked in air. "It means *the end*."

"That's not even remotely funny," I said.

Mars seemed surprised. "I'm not being funny. In Scouting, a dot in a circle means *end of the trail. Gone home*."

For probably the first time in our lives, we sat in complete stunned silence.

Bernie was first to speak. "Unless she was a scoutmaster, I'd say it was highly unlikely she would have taken her last moments to draw that symbol. It has to mean something else."

"Humphrey," I said softly, "please give this some thought. You were so close to Lark. Maybe you can figure out what she meant to tell us."

"And maybe you should talk to Wolf and explain everything to him before they take you in for questioning," suggested Bernie.

"I had the same thought," said Mars.

"But not without Alex German," said Nina.

It was my turn to wince. I still hadn't run into Alex since the day I broke off our relationship. Old Town wasn't huge, but it was big enough to avoid someone if you made an effort. Alex's turf was his office and the courthouse, places I didn't go often anyway, so that had been easy. But I would never stand in Humphrey's way just because of a little embarrassment to me. Alex was the best criminal attorney in Old Town, and we all knew it. "You'd better call him now before someone else is accused, too, and snaps him up first."

I held out my hand for his cell phone and dialed Alex's number for him.

We listened to Humphrey's end of the conversation. When he hung up, Humphrey was paler than normal. "He said he'd been expecting my call."

"Either someone else saw you, they have the fingerprint results back, or Mrs. McElhaney is a bigmouth," said Mars. "Is he coming here?"

Humphrey nodded. "This afternoon. I hope that's okay."

Nina smirked a little. "You're finally going to have to face him, Sophie."

"Actually, I'm not. I have the DIY Festival to take care of and I'm already running late."

Nina gasped, "I forgot all about that! I promised to go to Paisley's tent."

I rose from my seat and headed upstairs to shower and dress.

I confess that even though I was running late, I took a little extra time with my makeup and attire. I had no interest in getting back together with Alex. None whatsoever. But everyone wants to look good when they run into an ex. There's just that awful and probably really wrong hope of sparking a tiny hint of regret. I was the one who broke it off, but that fact didn't diminish the desire to look my best. I pulled on black jeans and a black V-neck top to appear thinner, a cropped black jacket with white threads running through it, and a chunky gold link necklace. I added bold gold earrings.

I hurried back down the stairs. Mars whistled at me.

"Very funny. Where are Nina and Bernie?"

"She went home to dress."

"She wasn't afraid to go home by herself?" I asked.

"Bernie went with her. They took Muppet and Daisy, as well as the Taser I gave you. After being away for so long, I think she really wants to get back to normal in her own home as soon as she can," said Mars.

"I can't blame her." I grabbed my purse and clipboard. "Good luck with Alex," I said to Humphrey on my way out the door.

I had barely approached the tents when several people rushed toward me. They waited politely in line while I took care of their problems. Fortunately, most of them were minor, until Greer Shacklesworth pulled me aside.

"Sophie, it's not like me to complain," she said.

Did she always begin that way? Was she under the impression that declaring she didn't complain somehow negated the fact that she *was* complaining? I smiled as sweetly as I could.

"The people in the tent next to mine have plastic coverings on their tables."

I blinked at her. Was she kidding? Judging from her expression, I was fairly certain that she was serious. "Maybe they're doing something messy and need a surface that's easy to clean."

"It looks trashy. And that's not all," she continued. "They're eating something made with garlic. I know now why it keeps vampires away. It keeps buyers away, too."

I tilted my head and made no secret of how ridiculous I thought her complaints were. "There are no rules against plastic on the tables or against eating garlic." I was sorely tempted to suggest that she worry more about herself and butt out of everyone else's business. Instead I checked my watch. "So sorry. I have to run."

In general, I don't like to make enemies, especially over something so utterly ridiculous. But when I left Greer, I suspected she would not be eager to help me if I was in a pickle.

I headed for Market Square, passing Paisley's tent on the way. Nina waved at me, but I could tell she was excited about a very pregnant lady who was looking at one of Paisley's adorable rocking chairs.

Dulci Chapman was scheduled next in the demonstration tent. She grabbed my arm as soon as I walked up to her.

"Can you help me move all this stuff into the tent as soon as Mr. How-to-install-a-toilet finishes? Emery promised to be here to give me a hand, but he hasn't shown up yet."

"Sure, no problem."

Furrows formed on Dulci's forehead. "I'm a little worried. This isn't at all like Emery. He's not answering his phone, either."

"He probably got hung up at work," I said.

"He's a pathologist. It's not like he gets a lot of emergencies," she said drolly.

Her phone rang just as the applause began for Mr. How-to-install-a-toilet.

While she talked, I carried a clock, a framed calendar, a chalkboard, a framed list of emergency and neighbor phone numbers, and a shopping list pad under the tent.

Dulci was still on the phone, but she managed to haul a couple of wire baskets and a key holder rack inside. After thanking someone, she disconnected the call. "No one knows where he is!"

She straightened her shoulders, took a deep breath, and walked out in front of her audience. I had to give Dulci credit, even though she was worried about her husband, she didn't show it. I doubted that even one person in her sizable audience would have guessed that she had a problem. She discussed the various items people might need in a home control center, then demonstrated how she goes about mounting each item on the wall.

I had places where I kept things, but I loved the idea of everything being in one spot and out of the way, yet visible at a glance. No more pawing through junk drawers or piles of mail. It was pure genius.

About halfway through, her husband, Dr. Emery Chapman, showed up, puffing like he'd run all the way to Market Square. He was a large man, tall and broad-shouldered with a significant belly that hung over the belt of his low-slung trousers. His round head was bald on top. The traditional horseshoe of hair in the back and on the sides was cut short and beginning to gray. Sweat peppered his brow and his complexion was an unhealthy ruddy shade. "Hello, Sophie. Terrible business about Lark."

He'd heard, of course. Everyone had. But he'd also been on the trip with Lark and he was a local pathologist. I assumed unusual deaths like Lark's were quietly discussed in pathology offices.

"It's just awful," I agreed. "Do you need to sit down?"

He pulled a handkerchief out of his pocket and wiped his forehead. "No, no. I'll be all right. I got held up at the hospital. You know how it is when you're hurrying to get someplace. Everyone stops to ask you something that could have waited until later."

"I love this home command center idea," I whispered.

He gave me a sideways glance that indicated he was not overly fond of it. "Umm," he grunted. "Dulci is very organized. I don't dare step out of line." He smiled at me when he said it.

When Dulci finished, Emery and I helped her gather her items. But members of her audience gathered around her, asking questions. I overheard several people ask what she would charge to install a home command center for them.

"Sounds like Dulci might have a new business," I said to Emery.

"I never imagined that. It's so simple, just hang everything on the wall." He squinted at the crowd around her in wonder.

"I'm glad we have a minute to talk," I said. "I was wondering if you picked up on anything unusual about Lark on your trip."

"Dulci and I have discussed that. I wish we had. If only she had confided in us, let us know if she was in some kind of trouble. We really didn't notice anything out of the ordinary. She was polite and cheerful." He shrugged.

"Did she talk about her children?" I asked.

His eyebrows shot up. "Yes, of course. You can't get a group of parents together without discussing children. Are they suspects?"

How to answer that? "I don't think so, but I don't really know."

"She's very proud of them," he said, "and of her six

grandchildren, as you might imagine. She did say she worried about her daughter. It must be rough raising so many small children at once. I remember joking that her daughter needed Dulci because she would have the little ones scheduled down to the minute. We could tell Lark was used to handling babies when one was thrown at her."

Chapter 14

Dear Sophie,
I have an ordinary navy-blue lamp that works fine and is a great size. But it doesn't fit our décor and Hubby thinks it should go. I'm sort of sentimental about it, but that blue is so bold! It looks like it came from the 70s, which it did.
                    Stuck in the 70s in Blue Canyon, California

Dear Stuck in the 70s,
Paint it a neutral color like gray, cream, black, or gold, whatever fits your décor. Then buy a crystal finial for it. Hubby won't even recognize it anymore and you'll have a new lamp for next to nothing!
                                              Sophie

"Thrown?" I gasped in horror. "Why would anyone throw a baby? Was it all right?"

"On the morning of our departure, we were all lining up outside of our hotel to board the bus for the airport. You know how it is, the bellmen are bringing down everyone's luggage and people are buying last-minute gifts. A sickly looking woman in rather shabby clothes ambled toward us, carrying a baby. I expected her to ask for money, but she shocked the entire group by tossing her baby at us and taking off at a clip that let us know she was not at all ill. Of course, everyone's attention was on the baby and the woman who had abandoned it."

He cleared his throat. "I thought she hoped one of us might take it home. Maybe she couldn't afford to feed it and believed it would have a better life elsewhere. All these notions just bombard you when something so odd happens. Well, it was Lark who caught the baby. She just stepped forward and reached out and that baby flew right into her arms. I've never seen anything like it. In fact, I remember wondering at the time if the woman had targeted Lark. A couple of the men in our group ran after the woman, but she disappeared fast."

"What did you do with the baby?"

"It was a doll."

"A doll? Why would anyone do that?"

"Apparently, it's a common scam. A woman who looks somewhat ragged throws the doll at a group of tourists. The tourists think she has thrown a baby and they all rush to catch it. Meanwhile, she has an accomplice in the crowd who steals unattended purses and bags."

"That's awful. Were any purses missing?"

"Luckily not. I think something went wrong. Maybe the accomplice was waylaid. Thankfully, their scam didn't work. But it was Lark who caught that baby when it flew through the air. Everyone talked about it on the flight home. What a way to end our trip!"

"I'll say! I'll have to tell Paisley about it. Did you notice Lark with anyone who wasn't on the tour?"

"You should ask Dulci. She spent more time with Lark. While they were out touring on the bus, I was attending the symposium where Nina's husband spoke."

"Did anyone take a special interest in her?" I asked.

"Peter Chryssos often ate meals with her. They were the only two in our group traveling without spouses, so I don't think one can read anything special into that."

Dulci joined us, beaming and bursting with energy. "Look at all these requests I have. One woman said I'm like Alexandria's Joanna Gaines! I consider that a compliment of the highest order. How much do you think I should charge?"

I had no idea. "How long does it take you to set one up?"

"There's an idea," said Emery. "Do it by the hour."

"I think I'd rather set a fee," mused Dulci.

I congratulated her on her success and excused myself.

As I walked away, Dulci called my name. She bounded after me, even though she was wearing high heels. I would have fallen flat on my face.

"I know how busy you are with the festival, and it's going so well! But would you have time to stop by, maybe for coffee tomorrow morning?" She turned and looked at her husband, "After seven?"

"Sure. Is everything okay?"

Dulci chewed on her lower lip. "I'm not sure."

"I usually walk the dogs in the morning. We could meet for coffee on the waterfront."

"I'd rather talk at my house, if that's okay. Bring the dogs with you. Come to the side door, through the gate. I'll see you then!"

I watched her run back to her husband. How did she do that without falling? When I turned around, I quickly changed my planned route because I spied Greer looking my way. She undoubtedly had another complaint to register. Now that she was out of her tent, I headed directly there to see exactly what she was selling that she thought was so much better than anyone else's.

A young woman sat in Greer's tent, intently studying her phone. I was so stunned by what I saw that I double-checked my list to make sure I had the right place. Sure enough, it belonged to Greer. She was turning everything gold. And I mean everything. A white platter showed off golden Oreo cookies. Only the white in the middles had been spared gold spray. A small sign next to them said in an ornate script, EDIBLE!

There were gold action figures, gold picture frames, gold keychains, and a gigantic gold mantel. I had to admit that the before-and-after gold-colored jewelry was impressive. The silver bracelet that demonstrated how it looked *before* was tarnished so badly it looked like it had been in a fire. But the identical bracelet next to it gleamed like it was brand-new, except it was no longer silver. It was gold. I would have sworn it was the real thing. Next to it were assorted bracelets for sale, including ones with coin charms like the one Greer had been wearing.

For those who didn't want their homes looking like Midas had decorated it, she offered a selection of modern shelves, lamps, clocks, and dishes with a simple, but trendy streak of gold. I did a double take as I walked out. Had that really been a gold dishwasher? I went back to check. It was!

I liked gold. But for the first time in my life, I realized that a little bit went a long way.

At two in the afternoon, I wanted to check on Mochie and the dogs. And I needed a little break for lunch, but I was worried that Alex might be at my house. And then, in a moment of total panic, I realized I hadn't arranged for anything to serve Alex when he came to talk to Humphrey. I had been so busy with the DIY Festival that I hadn't baked a thing.

There hadn't been a reason to bake, of course. I hadn't anticipated houseguests, or meetings with lawyers, or the possibility I would be hiding fugitives from the law.

I stopped in the middle of the sidewalk, doing a mental inventory of my freezer. We had finished my supply of chocolate chip cookies the night Nina had an intruder. But I was fairly certain I had some bourbon blondies with chocolate chips just waiting to be thawed. I realized suddenly that I was blocking the sidewalk, so I stepped aside, next to a show window, and pulled out my phone. I texted Mars: Please take bourbon blondies out of the freezer to thaw. Serve with coffee when Alex comes.

No sooner had I pressed the arrow to send the text than I felt someone standing in front of me. I looked up from my phone. It was Alex. I could feel a flush of red rushing into my face and hoped my makeup would hide it, but I didn't think I would be that lucky.

"Hi, Sophie." He leaned over to kiss me on the cheek.

I was startled at first, but then I thought maybe that was a good sign. If he was angry with me for the way I abruptly broke up with him, he probably wouldn't have kissed me. "Alex!" I smiled, a little unsure of just how this would go. "You look great!"

That wasn't just empty flattery. The last time I had seen him, he had been released from the hospital and was recovering from a nasty beating and broken bones. I felt a twinge of guilt. It wasn't as though *I* had beaten him, but he probably wouldn't have gone through that if I hadn't insisted on delving into a crime that had already been solved. To my credit they *had* convicted the wrong person, but Alex had warned me to stop pursuing the case. He had every right to hate me.

"Good as new, well, mostly," he said.

He'd been in the military and it had showed in his posture, the way he wore his hair, and even extended to his rather bland choices in the way he dressed. He'd let his hair grow out. Not a lot, just enough to see some waves and a few curls at the nape of his neck. He seemed softer somehow.

"I like your hair," I said.

Self-consciously, he ran his fingers through the loose curls. "I, uh, had a lot of time to think when I was recuperating. It sort of reset my way of thinking. My assistant says I'm not as rigid anymore, that it took a good knock to the head for me to learn to go with the flow. I guess that means it wasn't all bad."

It was unbelievably awkward even though Alex was being very sweet. "I'm sorry," I said. "I'm so sorry."

He nodded. "I'm heading over to your house right now to speak with Humphrey."

"I think he's going to need you."

Alex took a deep breath. "I expected he would. Good seeing you, Sophie."

I tried not to show the relief I felt that the horrible first encounter was over. I wanted to tell him to remind Mars to put out the blondies and serve the coffee, and I wanted to beg his forgiveness for having caused him to be in a coma and beaten to a pulp. So I said, "Good seeing you, too, Alex."

He managed a wan smile and walked away.

Only then, as I watched him grow smaller and disappear among the people on the sidewalk, did it occur to me that he was doing it again! What had he said? He *expected* Humphrey would need him. Why? How? Alex German knew something! It had to involve Lark. No, no, no. I was not going to let him hold some kind of confidence again. Did he know who murdered her?

I had been so upset about facing him that the tips on my

ears still burned. The festival could roll on without me for an hour.

I hurried down the street, planning to go home, and realized that it wasn't my day. Greer was heading straight toward me. There was an unmistakable glint of determination in her eyes. I forced a smile at her.

She did not smile back. She came at me with fury. "You know I never complain about anything. It's just not me. I believe in live and let live. But Natasha is putting on a show in her tent that's blocking traffic and distracting everyone."

Natasha had a tendency to try to steal the show, so I couldn't say that came as a surprise. I gazed at Greer for a moment. She was as beautiful as Natasha. A different type with her blond hair and upscale casual look that seemed as though she'd just thrown it on, but everyone knew she had carefully pieced it together. Could she be competing with Natasha for something?

"Then why don't you do the same? Show people how you dye everything gold?"

She looked as though I had slapped her. "I don't dye," she said snottily.

"Sorry." I wasn't, but it was the polite thing to say. "I'll go check on Natasha." I glanced at my watch on the way. I was going to miss Alex's discussion with Humphrey.

Greer was right about one thing, there was a huge group of people clustered around Natasha's tent. She had decorated one side with beautiful summer baskets, wreaths, and garlands. The other side featured Christmas. She couldn't have wedged in one more ornament. Although the clutter was overwhelming, I had to hand it to her. There was DIY eye candy from the bottom of her tent to the very top where a chandelier was decorated for Christmas.

In the front, she had set up a table, and was demonstrating how to make a wreath. Her half-sister worked be-hind her, selling people decorative items that filled the tent.

I watched as she explained which ribbons and glues to use.

Suddenly, panicked screaming began.

Chapter 15

Dear Natasha,
My eight-year-old daughter has her heart set on a
fancy princess bed with drapes on it, for heaven's
sake. I don't know where she gets these ideas.
There's no way we can spend that kind of money
on a canopy bed that won't be cool enough for her
in a few years. Suggestions?
Not a Queen but the Princess's Mom in Palace
Garden, Rhode Island

Dear Not a Queen but the Princess's Mom,
There's a very easy solution. Mount drapery rods
on the ceiling around the bed using ceiling curtain
brackets. Hang inexpensive gauzy drapes that she
can open and close!

Natasha

The screams were a pitch only small children can manage. The kind that drills right into your brain.

People backed away, revealing that Oscar had managed to glue himself to no fewer than three of his brothers.

They all squealed and desperately tried to tug away in every direction, which only resulted in more screams and anguished crying.

I had no idea how to move four little boys in the same direction, when they were glued to one another in such an awkward way. "Would someone please go get Paisley?" I shouted.

Thankfully, one of the vendors showed up with a cart. Four of us lifted on the count of three and placed them into it. We rolled them to Paisley, who finally heard their screams for Mommy as we approached.

"Oscar! What have you done now?" Paisley asked.

"He glued us together," cried one of the boys.

"Give it to me right now." Paisley held out her hand.

Oscar held the glue in his hands against his right cheek. It was a cyanoacrylate type of immediate glue just like the ones Natasha had been using in her demonstration. Paisley tried to take it from him, but it was glued not only to his right hand and his left, but also to his face. He had stopped screaming but his brothers continued to screech as they frantically tried to separate themselves from one another.

Fortunately, someone had called the EMTs. The boys stopped crying and stared wide-eyed the minute they saw the EMTs in their big yellow gear, clonking along in heavy boots.

It made me smile. I assumed they would be fine and now they were having the experience of a lifetime. They were being rescued by heroes. The crowd actually broke out in applause, something EMTs never got but richly deserved.

Dr. Chryssos arrived on the run. He raised his hand in a wave but got right to work on the boys. I could hear him asking them who their favorite superhero was.

That resolved, I walked back toward Natasha's tent.

The one next to her belonged to the mother of her half-sister. Like Natasha's mother, she was a free spirit who believed in the power of stones and potions. I was pleasantly surprised by the beauty of her creations. In fact, so much so that I bought a lamp made out of amethyst geode crystals on the spot.

While she wrapped it up, I admired the quality of the items she carried. She had the ubiquitous salt lamps and chunks of minerals said to bring luck and cure ills. But there were also tall golden obelisks lighted from underneath, drawer handles embedded with glistening white quartz, and stunning slices of rich blue agate with a touch of gold leaf on the edges that were framed as art.

"I'll keep the lamp for you until you finish up here. You chose the right thing, honey. It will bring tranquility and calm to your home. You could use that."

"How are things going with Natasha?" I asked.

She lowered her voice. "She has money issues. Bless her, she hasn't charged us a penny for staying in the apartment over her garage, but it's time for us to carry our own weight. That's one reason I was excited about this festival. I've had enough orders that I think I might be able to open a little shop. Rents are high in Old Town, but the shabbier the place, the better. I love quirky old buildings. We'll be looking for an apartment, too, so if you hear of anything, let me know. Natasha had a Realtor come by to look at the place, a Cal Bickford. I remember the name because it's the same as the lady who died."

"He's her brother-in-law."

"Small world, isn't it?"

A couple entered the tent and we could hear the wife exclaiming about the blue agate. I whispered, "Good luck!" and got out of the way.

I checked my watch. I had most certainly missed the discussion between Humphrey and Alex.

The rest of the afternoon passed without crisis. I was relieved to go home at six. The days were getting longer and the air felt light and summery. On my way, I passed Lark's house. Paisley was still there, shutting down for the evening.

"How are the boys?" I asked.

She gave me a grim look. "You'd think nothing had happened to them. They were so thrilled with the EMTs that the four who were stuck together now want to be EMTs when they grow up."

"It's amazing how resilient children are. How is Thomas doing? It must have been hard on him to find his grandmother dead."

"He's been very quiet about it, which worries me. I'm glad Bennett is around. He's great with the kids. I've asked him to feel out Thomas."

"Let me know if I can be of any help." I collected my new lamp and hurried home, ready to sit down with a cup of hot tea and relax.

Mars opened the kitchen door for me when I arrived. Nina held out a bowl of spring sugar snap peas. "We needed a pre-dinner nosh and these are so good!" she said.

Daisy and Muppet ran to me and demanded attention. I set the lamp down and obliged them.

I sniffed the air. "Something smells wonderful!"

"Francie made lasagna," said Nina. "It's just about ready."

"Francie? She very rarely cooks," I said. "What's the occasion?"

Mars laughed. "She wanted to hear what went down between Alex and Humphrey. She was hilarious, trying to listen in while pretending she was cooking."

"She'll be back any minute," said Humphrey.

"So what happened?" I asked, dying to hear about it.

"We'll tell you over dinner," said Mars.

I went upstairs and changed into soft old khakis and an oversized white blouse. I rolled the sleeves back and laughed when I looked in the mirror. Greer had been so elegant. I looked like I'd been cleaning house! I swapped the shirt for a V-necked cotton sweater and looked more like myself.

I padded downstairs in my bare feet, ready to eat lasagna.

Nina threw a cream and blue tablecloth on the table, and I set out blue earthenware plates with a rustic country pattern around the edges. Mars poured wine into handblown Italian wineglasses in faint shades of blue, green, and gold. Humphrey set a salad bowl and a loaf of French bread on the table. Slices had been partially cut into the bread to insert garlic and butter to flavor it while it baked. The scent was heavenly.

I retrieved rustic wood candlesticks in a cream color and was lighting them when Francie arrived. She didn't bother knocking. She walked right in, her golden retriever, Duke, leading the way.

We fed the dogs and Mochie, then sat down to eat.

"Well?" I asked. "What did Alex say?"

Humphrey took a deep breath. "I am the trustee of a spendthrift trust for Lark's children."

Of all the things in the world that he could have said, I never would have expected that.

"I can turn it down, of course, but I won't. I'm"—he paused for a moment, like he needed to pull himself together—"comforted that she thought so much of me."

I was glad in a way. It made up, at least a little bit, for turning down his marriage proposal. Whatever her reason had been, it wasn't that she didn't trust him or think highly of him.

"I understand her children are quite upset by this turn

of events," he said. "The daughter's husband was on the verge of filing a challenge to the will and the trust, but the will contains a provision that anyone who files a challenge will be excluded from the will. Apparently, that stopped the husband in his tracks."

Frank had been busy. "Paisley and Bennett seem very nice," I said. "Once they get over the shock, maybe they'll come around and be cooperative about it."

"I'm meeting with them tomorrow at Alex's office," said Humphrey. "I dread it. I expect they'll be angry. Alex said to brace myself and to remember that I didn't set this up. I didn't even know about it. They should direct their anger at Lark, not at me."

Francie sipped her wine. "I think it was brilliant of Lark. That husband of Paisley's would have run through her money before she knew what hit her. And worse, if she had the moxie to divorce him, he probably would have gotten half her money. Lark knew what she was doing."

"I wish she had talked with me about it," said Humphrey.

"You can still get out of it," said Mars.

"It's not that, I'm happy to do it. It's the last thing I *can* do for Lark. But I would have liked to know what she expected. You know, how generous she wanted to be and under what circumstances."

"Maybe she planned to speak with you about it," I said. "I'm sure she didn't expect to die when she did."

It was the wrong thing to say. Everyone fell silent until Francie asked, "What do we know about her death anyway?"

"Maybe we shouldn't talk about that right now," Nina said, gesturing toward Humphrey with her head. "This is delicious, Francie! I had no idea that you could cook."

"It's nothing. I haven't made lasagna in years. It was

one of my husband's favorites. There was a time when I could make it while wearing a blindfold with my hands tied behind my back."

"You really ought to enter it in a local cooking competition." Nina reached for another slice of the bread. "I bet you would win!"

"If I thought I could beat Natasha, I'd do it just to put her in her place for once."

"It's all right, Nina," said Humphrey. "I'd like to talk about Lark. No one wants to catch her killer more than I do."

"We don't have much to go on," I said. "The killer tried to make it look like an accident. But wasn't successful."

"He or she was probably in a hurry." Humphrey pulled a sheet of paper from his pocket. "We know the crime was committed after I left. Dawn was at five forty-three. It was still dark when I left so it must have been around five in the morning. What time did you find her, Sophie?"

"I wish I had checked my watch. Dawn was breaking when I left the house, but I bought a coffee and a Puppucini first. And then I checked the inside of Lark's house when she didn't answer the door. It was probably eight o'clock or so. But Frank, Paisley, and the kids had been there for a while and they would certainly have noticed someone coming out the gate or the front door of Lark's house."

Humphrey's fork clanked as it fell on his plate. "If I had only gone back. Her killer arrived in the dark, knocked on the door, and Lark opened it, expecting me. If I had gone back, she would be alive." He touched the fingers of his right hand to his forehead, covering his face.

"Or you would both be dead," said Mars.

"Mars!" I scolded.

"It's true. Humphrey wouldn't have expected to find a

murderer in Lark's house. He wouldn't have been armed or prepared in any way. He would be dead today, too, if he had gone back."

Humphrey dabbed at his eyes with a tissue. "Mars is right. I wouldn't have been of any help to Lark."

In an effort to change the subject at least a little bit, I asked, "What did Alex say about Wolf looking for you?"

"He called and set up an appointment with Wolf. We're meeting with him tomorrow. Alex doesn't seem too worried about it though he did say it would look better had she accepted my proposal. At least it will explain my DNA on the coffee mug in the sink."

And his fingerprints all over the house, I thought as I helped Nina clear the dishes.

Mars rose and fetched vanilla ice cream and a hot apple crisp that he had popped in the oven when I wasn't looking. Everyone moaned, but that didn't stop us from eating it anyway.

"Who baked this?" I asked.

They burst into gales of laughter.

Finally, Mars said, "You did. I found it in the freezer today when I was looking for the bourbon blondies, which were quite tasty!"

It lightened up our mood. Humphrey went home, no longer afraid the police would collect him and haul him off to jail. Francie and Duke took a share of the leftovers home with them. I washed dishes and went up to bed earlier than usual, leaving Nina and Mars to negotiate which movie to watch.

I was used to sleeping until a normal hour in the morning because most of my events took place in the evening. But little Muppet had other ideas. She jumped on my bed, annoying Mochie and Daisy, and most of all me. When I tried to roll away, she weaseled her cold little nose under the blankets and the pillow I was using to defend myself. I finally gave up. At least she let me sleep until dawn.

"Tonight," I said to Muppet firmly, "you are sleeping with Nina!" I considered opening the door to the guest room where Nina slept and leaving little Muppet there, but it was too cruel. Maybe Muppet really needed to go out. Besides, I was supposed to meet Dulci at seven.

I forced myself to get up and shower. I dressed in a pair of black jeans and a red top. I added small garnet earrings, and looped an abstract scarf around my neck to dress up my casual look. A little makeup, a slash of red lipstick, and comfortable walking shoes, and I was ready to go.

Mochie demanded food by lifting his bowl and letting it thunk on the counter. I fed him a can of salmon for cats. When he was satisfied that he wouldn't starve, I latched halters and leashes on the dogs, and packed the house keys, phone, and a little cash in my pocket.

I took care to lock the door behind me just in case the intruder was still about. Not that a locked door had stopped him before. Still, maybe he would make noise, as he had in Nina's case. There was no point in making it easy for him.

I shivered in the cool morning air. The dogs didn't seem to mind. Daisy and Muppet followed scents along the sidewalks. I steered them toward Dulci's house. In the back of my mind, I was planning to stop for a couple of Puppucinis on the way home as a reward for them.

We reached Dulci and Emery's house. I looked at it from across the street. It was three stories with dormer windows on the top floor. There was probably a basement, too. The front door was recessed. A lush white wreath hung on it, standing out in the subdued light. I guessed from the newish brick and lack of a historic marker that it had been built in the last few decades. To my untrained eye, the architecture appeared to be historically accurate. The house fit on the street as though it had been there for centuries. We crossed the street and walked by the walled garden on the side of the house. An ornate iron gate permitted passersby a glimpse of the garden and the house. The dogs pressed their noses against the gate and sniffed.

I tried the knob. The gate swung inward to a patio. I guessed the two double French doors probably opened to the living room. A wrought iron table and a set of garden chairs sat in the center of a brick patio surrounded by pots of flowers and a garden that ran along the brick fence. Dulci had planted bright red geraniums and violet petunias. A white dogwood tree in the corner still had some blooms on it and just to the side of it were two elegant high-heeled shoes with a woman's feet in them.

Chapter 16

Dear Sophie,
I have linens for twin beds, double beds, and a king-size bed. Making beds at my house is a nightmare. I can never find all the matching pieces for the correct size bed. There has to be a better way.
Linen Queen in Bedlam Corner, Connecticut

Dear Linen Queen,
There is a better way. Simply store matching items together by folding them and sliding them inside one pillowcase. You'll be able to tell the size of the bed from the package, and if you can't, then store them on different shelves in the linen closet. Now you can grab and go!
Sophie

I stared at the shoes, thinking I was seeing things. The dogs pulled me toward the shoes. I leaned to my left, trying to get a better angle so I could see more.

The dogs bolted toward the woman on the ground,

pulling me along. It was Dulci. She lay exactly as Lark had lain, on her abdomen, her head turned to the right. She was fully dressed. Either she had been there all night, or she had dressed for the day this morning. I tried to remember what she had worn the previous day. A red dress, I thought, but I couldn't be sure. She was wearing a cream blouse with a fancy gold, brown, and red design on the fabric that reminded me of horse reins, with brown slacks this morning. Earrings set with rubies and diamonds graced her ears and she wore a hefty gold coin pendant surrounded by a gold rope. A stepladder lay beside her as if she had fallen.

I closed the gate so the dogs wouldn't get out when I dropped their leashes to check on Dulci. If this was a crime scene, their presence, and mine for that matter, was a problem. But what if she wasn't dead? I released the leashes and knelt next to Dulci.

"Dulci?" I said. I picked up her hand. It wasn't very cold. She hadn't been out here all night. I couldn't feel a pulse, so I reached for her neck where it would be stronger. Still nothing.

My fingers trembled as I dialed 911 and reported the situation. Rats! I didn't know Dulci's house number. I grabbed the leashes that were dragging along behind the dogs and the three of us ran out the gate to the front of the house. I reported the house number to the dispatcher.

A squad car pulled up immediately and Wong stepped out.

"That was fast!" I said, disconnecting the call.

"I happened to be on the next block over. "What's up?"

"It's Dulci. I found her lying on her brick patio."

"Is she hurt?" asked Wong.

"I think she's dead," I whispered.

We ran around the corner to the spot where Dulci lay. I had to give Wong credit, she could move a lot faster than me.

Her radio crackled and in a matter of minutes, EMTs arrived.

I always felt better when I saw them. If there was any hope of reviving someone, they knew how to do it. Wolf strode in and cast a look at the dogs, but he didn't throw us out.

"She's positioned exactly like Lark was." I said, skipping the niceties of polite society, like saying *good morning*.

In a matter of minutes, he was on his radio requesting a medical examiner, and I was reeling from déjà vu. Except for the fact that it wasn't her grandchild who discovered her body, everything seemed to be an exact repeat of Lark's death. Even the people responding were the same, right up to Dr. Chryssos, who walked through the gate.

"Sophie," he said warmly, furrowing his brow, "I didn't expect to see you here."

Wolf watched him impatiently. "Over here, Chryssos."

The doctor pulled on disposable gloves and kneeled on the ground next to Dulci. Everyone grew quiet.

He stood up and peeled off his gloves. "Preliminarily I'd say she died very recently, within the last couple of hours. The similarity to Lark's death is eerie. Someone hit her on the back of the head, much as in Lark's case. Did you ever find the weapon?" he asked Wolf.

"No." He said it curtly, as if he was upset that he didn't have it.

The EMTs packed up and left.

"Was the gate unlocked?" Wolf asked me.

"Yes. I was supposed to be here for coffee this morning. I assumed Dulci left it open for me. . . ." My voice trailed off.

Wolf slid on a glove, not unlike the doctor's, and tried the handle of one of the French doors. Like the gate, it opened easily. "Did you go in the house?"

"No."

He spoke into his radio and looked straight at me. When he was through, he motioned to me to follow him out the gate. "Tell me what happened."

I relayed the whole thing, not that there was much to tell.

He patted Daisy and Muppet. "You were supposed to meet Dulci here this morning?"

"Yes. She asked me to stop by for coffee this morning after seven. She didn't say why, but when I asked if something was wrong, she said she wasn't sure."

"Any idea what that could have been about?" he asked.

"Not a clue. But she did look back at her husband. I got the feeling that maybe she didn't want him to know she was meeting with me. There was something about the way she said it. I don't think she wanted me to set up a charity event for her."

"Something might have come to her about Lark's death. But she didn't want Emery to know," he mused. "All right. If anything else occurs to you, let me know."

And just like that, I was dismissed. I really wanted to go into Dulci's house to look around. But I had the pups with me, and I was fairly sure they wouldn't have let me in anyway.

We walked slowly to Bean Time. Daisy pranced with excitement. She knew there was a delicious Puppucini in her future. Muppet watched her, clearly confused.

I took my latte and their treats to an outdoor table. They licked their Puppucinis with gusto while I sipped my latte and looked around, feeling a little numb. It was a gorgeous spring day. The sun was shining, and the air was crisp and dry.

Dulci had planned to make an aspirational word wall for her grandchildren. She was going to start a new business setting up home command centers for busy families. And now she was gone. In the blink of an eye, all her plans and dreams, her entire life had come to an abrupt end. What was it she had wanted to tell me? Something about the trip? Something about Lark?

And then it dawned on me. Nina was next. If it hadn't been for Muppet, I would have found Nina lying on the ground outside her house yesterday morning. I jumped to my feet, alarming the dogs. I quickly gathered the empty cups, tossed them in the trash, and took off for home, walking as fast as I could.

I'm ashamed to admit that I was the one panting when we reached my house. The dogs were psyched about our fast walk.

I entered through the kitchen door, which was not locked. Bernie was flipping French toast and Nina was wandering around in a bathrobe, clutching a mug of coffee.

"We have to keep the doors locked," I said. "Where's Mars?"

"Right here," his voice came from the foyer. Mars walked into the kitchen still towel-drying his hair. "That's some snazzy bathroom you had installed, Soph. Bernie, you really ought to think about renovating some of the bathrooms in your house. You can start with mine."

I unfastened the harnesses.

Bernie handed him a plate of French toast. "It's not a bad idea at that." He frowned at me. "Have you been running? Why are you breathing so hard?"

"I'm just glad to see you all here. Especially you, Nina." I plopped into a chair by the fireplace in a most unladylike manner. "Dulci is dead."

My words brought everyone to a halt. They stared at me and then everyone asked questions at the same time.

Thankfully, Bernie brought me a mug of English breakfast tea. I sipped it. He had made it just the way I liked it, with milk and a little sugar. I thanked him and told them what had happened.

"I can't believe this," said Nina. She gasped. "If it hadn't been for Muppet, that would have been me!"

She looked for the little dog and swept her into her arms. "You saved me!"

I had a feeling that after all the animals Nina had fostered, this one was going to be a failed foster. I knew I wouldn't be able to give up Muppet.

"I guess that means Humphrey is off the hook," said Mars.

"He went home last night," Nina pointed out. "He doesn't have an alibi. He could have killed her."

Mars gave her a look. "I seriously doubt that he has secretly been seeing her or that he proposed to her."

Nina snickered. "Well, this *is* Humphrey we're talking about. He's been known to do wacky things."

I was glad they were bickering, but the full impact of Dulci's death hadn't dawned on them yet. Two women were dead. The only survivor was right in front of me. Someone would be after her. I bent forward, toward Nina. "What happened in Portugal?"

She stared at me. "You make it sound so sinister. Nothing special happened. It was just a trip like any other."

I could see from the expression on Bernie's face that he understood. "Did the three of you meet anyone there? Have lunch with a stranger or tea at someone's house?"

"I don't think they do afternoon tea in Portugal, Bernie. But in answer to your question, we stayed mostly with our group."

"Except for the day you got lost," Mars said.

Nina shrugged. "That wasn't any big deal. I'll admit I was a little panicked for a minute when I couldn't figure out the way back to the hotel, but the cab took me back and all was well."

"What about the baby?" I asked.

"What baby?" Nina asked. "There was no baby. There were only adults on our tour."

"The one that was thrown at you." I drank my tea, hoping her version might differ slightly from Emery's and reveal something.

"Oh, that." She shook her head. "It was nothing but a ploy to divert attention while they picked pockets and purses."

Mars was incredulous. "Was the baby hurt?"

"It's not a real baby, Mars," said Bernie. "It's a doll, but they wrap it up in swaddling so that it appears to be an infant. I can't believe they're still pulling that old trick."

"I would fall for it," said Mars. "You'd have to have a heart of stone not to try to save a baby."

"And that's why it works. Who's ready for French toast?" asked Bernie.

We all pitched in and within a matter of minutes, we sat down to eat breakfast. Bernie's classic French toast with butter and maple syrup tasted heavenly. He had made a fruit salad to go along with it and had tossed in pomegranate seeds which were sweet and burst in my mouth.

I had to bring us back to protecting Nina and figuring out what had happened to them on their trip. "Nina, are you in any organizations with Dulci and Lark?" I asked.

"I don't think so. I didn't know them very well before the trip," she said.

Their trip had to be key. But Nina didn't seem to think anything unusual had happened.

As if he was reading my mind, Bernie asked, "Is it possible that you, Lark, and Dulci saw something that you shouldn't have?"

Nina helped herself to another slice of French toast. "Like what?"

"A murder," said Mars.

Bernie flashed him a look. "I'm serious. An altercation? A strange meeting between a fellow traveler and someone else?"

Nina stopped eating for a moment. "We drank wine, ate tapas, saw sunsets, looked at architecture, went to art museums . . . I promise you we didn't see anything peculiar."

Mars sighed. "All right, then. We don't leave Nina alone."

Nina looked at each of us. She broke into a smile, "Aww, y'all are just being silly."

"Then why have you and I been staying here?" Mars asked, making his point quite clearly.

"Because I would sleep better if I wasn't alone. But you don't have to babysit me."

"I think we do," I said. "The murders took place early in the morning, shortly before dawn, when it was still dark outside. So we need to be most vigilant then."

"You can come to work with me," said Bernie.

"Maybe you shouldn't work at Paisley's tent anymore," I said. "I know there are a lot of people around, but there's no point in tempting fate by having you out in the open where the killer can find you."

"Now stop it!" cried Nina. "You're scaring me."

"Good," said Mars. "You need to be careful."

It was almost noon when I arrived at the festival. I felt like vendors swarmed out of their tents to question me. Most of them didn't have problems. They had heard rumors and were curious about Dulci. They wanted to know if she had really been murdered and whether there was any truth to the rumor that she had been left for dead in the exact same way as Lark.

Humphrey found me, his pale face rosy around the edges and the tips of his ears practically blazed. "This has to be the worst day of my life."

"Your visit to the police was a bomb?" I asked.

"How do people who actually break the law manage to cope? I haven't done anything wrong, but I was a wreck. The only bright side was that I knew Wolf. He was calm and polite but I was so nervous I thought I was going to faint!"

"You must have passed inspection. They didn't arrest you," I said cheerfully, hoping to make him feel better.

"They might. Paisley's husband, Frank, went to the police and told them I had manipulated Lark and convinced her to give me power over all her money! Me! I've never even contemplated doing anything like that. I loved Lark." Tears welled in his eyes. "I'd have done anything for her. She was strong and independent, and I'm not some swindler who runs around cheating people."

Poor Humphrey was so agitated that his hands shook.

"Anyone who knows you realizes that. I'm sure Wolf took your character into consideration."

"Character! Yes, that's it. I'm not some bamboozling lothario. I have character and morals." Humphrey's chin lifted a bit. He sucked in a deep breath. "I'm on my way to meet Lark's children. Wish me luck?"

I pecked him on the cheek. "You'll do fine. Remember that they had a big shock when Lark died so they're fragile right now. They might say things they will come to regret later on when they get to know you."

At that moment, Natasha rushed up to us. "Is it true?"

"I presume you're talking about Dulci?" I asked.

"Dulci . . . Someone phoned the funeral home about Dulci this morning and the police asked me about her," said Humphrey.

Natasha shrieked and clasped a hand to her throat. "What is happening here?"

"Who is Dulci?" asked Humphrey.

I explained what had happened to her.

Natasha was horrified, but Humphrey appeared to feel better.

"I don't have an alibi for her death, but I didn't know Dulci." Relief washed over his face. "I'm really sorry she was murdered. Truly. I wouldn't wish that on anyone. But on the list of suspects, I believe I just tumbled way to the bottom. It had to be someone who knew both Lark and Dulci."

Natasha backed up a step. "You're a suspect? Well, don't come to my house." Natasha scurried away as if she were afraid of Humphrey.

I smiled at him. "Don't mind her. But I think you're probably right about not being the prime suspect anymore."

"Thanks, Sophie."

I watched Humphrey walk away and disappear into the crowds of people. I hoped Paisley and Bennett wouldn't be too hard on him.

An hour later, Wolf tracked me down. He handed me a cold drink, which I suspected was a peace offering. I wasn't far off. He asked me questions about Dulci again. The only problem was that I didn't have any different answers.

"How is Emery taking Dulci's death?" I asked.

"He's completely broken. He can barely function."

"I trust he had an alibi?" I asked.

"He left early for the hospital. It checks out. Several people saw him."

Wolf frowned at me. "Keep an eye on Nina."

He walked away and I couldn't help looking around at all the people walking past, laughing and going about their day. Had one of them murdered two women?

I spent the next few hours scurrying between tents and checking to be sure the people who would be doing live demonstrations hadn't forgotten. By six o'clock, when the tents closed for the day, I was bushed and ready to go home.

Chapter 17

Dear Sophie,
I've moved into a new apartment and I'm on a
tight budget. Every night I come home to a cold
house. I have blinds and hardwood floors, but
something is missing. How do I cozy it up?
Clueless in Cold Spring, New York

Dear Clueless,
Curtains! Even if you never close them, they will
add warmth to your apartment. Look for them on
sale, on eBay, or use shower curtains! Some are so
pretty that no one will know. Scour sales for a
good-sized rug and the rest will be easy.
Sophie

Nina hadn't left my house the entire day. She spent the evening closing curtains and peering out of them. Bernie stayed over in a guest room, just to be on the safe side, in case someone got past Mars.

When we went to bed, I made sure barky little Muppet

slept in Nina's room. That way she wouldn't wake me up, but she would bark if anyone came near Nina in the night.

As tired as I was, I couldn't sleep. Mochie and Daisy drifted off right away, but I lay awake in the dark with my window open a crack, listening to the sounds of the night. An occasional car drove by. I drifted off but woke at every little noise. By four in the morning, I was done tossing back and forth. I slid on a bathrobe and walked down the stairs barefooted. The hardwood floor was cold on my feet. I walked as quietly as I could. Mochie raced down the stairs on silent cat feet. But Daisy's paws were heavy, and the stairs creaked with her every step.

The foyer was dark, but I thought I heard someone whisper. Chills ran through me. I sidled into the kitchen, reaching for anything heavy, like a bottle of olive oil. Something moved in the corner and I realized that three shadows sat at the banquette in the corner. I screamed like I was under attack.

"Soph! Soph!"

Was that Mars? I peered into the darkness. Nina, Mars, and Bernie sat around the kitchen table.

I reached for the light switch. "What's going on?"

"No!" they all cried in unison.

"We had a long discussion about this," said Mars. "No lights. We want the killer to think we're all asleep. If he sees shadows moving around the house, he'll walk away."

"We'd rather deal with him now," said Bernie.

I put on the kettle for tea. "You know, both Dulci and Lark were killed after the men in their lives left the house. That does suggest that he watches the house and waits."

"And both times, they left early in the morning, before dawn," said Nina.

I was too fidgety to sit and wait. I mixed batter for an

upside-down skillet cake with pears, then brought a bowl of pears to the table and peeled them while we talked.

"Who else from Old Town was on the trip?" asked Mars.

"Whitney Rutherford."

I didn't need to see Nina to know she was making a dour face.

"The travel agent?" asked Mars.

"I think she probably booked enough seats to get herself a free trip. Isn't that how it works? She brought along her son, who was an absolute pill." She spoke in an annoying pitch. " 'I don't want to go there. I don't want to do this. I don't want to eat that.' He's awful!"

"Teenager?" asked Bernie.

"Twenty-six!" said Nina. "As far as I can tell, he's currently unemployed. I think Whitney wants him to get in the travel business like her, but he's so unfriendly that I can't imagine anyone booking travel through him."

"Short, blocky fellow?" asked Bernie.

"Yes. Do you know him?"

"He comes to the bar in The Laughing Hound once in a while. He's always alone. I think he tries to pick up women but doesn't have much luck."

"Sounds about right," said Nina. "That cute Doctor Chryssos was on the tour, too. He spent most of his days attending the pathology symposium, but he came along on a few of the outings. Even my husband went to see the Sintra National Palace. Other doctors were there with their spouses from all around the country. My husband and I had drinks with some of them, but it was mostly standard socializing. You know—where are you from? Do you have children? They show pictures. You tell them how beautiful their kids are. And after that, you wave when you pass by them in the hotel or on the street."

I looked out the bay window into the predawn darkness wondering if the killer was out there. Did he know where Nina had gone? It wasn't a secret that we were friends. A lot of local people would guess that she might be at my house.

While my friends talked, I preheated the oven, then rounded the island to the stovetop where I warmed a skillet and added butter and brown sugar. It was a little odd working in the dark, but my eyes had adjusted enough to see what I was doing. I laid the pear slices in the melted sugar, poured the batter on top, and slid it into the oven.

"It's almost time," Bernie said.

"Maybe I should dress and pretend to leave," said Mars. "I'll circle around and come in through the alley."

"You will not!" Nina said in a very firm tone. "I won't have you killed while I sit inside, safe and sound."

"It's interesting that you were the only one who was asleep," I said. "Lark and Dulci were up and dressed, ready for the day. They must have turned on lights. He would have seen them."

"Maybe he wasn't waiting for the men to leave," mused Mars. "Maybe he was waiting for them to turn off security systems and alarms."

"Some people think Lark let her killer in," said Bernie.

"This is terrible. It's like living in a horror movie!" Nina ranted. "We're sitting ducks waiting for someone to knock on the door."

"Nina," said Mars in a calming voice, "what else do you, Lark, and Dulci have in common?"

"None of us have a dog."

It wasn't the answer I expected but it was certainly true.

I pulled the pear upside-down skillet cake from the oven and let it sit while I whipped fresh cream. As the sun rose in the sky, we ate the cake and celebrated the fact that nothing had happened.

We went over our schedules, arranging them so Nina could leave the house but wouldn't be alone. Mars, who could work from home easily, got the lion's share of the time, but it didn't seem to bother him one bit.

He and Nina would walk down to The Laughing Hound for lunch with the dogs. They could eat on the outdoor terrace in back.

Half the cake was left on the platter when Bernie went home. Mars yawned and slinked off to the family room. Nina muttered promises of helping to clean up after she took a nap and disappeared up the stairs.

I needed to bring a dish to Emery. He had children and grandchildren, and probably all kinds of other relatives who would be arriving. If I knew the Old Town community, he would be swimming in casseroles and ham biscuits. It was early in the day and I had a little time now that everyone else had gone to bed. I mixed together the ingredients for Chocolate Mayonnaise cupcakes and poured the batter into a cupcake pan.

While the cupcakes baked, I beat a creamy chocolate frosting. They didn't take long to bake, so I pulled them out of the oven and placed them on a baking rack. The cupcakes needed to cool before frosting so I dashed upstairs, showered, and dressed in a summery periwinkle dress that looked odd with Keds, but I had to be sensible about all the walking I would do.

Careful not to get frosting on my clothes, I piped icing on the cupcakes and popped them into a disposable aluminum pan with a clear top to protect them from the elements while I walked over to Emery's house. My recipe made two dozen and they didn't all fit in the pan, so I stashed a few in the freezer for us to eat later.

I figured Mars and Nina could take care of the dogs and Mochie, who were happily sleeping at that moment, and left the house, locking the door behind me. Nina hadn't been much help in understanding why someone might have killed Dulci and Lark. I believed what she was saying, but someone had to know more. I intended to have a few chats, namely, with Dulci's husband, Emery, the good Dr. Chryssos, the travel agent, and Lark's son, Bennett.

Emery and Dulci's house was silent when I approached. Granted, it was early in the day, but somehow I had envisioned crowds of people coming and going already.

I tapped the knocker and waited for a response, the cupcakes getting heavy in my arms.

Emery opened the door looking ragged. His usually ruddy face was pale. The bags hanging under his reddened eyes were a sickly gray. He wore a T-shirt with a worn unbuttoned flannel shirt over it, leaving room for his ample belly to protrude.

"Sophie!" he gasped. He seized my arm and tugged me into the house. "I was afraid you were the police again. They'll be back. I know they will."

I had planned to say how sorry I was, to express my condolences, but I found myself asking, "Did you get any sleep last night?"

He ignored my question. "Tell me what happened."

"I'd like to put this down," I said, indicating the cupcakes. "Which way is the kitchen?"

He led me through a long hallway to a white kitchen. The handles and knobs were all brushed pewter, bright enough to match the gleaming stainless steel appliances. Every corner displayed Dulci's handiwork. She could have bought some of it, but I suspected she had made most of the décor herself, from the farmer's market baskets on the wall to the home control center.

I slid the cupcakes into the refrigerator. "Should I make you some coffee?"

"Keurig," he said, evidently assuming that needed no further clarification. He led me to two chairs in the family room off the kitchen and positioned his so that it faced me. He leaned forward toward me. "Tell me what you know."

There wasn't much to say. I weighed whether or not to reveal that something had troubled Dulci and that was the reason she had asked me to come. But in the end, I decided it was far more important to provide all the details possible in an effort to find her murderer. Besides, Dulci was gone now and the very thing that had prompted her to ask me to come might have been the very same thing that led to her demise. I told him about finding her on the patio, about the ladder and her high heels. "Dulci had asked me to meet her here. I was under the impression that something was troubling her?" I ended my statement a pitch higher, hoping he would perceive it as a question.

He sat up straight and rubbed his jawline. He looked past me as though he was thinking. "Did she give you any clue what it was about?"

"Nothing. She was in a hurry. I thought it might be related to Lark's death. Did Dulci have any ideas about who might have killed Lark?"

"If she had, I have to presume that she wouldn't have opened the door to the murderer."

"Opened the door?"

"We have an alarm system. A good one." He massaged his forehead. "This is my fault. All my fault. We'd been talking about adding cameras. You know, the kind that shows who is at the door. You can see on your phone who is at the door and even speak to them, so burglars don't know that you're actually in a restaurant." He closed his eyes for a moment, then rubbed them with his thumb and middle finger. He pulled a handkerchief from his pocket and dabbed at his eyes. "But what with the trip, I never got around to ordering them."

"But that's not your fault," I said soothingly. "Are you saying that you think burglars killed Dulci?"

"I turned off the alarm when I left the house in the morning. It was around five. I like to be at the hospital early. It gives me a chance to get organized before everyone starts coming in and things get busy. It was still dark outside, but I didn't turn the alarm on and apparently, Dulci didn't either. It was off when the police called me, and I came home. There's no sign of forced entry, so they think she opened the door and let her killer in."

Chills ran up the back of my neck. "That's exactly what happened to Lark."

Chapter 18

Dear Natasha,
I watch your show every day. But you don't do much with furniture. I found a lovely chest of drawers for my little boy, but it's so plain. He's crazy for dinosaurs! How can I dress it up without drawing dinosaurs?
Unartistic Mommy in Paint Rock, Texas

Dear Unartistic Mommy,
Buy inexpensive dinosaur molds, fill them with polymer clay, and bake. When they have hardened, paint them bright colors and adhere your new dinosaurs to the chest.
Natasha

"Do you think he was out there, waiting for me to leave?" asked Emery.

"It's entirely possible. Did Dulci and Lark have a connection before the trip? Do they belong to the same club or have the same hobby?" I asked.

"They knew each other. We socialized together. I knew

Lark's husband. He was also a pathologist and that sometimes brought us together at various functions. Dulci
doted on our grandchildren and spent a lot of time with
them. She volunteered at the hospital gift shop one day a
week and she belonged to a crocheting group. I don't
know if Lark was involved with any of those things."

I hated to pose this question and was certain Wolf must
have, but he certainly wouldn't share the response with
me. "Do you know of anyone who would have wanted to
kill Dulci?"

He looked away again and shook his head. "She was
kind and thoughtful." He smiled wryly. "Our daughter
asked yesterday, 'Why would anyone want to murder Mom?
She was so boring!' It sounds so unkind, but I know what
she meant. Dulci wasn't involved in anything controver-
sial. She focused on her family and friends."

"I'm so sorry, Emery," I said.

"I didn't know the trip to Portugal would be our last
trip together. We had a delightful time. I just can't believe
she's gone. Who would do this to her?"

"Emery, think back to your trip. Did anything odd happen? Did Dulci return from a bus tour and tell you a weird
story?"

His brow furrowed. "You think someone followed us
back from Portugal just to murder Dulci? That's absurd."

"On its face, I guess it is. But Dulci's and Lark's deaths
were remarkably similar. And Lark was murdered less
than twenty-four hours after you returned. I can't help
thinking there's some connection. Don't you find it odd
that the killer bothered to place a ladder next to each of
them even though it was dark outside and there's not a
chance that either of them was planning to do anything re-
quiring a ladder?"

His eyes narrowed. "I see what you mean. Dulci was always climbing on ladders to decorate the house. Every

Christmas I begged her to wait and have our handyman do it for her. She never listened. So I didn't give the ladder any thought at all."

"What happened in Portugal?" I pressed.

He gazed at me blankly and at that moment, the front door burst open and a young woman's voice called, "Dad? I brought breakfast!"

Emery bolted from his chair. "Becky!" He strode toward his daughter and hugged her. Both of them cried.

It was time for me to get out of their way and let them grieve. As I walked past them, I encountered a nice-looking young man who introduced himself as Pat. "The son-in-law," he clarified.

I offered my condolences and left.

Chapter 19

Dear Natasha,
I have leftover wallpaper that's too beautiful to throw out. You're so clever about these things. How can I use it?

          Wallpaper Diva in Wall, South Dakota

Dear Wallpaper Diva,
The best place for wallpaper is in the trash. It went out of style forty years ago.

          Natasha

I still had some time before the DIY Festival opened for the day. The vendors were arriving, buying cups of coffee and goodies from the local bakeries. I hoped Paisley might be at her tent, refreshing her stock of furniture, so she could tell me where to find her brother.

I stopped to buy some lattes as bribes, to smooth the way into talking with me. When I arrived at Lark's house, the first thing I noticed was that the crime scene tape had been removed. The front door was open. I could hear Paisley inside, crying, "But I don't want to sell."

The front door closed. Even a latte wouldn't smooth over that. Was she arguing with Humphrey?

The door opened and her brother, Bennett, bounded out as if all he wanted in the world was to get away.

"Bennett?" I said.

He turned to look at me.

"Sophie Winston," I said. "I was hoping to talk with you. Latte?"

We could hear raised voices inside the house.

"Sure, thanks. I'm sorry. You were a friend of my mom's, right?"

"Yes."

He nodded. "Paisley said you were very helpful the day Mom died." He glanced at the house. "Would you mind if we walked somewhere? Anywhere, really."

"Who is arguing with Paisley?" I asked as we walked toward Market Square.

"Frank. Who else?"

"I gather he'd like to sell the house?"

We settled on a bench near the fountain where the sun shone on us.

"He, um, he's good at running through money." Bennett took a swig of his latte.

A rather amusing assessment given that Bennett was a professional gambler. He probably went through money very fast himself. "I presume that's the reason Lark arranged for a spendthrift trust?"

"You know about that?"

I nodded. "Humphrey and I grew up together. He was a good choice. I'm sure he'll be fair and reasonable."

"I knew about the trust, too. Mom didn't tell Paisley because she blabs everything to Frank. I can't blame Mom for not telling her. Look how he's fighting to sell the house. He should be leaving that up to Paisley and me. It's wrong of him to be putting Paisley through this right now. Mom just died! The house can wait. Everything can wait. We haven't even buried her yet."

"I'm so sorry, Bennett. We all miss Lark."

"Frank thinks your friend, Humphrey, murdered her," he blurted, looking straight ahead.

"I think that's highly unlikely," I said carefully. Could they know that Humphrey had proposed to Lark?

"I don't know anyone else who would have knocked her off."

I didn't say anything. In my heart, I knew Humphrey couldn't have killed Lark, but that wasn't anything that would convince Bennett. "I don't think Humphrey had anything to gain from Lark's death," I pointed out.

"Probably not." Bennett stared at the latte in his hands. "Paisley has always been a pushover. She has such a kind heart and can't imagine that anyone would be cruel or unfair," he said. "She's still so naïve. I'd have thought she would outgrow that as she got older. But she's still the same Paisley who believes everything. You know those women who get sucked into sending money to men they meet online? Paisley could be one of them." He shook his head. "It's part of what makes her so sweet. I just wish she weren't so easily duped."

"I gather you're not keen on Frank?"

"I suspect I'd like him better if he weren't related. But I didn't get a vote in that." He smiled at me sadly.

"Do you know of anyone who might have wanted to kill Lark?" I asked.

"It has occurred to me that someone might have figured out who she was and intended to burglarize the house. They might not have intended to kill her."

"Who she was? What do you mean?" I asked.

"Mom's dad was a world-class jeweler. Not the kind you see in the mall. The kind that the überwealthy come to when they need a gift. He designed one-of-a-kind jewelry.

Museums sometimes commissioned him to clean up or restore or even make molds of historic pieces. His jewelry was worn by movie stars and royalty. After my dad died, Poppy, my mom's father, moved here from New York to live with her. Maybe someone thought there was a stash of gemstones or gold in the house."

"Where is Poppy now?"

"He died a few months ago."

I gasped.

"Natural causes. No one murdered him," he said calmly.

"I knew he had moved here, but I had forgotten all about him," I said.

"She took care of him for a couple of years and when he died, she decided to take a long vacation to get away and relax a little. Focus on herself again."

"Was she worried about anything?"

He snorted. "Besides Paisley and her brood?"

"Is there anything to worry about or was she just being a mom?"

He turned his head and eyed me as though he was trying to figure out just how much to reveal about their family dynamics. "Both, I guess." He winced a little. "Frank thinks he has the world figured out. He thinks he's smarter than everyone else."

"Is he?" I asked.

Bennett snorted. "Definitely not. I knew another guy like that. He dropped out of college after a few weeks because he said there was nothing they could teach him. At the time, I thought maybe he was some kind of savant who really did know more than the rest of us. Today he slings burgers at a fast-food joint. Don't misunderstand me, there's nothing wrong with that, but it's not what you'd expect of a genius."

"Frank has an inflated opinion of himself?" I asked.

"That's a good way of putting it. For instance, he didn't

graduate from college, much less law school, but he thinks Mom's lawyer, Alex German, is an idiot. Frank thinks he knows more about the law and wants to challenge the trust."

"How do you feel about that?"

"Annoyed. I'm going to have to pay some lawyer to get rid of what will ultimately be a nuisance filing. But that's how Frank is about everything. He's so certain that he can manipulate any situation in which he finds himself, when the sad truth is that he not only spins his wheels but often digs them deeper into the mud and then has to get himself out of trouble. Of course, you understand that it's never his fault. It's all of his making and his crazy ideas, but everyone else is stupid and out to get him. Did Mom tell you that he and Paisley are being sued?"

"No! What for?"

"As I understand it, a guy named Walter Wicklin was getting a divorce and went to Frank for advice on hiding his assets. Wicklin claims Frank suggested transferring his savings into Frank's name so the wife wouldn't find the money and, even if she did, then she couldn't have it. Frank claims Wicklin gave him that money as payment for his services."

"If Wicklin is right, that would be a scam on so many levels!" I exclaimed. "Do you think Wicklin is telling the truth?"

"Let's say I'm very much afraid Wicklin is telling the truth. It sounds just like the disordered and confused ideas that Frank gets."

And then before I thought it through, I blurted, "How can Paisley stay with a man who would do something like that?"

Bennett shot me a look and said in a dull tone, "Because she loves him."

"Ouch. That sounded bitter."

"Not so much bitter as frustrated. What will it take before she sees Frank for what he is?"

Again, I found that somewhat ironic coming from a gambler. Gambling wasn't illegal, of course, but a little cloud of swindler hung around the avocation of gambling.

"Frank isn't malicious," he said. "Paisley wanted to go into business with me, but I bailed as soon as Frank was involved. He doesn't think like a regular person. The ideas that he put forth scared me. It was a legitimate business, but Frank was making it into something shady. I wanted no part of it."

I was itching to come right out and ask him if he thought Frank could have killed his mom, but it just seemed rude. "I get the impression they're in need of money. They have such a big family."

Frank tossed the empty latte cup into a nearby wastebasket like he was shooting a basketball. "Mom was one smart cookie to protect Paisley's inheritance." He sighed. "I feel like Mom is still in Portugal and she's going to come home tomorrow or next week. I can't wrap my head around the fact that she's gone." He shot me a funny look. "Are all those people waiting to talk to you?"

"Huh?" I looked over my right shoulder. A line of vendors had formed. "I'm afraid so."

He stood up and reached out his hand for me to shake. "Thanks for listening to me drone on about the family."

"It was my pleasure. If there's anything I can do, just give me a call." I handed him my card.

He walked away and was immediately replaced by a vendor whose wallet had been stolen. I headed straight to his tent with him, and called Wong, who showed up promptly. While she peppered him with questions, I gazed around the tent. He had created all kinds of clever storage solutions for everything from socks and shoes to paper towels and spices.

I was on my hands and knees when I felt a tug on my jacket. Thomas, Paisley's oldest child, had crawled under a display table behind me.

"What are you doing?"

"I'm looking for a wallet."

"Can I look with you?"

"Of course!"

Three minutes later, Thomas asked, "Is that what you're looking for?"

Sure enough, a man's wallet was barely visible, wedged between two cardboard boxes where it had probably fallen. I reached for it. Trust a kid to see what all the adults had overlooked. "Found it!" I said in a loud voice. I handed it to Thomas. "How about you give it to Officer Wong since you're the one who spotted it?"

I was still on the ground, crawling backward, when I heard Officer Wong ask, "Is this your wallet?"

Thankfully, everything was there. The vendor handed Tommy a twenty-dollar bill.

Tommy's eyes grew large. For five seconds I could see the excitement in his face. And then, he handed it back to the vendor. "Thank you, sir, but I don't deserve this. I'm glad I could help you."

With all the grown-ups watching in awe, Tommy smiled and left the tent. I could hear people saying, "Are you kidding? I would have taken the money!"

The line of people I had seen earlier had followed me. I took care of their problems in fairly short order and was surprised when no one else demanded my attention. I spotted Tommy sitting on the front steps of Lark's house.

I went over and sat down next to him. "It was very nice of you to find the man's wallet. And quite noble to turn down his reward."

"My nana said the real reward is in helping someone else."

"Your nana was very smart."

"I miss her." He let out a little sigh. "I used to come over here and stay with her. All by myself, without my brothers."

I could imagine what a treat that must have been for him. Behind us, inside the house, I could hear Paisley's shrill voice, "You had no right! Those are *my* family heirlooms. Not yours to sell. I can't help it if your family sold everything they ever treasured. Now where is it?"

Chapter 20

Dear Sophie,
I love, love, love wallpaper. My husband had to
scrape wallpaper off the walls for his mother when
he was a teenager and swears he will never, ever
put up wallpaper! How can I get the effect without
wallpaper?
        Sad Plain Walls in Walla Walla, Washington

Dear Sad Plain Walls,
Don't despair. If you are an artist, you can paint a
mural. If not, try a stencil to paint a pattern across
the wall. Or use masking tape to create a pattern,
paint, remove the tape, and voilà!
        Sophie

It couldn't be good for Tommy to be hearing their fight.
"Where are your brothers?" I asked.
"Inside."
"Why aren't you inside?"
"I don't like hearing my parents argue."

I couldn't blame him for that. "Your mom told me that you're homeschooled."

"Yeah."

"What grade are you in?"

"Seventh."

That didn't sound right. Tommy couldn't be older than ten. "How old are you?"

"Ten. But I'm a fast learner."

"You must be pretty smart."

He shrugged.

"Then shouldn't you be studying?"

"I have the week off because my nana died. My paw-paw died last year and my grandpa, too. I saw my nana dead, so I get time off from school to think about dying

I was pretty sure that wasn't what he was supposed to be thinking about. "Wow. That's a lot of dying. I'm really sorry." I had no idea how to help a child work through the tragedy of death, let alone so many. All I could think of was to do something happy, something that would cele-brate the fact that Tommy and I were still alive. "Do you like ice cream?" I asked.

"Sure. Everybody likes ice cream."

"Let's ask your mom if we can go get an ice cream cone."

He brightened up. "Okay!"

I stood up and tapped the knocker on the front door. Paisley answered, her face flushed with fury. I got the feel-ing she was ready to yell at Tommy, but she bit back the anger when she saw me.

"Sophie. Is there a problem?"

"Not at all. I just wondered if I could take Tommy to get an ice cream cone."

"Please, Mom?" he asked in the sweetest little boy voice.

She placed her palms on the sides of her face. "I think that would be wonderful. You behave now, Tommy. Do you hear me?"

"Yes, ma'am."

The smile that appeared on his face filled me with joy. Just like Lark had told him. Doing something for someone else was its own reward.

He tugged my hand and marched hurriedly toward the ice cream shop. He knew exactly where it was. He didn't linger, viewing all the options, either, like I did when I was a kid. He immediately ordered one scoop of bubble gum and one scoop of chocolate mousse in a sugar cone.

He didn't talk much on the way back because he was busy licking his ice cream cone. But I noted that Whitney Rutherford was at work in her travel agency and planned to return.

Tommy was licking his fingers by the time I dropped him off. Paisley was seated outside in her tent and several people were admiring her clever painted furniture. She seemed much calmer and gave her son a big hug. "Did you thank Sophie?" she asked him.

"He did," I said.

"That's my boy." She ran her fingers through his hair.

"Do you have any children?" Tommy asked me.

"No, I don't."

"Tommy! Are you thinking of leaving me for Sophie?" Paisley teased.

"I thought maybe we could give her Oscar."

"Now there's a good idea," said Paisley. "Maybe she'll take Daddy, too!"

I knew they were joking, but having witnessed Oscar's handiwork, I quickly declined the generous offer and left them laughing.

I hurried back to North by Northwest Travel. A bell chimed when I opened the door and walked in.

Whitney Rutherford rose from her seat. I suspected her hair was naturally curly, but the slightly too orange blond color probably came from a bottle. She was fond of food and a regular at The Laughing Hound. Her taste in clothes leaned toward soft materials, which were undoubtedly comfortable, but had a tendency to cling to her rolls. She picked up an expensive purse that occupied the client chair in front of her desk. I recognized the label. It had seen better days. The smooth wine-colored leather had weathered and bore scratches from use.

"Sophie! How nice to see you. Planning a trip?"

"Sometime soon, I hope. Nice bag."

Whitney stashed it on the floor. "I love that old purse. The poor thing is so beat up that I really need to let it go now. I bought a new one for the trip. I'm so mad at myself. I warn my clients about thieves and pickpockets all the time. But when we landed here, I knew I would need a free hand, so I slipped my purse into the blue bag the tour company gave each of us. I guess I was tired, and I stupidly handed the blue bag that contained my purse to my son so I could pull the luggage off the baggage carousel. Honestly, I could just shoot him. He set it on the floor and surprise, surprise, it was gone."

"Oh no! I hope you didn't have much money in it."

"Several hundred dollars in traveler's checks. Thank heaven for that. I can get it back. But the rest of the things are so annoying to replace. Passport, driver's license, cellphone. It's a nightmare."

"I'm so sorry. And how ironic that it happened to you right here at home."

"Isn't that odd? When we're abroad we're looking at churches and spires, and such interesting things that we forget to be alert. But it happened to me right here. So what can I do for you?"

"I really wanted to ask you about the trip to Portugal."

She gestured toward the chair. "It was fantastic. I recommend it highly. I guess Nina has told you all about it. It's three weeks long, which gives you plenty of time for sightseeing on your own or just lounging at the beach in addition to all the day trips."

I spoke in a soft voice, knowing I was going to disappoint her. "I understand you and your son were there with Nina, Dulci, and Lark. I'm sorry. I'm not interested in booking a vacation right now, but I would like to know if you noticed anything unusual on your trip."

She blinked at me and said very firmly, "There is no connection between Lark's and Dulci's deaths and the trip. None, none, none. Detective Fleishman has already been in here pelting me with questions. I really don't understand why anyone would think there was a link between the trip and their deaths. It's not like they died during their vacations."

I understood her reluctance to think along those lines, so I threw the ball in her court. "Then why was Lark murdered the night she returned?"

"How should I know?" Her voice was shrill.

"I gather you went on the bus trips during your stay in Portugal?"

"Of course. I need to know what my clients can expect."

"Did you see anything peculiar involving Lark, Dulci, or Nina?"

"Why don't you ask Nina?"

"I have. I need an unbiased opinion. That's why I came to you." I tried hard to sound like I was flattering her.

"I see. Well, I can't say I saw anyone sinister following them around. But I did notice that Lark was coupling up with that Dr. Chryssos. He's so handsome. If I hadn't had my son with me, I might have been interested in him myself."

I smiled to encourage her. "Did they go off anywhere by themselves?"

"There were some days when they didn't take the bus tour. I assumed they wanted to enjoy the beach."

"Did Lark visit any of Frank's relatives during the trip?" I asked.

Whitney seemed surprised. "Does he have relatives in Portugal? I know his father died about a year ago in that horrible accident."

"Car accident?"

"In a manner of speaking, I guess. It was a hit-and-run. The poor man was crossing the street when he was hit by a van. I haven't followed up on it, but I don't think they ever found out who did it."

"How awful!" But it surely didn't have any bearing on Lark's death. "If you think of anything, please let me know. We're worried about Nina."

Whitney gasped and I thought it was the first time she had seriously considered that someone else might be in danger. "She's not the only one. What about me?"

"Do you have a list of the people who were on the tour?" I asked.

"Yes," she said in an annoyed voice. "Wolf insisted I give him one. Said he would get a warrant for it if I didn't! But it's confidential, Sophie. I really can't share that information with you."

She probably wondered why I was sitting there not saying anything. I was debating whether to do a low-down dirty trick or not. Part of me knew it was wrong. But the other part of me wanted to find the killer to protect Nina. "Don't you think you should notify all of them?"

"Of what?"

"That two passengers have been murdered and another one managed to scare away a burglar or worse?"

When her eyes were big like that, Whitney looked much younger. "Any one of us could be next."

I presumed that some of the travelers were from Arlington or Fairfax. "And so far, they have all been in Old Town."

"Oh my gosh! You're right! I've been living the life of Riley, completely oblivious to the danger. What should we do?"

"Since I can't see the list of people involved, maybe you could phone them and ask if they saw anything."

"Yes. I'll do that." She thought for a moment. "No, I won't. One of them could be the killer. I'm not letting a murderer know I'm onto him."

"I can't blame you for that." I smiled at her. "Have a great day!"

I walked out and heard the lock on the door click behind me. It hadn't been nice of me to frighten her. On the other hand, I truly did not know if she was the killer's next target. So maybe I had saved her life since she would be on the alert now.

I dropped back by the DIY Festival. It was in full swing, with crowds of people strolling through. Plenty of them carried bags indicating they had purchased something. I spied Frank unloading an unwieldy table from his van and walked over.

"Can I give you a hand with that?"

"Please! If you could just hold this end and walk backward, while I hop in the truck and lower the other end, that would be great!"

I could see why Paisley had been attracted to him. Frank had a certain charisma. He flashed a white-toothed smile at me and whisked a hand through thick wavy hair, almost as dark as Natasha's. Tommy had inherited his dad's dark hair and brown eyes. In fact, they looked a lot alike.

I held on to the table as requested and in less than two minutes, Frank had it out of the truck and on a cart. It was covered with a thick moving blanket.

"Tommy told me that you lost your father last year," I said. "I'm very sorry. You seem to have had more than your fair share of deaths in the past couple of years."

"It was hard. He wasn't an old guy yet. I always imagined that he would be around well into his eighties. You know, the wizened little guy giving sage advice to great-grandchildren. I know what Paisley is going through right now. Losing a parent is earth-shattering. Paisley's father had been sick, and we all knew how it would end, so we were sort of prepared for it. But when it's so sudden, it's a big shock."

"I heard your dad was hit by a van?" I asked.

He glanced at me. "Paisley says you're friends with that Fleishman fellow. Well, no offense, but I hope he's a better cop than the guy who handled my dad's case because they never found the van or the driver."

Chapter 21

Dear Sophie,
I love the idea of a home control center but I'm on
a tight budget. How can I do it for less?
                    Mom of Six in Childwold, New York

Dear Mom of Six,
Go to your dollar store. Buy a clipboard for each
child's papers and hang them in horizontal rows.
Add a big calendar for appointments and a chalk-
board for daily events. Buy hooks for keys and a
basket for mail. If it looks disjointed, paint a bor-
der around the whole thing!
                                        Sophie

Natasha strode up to Frank and me. "May I have a word, please, Sophie?"

I excused myself and followed Natasha. "What's up?"

"I'm sick. You won't believe this."

We were still walking. "Where are we going?" I asked.

"To The Laughing Hound."

"Great! I'm starved."

She glanced at me. "You can't stay there."

"Why not?"

"You'll see." She pulled open the door and waved away the hostess.

"We have to make ourselves invisible," she said.

I snapped my fingers. "But I left my cloak of invisibility at home!"

"Shh." She sidled toward the bar. "Look for just a second, so you won't be seen. The table all the way in the back on the right."

I peeked around the corner. "Mars is here."

Natasha pulled me back. "Did you not notice who was with him?"

I looked again and stepped back. "Greer Shacklesworth."

Natasha crossed her arms. "What are we going to do about it?"

"We? Mars is a free agent. And Greer is very attractive. Good for him," I said.

"What's wrong with you?" she whispered. "Can't you see that she's seducing him?"

"What do you want me to do? Go sit next to him?"

Natasha eyed me. "That's not a bad idea. We could both pull up chairs and interrupt their little tête-à-tête."

"It was a joke, Natasha," I said.

"Um-hmm. Look at them now."

I peeked again. Greer was definitely getting closer and gazing into his eyes. Wow.

I stepped back. "We are not interfering. Let's get a bite to eat."

"Great idea!" Natasha walked into the room and straight up to the table where Mars sat with Greer.

I wasn't playing her game. I headed for the bar and tried to ignore her when she called, "Sophie! Look who's here!"

"Sophie!" Natasha's voice grew insistent.

Reluctantly I turned around and found Dr. Peter Chryssos smiling at me. He was seated at a small table, evidently having lunch.

"I believe someone wants your attention," he said.

My gaze flicked over to Mars. I hoped he wasn't on a date with Greer, because Natasha had already pulled up a chair and was gesturing wildly for me to join them.

"Are you eating alone, Dr. Chryssos?" I asked. "Would you mind if I joined you?"

"By all means."

"Thanks. I'll be right back."

I made my way to Mars's table and ignored Natasha's entreaties to sit down. After all, she had achieved her goal of disrupting Greer's intentions toward Mars, assuming she had any intentions. "Where is Nina?" I hissed at Mars.

"In the back with Bernie. Don't worry, we haven't abandoned her."

I gave him a thumbs-up and went to join Dr. Chryssos, who appeared to be eating a hefty grilled sandwich. "That looks good, Dr. Chryssos. What's in it?"

"Please, call me Peter, otherwise I'll have to call you Mrs. Winston. Bernie came up with this and named it the No Guilt Sandwich. It has bacon in it, which ought to cause me to feel guilty, but the rest is shredded chicken, avocado, and Havarti. So it's not all bad!"

"I'll have one of those," I told the waiter, "and unsweetened iced tea." When he left, I said, "I'm glad to have a chance to talk with you."

Peter raised his eyebrows and swallowed a bite of his sandwich. He wiped his mouth with a napkin and said, "I can't tell you anything about Lark or Dulci."

"Oh, but I think you can."

He gazed at me quizzically.

"I'm not interested in their medical condition. What I want to know is what happened during your trip."

He nodded knowingly. "It's very troubling. I've bought extra bolts for my doors."

"It's believed that they opened the door to their killer." As I spoke, I realized that narrowed down the field. I mused aloud, "Which means they had to know the person, at least well enough to not have felt fearful."

"Are you implying that it was someone on the tour with us?" he asked.

"I'm not implying anything, but now that you mention it, was someone on the tour disgruntled or angry with them?"

"Whitney Rutherford's son is a totally self-absorbed young man. Probably the rudest person I have ever met. I would go so far as to call him narcissistic. I'm not a psychiatrist but I think Lark and Dulci would have had to do or say something to trigger his anger for him to kill them. I wouldn't count him out, though."

"I heard you spent quite a bit of time with Lark."

"She was lovely. A very nice traveling companion. But don't get the wrong impression. There was nothing romantic going on. We were the only two without spouses, so we teamed up when it came to meals and such."

"Did she say anything to you about an incident? About going to visit anyone? Doing something that was off the itinerary?"

"She did a lot of shopping for her family. She showed me toy sailboats for the boys made out of cork and joked about a cork voodoo doll that she bought as a joke for her son-in-law. She said she had lit candles at the cathedral for her parents, her grandparents, and Frank's father."

"Was she Catholic?"

"I don't know. But it made her very happy. She seemed content, as though it had brought peace to her. I seem to recall her saying something about being relieved of a great burden."

I finished the last bite of my sandwich. "I hardly think anyone would have killed her over cork sailboats. Were you there when the baby was thrown?" I asked.

"That was something! I bit on that one hook, line, and sinker. I thought it was a real baby and I dodged forward to help catch it. Can I tell you how stupid I felt when it turned out to be a doll? Those people were pros. I've never seen anything like it."

"Did they steal anything from you?" I asked.

He shook his head. "I think one of the ladies lost her purse. She was frantic, but for the sake of convenience, her husband had put their passports and tickets in his inner jacket pocket, so the loss was mostly financial, although I believe he did get her cell phone. I saw them on the plane, so it didn't prevent them from going home."

"Did anything else like that happen?" I asked.

"Well, people try to sell you roses and whatnot when you dine outside but that couldn't be connected to Lark's death."

He took a big gulp of his iced tea. "So what happened with you and Wolf?"

I really didn't want to go into *that*. Luckily, his phone buzzed.

He glanced at it. "I'm very sorry to break this off, but I'm being summoned."

"Another death?" I asked, chills running through me.

He nodded. "Car accident." He bestowed a lovely smile on me. "Would you have dinner with me sometime?"

"Sure," I said. "I'd like that." He would probably ask about Wolf again, but I supposed that couldn't be avoided.

"I'll give you a call," he said, and he walked away.

I glanced over at the table where Natasha had joined Mars. He was gone, as was Greer. But Natasha and Nina watched me. I asked the waiter for my tab.

He looked at me in surprise. "Dr. Chryssos took care of it."

How had he done that? It was very generous of him. I walked over to the table where Natasha and Nina were.

"Well?" asked Nina. "How did it go?"

"No one who was on your trip recalls anything helpful."

"That's what you talked about?" asked Natasha. "No wonder you can't get a date."

"I have some good news," said Nina. "My husband is coming home. You won't have to put up with me much longer."

"I enjoy having you stay with me. But I know you'll feel better when you can be in your own home." I eyed Natasha. "How was your lunch?"

"Greer is definitely after Mars. She didn't even have the grace to stop flirting with him when I joined them. What moxie!"

Nina snickered. "I do hate to agree with you, but Sophie, this time Natasha is right. Greer is quite the operator."

"Thank you, Nina! Now, how are we going to stop this?" asked Natasha, looking straight at Nina.

"Oh, I didn't say that. If Mars likes Greer, then that's his business." Nina threw me a delightedly smug look.

"I am not getting involved," I said.

"Sophie!" Natasha whined. "I thought you were on my side."

I tried very hard not to make a face. Mars had been miserable with Natasha, why on earth would I help them get back together? I changed the subject. "Any luck on the house?"

Natasha's eyes welled up with tears. "It's a nightmare. Cal Bickford came over to look at it. Did you know that he's Lark's brother-in-law?"

"I didn't know that," said Nina.

Natasha nodded. "The house is worth a lot. I can't give it up. I just can't. I've spent so much time getting it just right. I refuse to walk away from it now."

How could I have been so stupid? That was why Natasha was so eager to reconcile with Mars. If he moved back into the house, her problems were over. How wicked of her! Part of me wanted to berate her, but there was just no point in that. "Have you applied for a loan to buy him out?" I asked.

"They turned me down," she admitted. "I don't know what I'm going to do."

I was glad I hadn't yelled at her. I would be very upset if I were losing my house.

"So you're going to put it on the market?" asked Nina, her eyes wide.

"How did I ever get myself into this mess?" Natasha moaned.

Nina and I knew the answer to that, but we had the decency not to say so.

I glanced at my watch. "I've been here way too long. Nina, do you want to come with me or stay here with Bernie?"

"I'll come browse through the tents."

"Spy on Greer's, will you?" asked Natasha as we walked out the door.

"Who's minding the store at your tent?" I asked.

"My sister."

"I'm so glad that you're getting along," I said.

"We do have a lot in common. We're still searching for our father."

Natasha had only recently located her half-sister through a DNA match. They not only shared a father, but he'd apparently had a type of woman that he liked. Both of them had earthy moms who believed in the power of stones and potions. "Have your moms met yet?" I asked.

"There's another headache that looms in my future. I've been able to talk my mom out of coming up here, but I can't do that forever."

"You have told her about your sister, haven't you?" Nina asked.

Natasha avoided eye contact. "Um, well, sort of."

"You haven't told her?" I gasped.

"Seriously, Sophie? How would you tell your mother that the man she married abandoned her and her child and waltzed off to marry someone else?"

She had a point. "I wouldn't be able to do that over the phone. I would drive to Berrysville and tell her face-to-face. It would be hard to do, but your mom would probably deal with it better than most people. Look at you. In the beginning it was horrifying to you. And now you like them."

Nina nudged me. I followed the nod of her head.

Wolf had shown up and was standing in front of Lark's house with his arms crossed over his chest.

Chapter 22

Dear Natasha,
I can't stand the tiles in the backsplash behind my kitchen sink. I've pried one loose, so I know that can be done. But what can I replace it with that won't cost a fortune? I can't afford a tile installer.
  Ugly Tile Has Got to Go in Pearl Beach, Michigan

Dear Ugly Tile Has Got to Go,
First pat yourself on the back for getting rid of that eyesore! You can always paint your backsplash. From a scenic vista, to flowers, or a checkerboard, your imagination is the limit. Just be sure to seal it. You can also buy beautiful stick-on mini-tiles in glass, stone, and mother-of-pearl. No one will ever suspect!

                                              Natasha

Trying to look calm and collected, I crossed over to Lark's house with Nina. "Is something wrong?" I asked Wolf.

Paisley glared at her husband. She held a green leather

box, of a type I had seen used for antique jewelry, complete with a brass snap and hinges. She flipped open the lid. White satin lined the interior, but it was empty.

Frank's face burned with fury. "I'll tell you what's wrong. A priceless family heirloom is missing. The police did a thorough search of the house and surprise, surprise, now the box it was in is empty."

Paisley winced, her brow furrowed. She spoke through clenched teeth. "Is that who took it, Frank?"

"Who else?" he said angrily.

Speaking softly, I asked, "Could this heirloom be the reason someone killed Lark?"

"No one knew about it," said Paisley.

Wolf raised his eyebrows. "Clearly the two of you knew. Probably Bennett, too?"

"Bennett!" spat Frank. "If Bennett got hold of it, it's gone by now."

"What was it?" I asked.

"Jewelry that my grandfather had made," said Paisley. "It makes me sick to my stomach that someone stole it. If they're professional thieves, they'll break it down into pieces and use it to make new jewelry so it can't be tracked. And if they're stupid kids, they may end up throwing it in the trash because they'll panic and be afraid of getting caught. I can't believe this is happening!"

"Who entered the house the day Lark died?" With angry black eyes, Frank directed his question to Wolf.

To his credit, Wolf remained stoic and unflustered. "I think it's highly unlikely that the police have anything to do with missing jewelry."

"Really?" Frank spoke sarcastically. "I want a list of those people and I want them all polygraphed. And if you don't do that by tomorrow, I will file a suit against the police department."

"Perhaps we should begin with a list of the non-official

people who have been in the house," said Wolf, sounding quite amiable.

Paisley nodded. "I can do that. It's mostly just family."

Of course, I couldn't help thinking of the day Frank had hauled Lark's possessions out to be sold.

"Let me know when I can pick it up," Wolf said. "In the meantime, I would recommend limiting use of the house by anyone except yourselves. There's a chance someone has moved it or hidden it elsewhere to remove later on."

"What are you implying?" Frank shouted.

"I'm not implying anything. Perhaps you'll find it tonight." Wolf walked away.

Nina and I followed him. "You seem awfully calm about this," I whispered.

Wolf shrugged. "If Frank and Bennett were ransacking your house, what would you do with something priceless that you wanted to keep?"

I gasped and stopped walking. "Are you kidding? You think Paisley hid it from them?" Now that I thought about it, that was exactly what I would have done in her shoes. Frank had been so busy carting Lark's possessions out to sell on the very next day after her death. I would have taken anything that was valuable and hidden it. "Of course! And now she can't come clean because Frank would run off and sell it. She didn't plan on anyone calling the police about it."

"Precisely."

"How did you know?" asked Nina.

"Let's just say it's not the first time I've seen this particular song and dance. Death is heart-wrenching, but it brings out the worst in some people. All they see is dollar signs."

"Does Frank have a criminal record?" I asked, hoping the answer would be *no*.

Wolf gazed at me for a minute. "It's all public record. I

don't see why I can't tell you. Frank doesn't but his father was well known to the police. Frank's uncle, too."

"Would they have murdered Lark?"

"No. Frank's father and his uncle have both passed away. With the exception of a few bar brawls, they weren't violent. Mostly they were engaged in fencing stolen goods."

I breathed a sigh of relief.

Nina shivered. "Imagine having them at your family holiday celebrations."

"They're small fry," Wolf said as though that were reassuring. "But they have some connections to worrisome felons."

"I guess that narrows down the suspects. Frank probably blabbed about his mother-in-law's priceless jewelry. Then Frank, or one of his unsavory friends, paid her an early morning visit."

"It's possible," Wolf murmured. "But it doesn't explain the attempted break-in at Nina's house or Dulci's murder."

"So you think they're all connected."

"It's a possibility," he said, neatly ducking my question.

"Do you have Dulci's autopsy results yet?" I asked.

"The same as Lark's, a bash on the head and bruising from a fall," he said. "Nina, have you thought of anything that might have happened to you in Portugal?"

"Not a thing. Across the board, everyone says it was a great trip and nothing untoward happened except for the doll being thrown at us, which apparently happens quite often and not just in Portugal."

He nodded. "That's the same thing I'm getting. If you hear of anything, let me know. Okay?"

He walked away and more than anything, I wished it were dinnertime and that I could round up my friends to mull over the situation. Poor Nina had to be scared out of her wits.

A white-haired woman with a broad grin walked toward Nina and me. She wore a long gauzy skirt and a blouse that revealed cleavage. It took me a moment to realize that it was Natasha's mother, Wanda. She had aged since I had seen her last. She opened her arms wide and crushed me in a big hug and then moved on to do the same to Nina.

"Sophie! Nina!" she cooed. "I haven't seen you in the longest time." Unlike her daughter, Natasha, Wanda Smith was about as down home as a woman could get. She had worked in a diner as long as I had known her. She gardened and loved animals. She believed in old-fashioned remedies that no one used anymore. I had once caught her in Natasha's backyard turning in circles under the moon sprinkling some herb around her.

"Let me have a look at you two," she said. "Oh darlin's, you're as pretty as ever. Now Sophie, I have to know. Did you get back together with Mars once Natasha tossed him to the curb? I knew he wasn't the right man for her, but I sure do like that fella."

Nina opened her mouth and gazed at me.

Natasha had lied to her mother about who instigated their break-up. I elbowed Nina. Natasha was, in the parlance of Desi Arnaz, going to have *some 'splainin' to do*. I wasn't getting in the middle of that mess. "We're still friends."

Wanda seemed disappointed. "Well you keep workin' on him, sweetheart. Now where might I find my daughter? She told me she had a booth here."

And in the tent right next to her daughter's was the woman Wanda's husband had married when he left Wanda.

Chapter 23

Dear Natasha,
I have a little bag of coins left over from travels
abroad. Some of them are really pretty. What can I
do with them?

In the Money in Coin, Iowa

Dear In the Money,
Leaving a small space between the coins, glue them
to a simple plastic hairband. Take a twisted gold
wire and snake it between the coins in a serpentine.
Now you have a gorgeous one-of-a-kind hairband!

Natasha

Natasha should have told her mother about Griselda Smith months ago when Natasha located her half-sister, Charlene. Wanda would have learned the truth in bits and pieces and had time to digest it all. I shouldn't criticize Natasha, I was equally good at putting off uncomfortable news. But now it was too late to ease Wanda into the truth.

The only bright side to the whole thing was that Griselda

and her daughter, Charlene, were about as nice as anyone could be.

There was nothing I could do about it now. Wanda was here. I exchanged a look with Nina. "Her tent is this way, Wanda."

"Everybody at the diner sends their best," said Wanda. "Your mom and dad were positively envious when I told them I was coming up for a visit. They said you're so busy that you never invite them, so I told them that I wasn't invited at all. I was just going to come on up here and surprise my baby girl."

There were going to be a lot of surprises. I stopped her. "Are my parents on their way, too?"

"Don't you worry, sweetheart. You dad is in a golf tournament, so this isn't a good time for them." She looked from side to side at the tents as we walked. "I'm so impressed with the clever things everyone has made. Did you see the tent where that woman turns everything into gold? What was that guy's name? Midas!"

"That's Greer. She has some remarkable things."

And then it happened. Wanda Smith saw Griselda Smith's tent. It beckoned her like a fish to water.

"Oh my!" Wanda said. "We have to stop *here*."

It was like watching a car accident in slow motion. Every fiber of my being wanted to prevent what was going to happen but it was already on a collision course.

"Hi!" Griselda reached out her hand to Wanda. "I'm Griselda Smith. What can I help you with today?"

Wanda took the outstretched hand and shook it. "Wanda Smith. You have such beautiful things." She gasped. "And herbs! The last time I was here, I like to never have found any horse chestnut. This time I came prepared. Where's your store in case I need anything?"

"Isn't that funny? We have the same last name," said Griselda.

I mashed my eyes shut, waiting for the worst.

But Wanda chuckled. "One of my husband's two million relatives!"

Griselda continued, "I haven't got a store yet, but I'm planning to open one as soon as I can find the right location. Rents run high in Old Town."

"Do you have a card or phone number where I can reach you? I don't know that I'll need you this trip, but I would feel so much better if I knew where I can buy the herbs I need when I come to visit my daughter."

My heart thundered in my ears. I could see the tension in Nina's face when she glanced my way. Any minute now one of them was bound to say something that tied Griselda to Natasha and the world might just blow up. Their world anyway.

Griselda jotted her name and phone number on a slip of paper and handed it to Wanda.

I realized I had been holding my breath and exhaled. Maybe, just maybe, the confrontation wouldn't happen at this moment.

But then Natasha swung into the tent saying, "Griselda, I just heard about a wonderful space for your store—" A moment of awkward silence followed. "Mom! What are you doing here?"

Wanda grinned and opened her arms wide for a hug. "Surprise!"

The two of them embraced and I could see Griselda looking at Wanda with a totally different expression. "You're Wanda?" she asked.

My job here was done. I could so easily have grabbed Nina and backed out, could have said goodbye, and been on my way. But I was riveted to the spot.

Natasha gave me a wide-eyed frantic look.

"Why don't the two of you go grab a cup of coffee," I suggested. "Maybe Charlene can watch your tent?"

Griselda folded her arms over her chest. "You haven't told her about us. Wanda doesn't know, does she?"

Wanda glanced at Griselda. "Know what?"

"I cannot believe that you haven't told your mother." Griselda looked Wanda straight in the eyes and said, "There's a reason we have the same last name. We married the same man."

Wanda's gaze flew from Griselda to Natasha. She turned around to me. "I know you'll tell me the truth, Sophie."

It wasn't my place to tell her everything that had happened. How Natasha was looking for her father and had found Charlene, her half-sister through DNA testing. And that led to Griselda, her mom, who was so much like Wanda that we had all been astonished. I simply nodded my head, leaving the long story to Natasha and Griselda.

Without another word, I tugged at Nina and left Wanda to tell her story of life with Natasha's father. I walked over to Big Daddy's bakery, bought a box full of croissants, cupcakes, and cookies, and then stopped by to pick up four mocha lattes. Natasha wouldn't touch any of it, but that was her problem. Nina and I carried it all back to Natasha's tent.

Charlene had joined the group by then. I handed her the goodies, kissed Wanda on the cheek, and left them to sort out their life stories, which would undoubtedly end where they always did—where was Amos, the man who had married Wanda and Griselda, fathered their daughters, and left them all without so much as a fare-thee-well?

Mars phoned Nina to say he was heading back to my house. He located us among the tents and the two of them walked home.

I thought about Wanda and Griselda through the rest of the day. As things wound down, I headed for the grocery store to pick up items for dinner. I had pork tenderloin in mind because it cooked fast and was always delicious.

Small red potatoes to roast in the oven, and a bundle of fresh green baby spinach as the basis for a salad. I stood quietly for a moment, thinking about a quick dessert, when the gossipy voices of two ladies nearby infiltrated my thoughts.

"I can tell you one thing, if I were Nina Reid Norwood, I would be quaking in my boots. She's the next one. What do you suppose they did on that tour?"

"I don't think it had anything to do with their trip. Unless, of course, it was Whitney's son. What's his name? Hutt! Who would name their child Hutt?"

"I understand it's a family name."

"Pity. It's not what you'd call melodious."

"Sounds like Hun, as in Attila the Hun."

They giggled. "Maybe it's the right name for him after all. Do you think he would murder someone?"

"All I know is that he was in my daughter's class in school and she was terrified of him. He was the original bully. Don't they usually outgrow that kind of behavior?"

The two women moved on, still chatting, but I had heard enough to make me wonder.

I stared blindly at the perfectly stacked boxes of berries. And suddenly I knew exactly what Bernie and Mars would love—a berry trifle. I added raspberries and blueberries to my cart and grabbed a bag of gingersnap cookies and some heavy cream.

As I walked home, I thought about the travel agent's son, Hutt. He had two things against him. Most importantly, he had been on the trip, which meant he knew the other travelers and had the opportunity to spy on them or at least learn about them. He also had access to their addresses through his mother and her computer.

But we were missing a motive. I could only think that he had been blackmailing them. But then why kill them? Wasn't it more profitable to keep the money rolling in? As far as I knew, he hadn't had any other connection to them. I would have to ask Nina. Maybe he volunteered somewhere and knew them through some organization.

Mars and Nina were lounging in the kitchen when I came home. Mars opened the door for me and took the heavy grocery bags out of my hands.

Mochie mewed and rubbed my ankles. Daisy and Muppet pranced, eagerly awaiting a petting session. I indulged them all.

Nina handed me a glass of wine. "To what do I owe this reception?" I asked.

But before anyone answered, the door opened and Bernie bounded into the kitchen. The dogs and Mochie started their excited fuss all over again. Nina handed him a glass of wine, too.

While sipping the delicious wine, I unpacked the groceries and we all fell to tasks for dinner. Mars and Nina helped Bernie cut the potatoes and I started the pork tenderloin. While the pork cooked, I turned my attention to slicing onions and chopping pecans for the salad, I told them all about the encounter between Wanda and Griselda.

"Hah!" Bernie chuckled. "I wouldn't want to be eating dinner with them tonight."

I had to agree. "The tension must be awful. They share a lot of interests, so I suspect they might end up being friends, but that will take some time."

Our timing was pretty good. I washed the berries for the trifle and spread them on paper towels to dry. I beat the cream so it would be ready, and whisked together cider vinegar, olive oil, and honey to dress the salad.

I took out a French farmhouse-style tablecloth in spring shades of blue, yellow, and green and set the table with Royal Worcester Evesham plates adorned with fruits and vegetables.

The potatoes came out of the oven, crispy on the outsides.

In minutes, Mochie and the dogs were fed, and we sat down to eat. The topic of conversation turned to the murders immediately.

Mars grumbled a little when he had to stop eating Bernie's crispy potatoes to retrieve a pen and a pad of paper.

"Before you start making your lists," I said, "I wanted to ask Nina about Hutt, the travel agent's son. Did you know him before you went on your trip?"

"I expect I had seen him around town. But he doesn't volunteer at the animal shelter or anything," she said, cutting into a juicy piece of pork.

"Then there's no reason for him to have tried to break into your house?" asked Mars.

"Of course not. There's no good reason for anyone to break in," insisted Nina.

"No cash on hand? No artwork or other valuables?" asked Bernie.

"Well, when you put it that way, maybe. But why choose my house? Natasha has all kinds of fancy stuff," said Nina. "And for that matter, you live in a mansion. If I were a thief, I would pick your house on the assumption that someone very wealthy lived there."

I chuckled. "The most valuable thing Mars owns is an autographed baseball."

"Not true," said Mars. "I have acquired a genuine helmet autographed by Joe Namath that happens to be worth five times what the baseball would fetch."

"Well, if you're counting that kind of thing, my husband—" Nina paused, holding her fork in the air. "Oh my gosh. How could I have forgotten? My husband has a little coin collection. As those things go, I don't think it's very impressive, but he does have a few gold coins that I suppose are worth stealing."

"I didn't know that," said Bernie. "I have an interest in numismatics myself. I've lived and traveled in so many countries that I started picking up interesting coins. As you say about your husband's collection, it wouldn't impress a major collector. We should get together sometime. I'd be interested in seeing what he has."

"Does anyone know if Lark, Dulci, or their husbands collected coins?" I asked.

None of them knew.

"Was anything in particular a topic of conversation during your tour?" Mars stopped eating and gazed at her inquisitively. "Perhaps Lark said something about her silver and then you told her about the painting in your living room?"

"Which painting?" Nina frowned.

"Whichever one is valuable," Bernie said patiently.

"We like them, but none of them are museum worthy if that's what you're getting at."

"You didn't talk about anything like cash or heirloom jewelry or your husband's coin collection?" I asked.

Nina didn't reply right away. "There was jewelry on display at the Palacio Nacional. I think that's what it was called. It's considered the Versailles of Portugal. The guide told us that they had loaned some pieces to a museum in Holland for an exhibition of crown jewels. Some clever person or persons managed to get by all the alarms, break the case, and steal millions of dollars of crown jewels, not just from Portugal. They've never found the missing jewelry or the culprit!"

"Was Hutt there?" I asked.

"I can't say that I took roll call, but I think he was," Nina said. "My husband and Dr. Chryssos even went on that tour. It's very impressive."

"Put Hutt on your list of suspects, Mars," said Bernie. "Maybe he was inspired."

"It would explain why Lark and Dulci let him into their homes," I said. "But if he was after their jewelry, why not try to enter the homes when no one was home? That way he wouldn't have had to murder anyone." Bernie had thrown some raw sliced apples into the salad. I speared one and savored the tart sweetness.

"He would have had to break in, which might be complicated. Or he was smart enough to do it in the dark of night so he wouldn't be seen," Nina suggested. She gasped. "Lark talked about her father being some kind of fancy jeweler in New York. She said something like 'he had a salon in his apartment where he met with super-wealthy clients to design one-of-a-kind pieces for them.'"

"Bennett mentioned that to me today, too. And Paisley and Frank were arguing about a family heirloom that her father made. It has gone missing. Paisley thinks Frank took it. Wolf thinks Paisley is lying to Frank and that she hid it from him," I said.

"Now we've got something!" Mars excitedly scribbled on his list. "Did Dulci have some kind of family heirloom that might have been valuable?"

Once again, no one knew. We all looked at Nina waiting to hear if she had heirlooms worth stealing. "I do have some jewelry that my grandmother left me, but nothing worth killing for. I would be sad if it were stolen, but it's more sentimental than valuable. If I tried to sell the pieces, I don't think they would add up to much."

"All right then, Sophie, you check out Dulci's jewelry situation," said Mars.

"She was just murdered!" Nina objected. "She can hardly go to Emery and ask snoopy questions about his wife's jewelry."

"She'll think of a way," he said, flashing me a smile. "I'm

sure Emery would like to find her killer. He'll understand if you tell him that's why you're asking him questions."

Mars was probably right. Emery hadn't balked a bit this morning. It might seem uncaring, but it was so important to find the link between the victims. Emery would understand that.

"Then there's Humphrey." Mars wrote his name on the list.

"I think you can strike him. The only motive he could possibly have had to kill Lark was that she turned him down when he proposed. Why on earth would he have come to my house in the middle of the night or murdered Dulci? No way."

"I have to agree with Nina," I said. "Trying to eliminate Humphrey would only be a colossal waste of time."

"Doesn't Dulci's death also eliminate Frank and Bennett as suspects?" asked Bernie. "If the theory is that they were after Lark's money, then why bother to kill Dulci?"

"It feels like someone has pulled the rug out from under us," said Mars. "Maybe we should go over the incidents. Is it possible that none of them are connected?"

"Aside from the obvious fact that all three women were on the same trip to Portugal, there is one thing that stands out in my mind—the ladders. It's so obvious that neither Lark nor Dulci was outside predawn in high heels climbing a ladder. That had to be staged."

"The killer thought he could fool the authorities into thinking their deaths were accidents? It sounds like we're dealing with someone who isn't terribly bright," said Bernie.

"Or he didn't think it through," said Nina. "Maybe he didn't plan to kill anyone. He saw Humphrey leave Lark's house, assumed in the dark that it was Lark, broke in—" She stopped abruptly.

"The theory is she let him or her in," I said, pointing out the loophole.

*   *   *

I cleared the dishes from the table and assembled our berry trifles. Nina poured a generous amount of raspberry liqueur into the dishes while I was working. In each individual trifle dish, I placed crunchy gingersnap cookies, followed by a good dollop of berries, then whipped cream, and repeated the process, ending with whipped cream on top of each one. I poured tea for me and decaf coffee for Bernie. Nina and Mars stayed with the wine.

The conversation abated when we tried the trifle. It was the perfect combination of flavors and textures. We had just finished when we heard a loud boom and felt the earth shake.

Chapter 24

Dear Sophie,
I'm doing a retro country kitchen with a turquoise refrigerator and curtains below the sink. My budget is shot but I need café curtains to finish the look. I can't find the right thing and I can't afford to pay big bucks to have them made.
                    It's Curtains for Me in Old Town, Maine

Dear It's Curtains for Me,
Place a tension rod in your window. Buy four to six (depending on the size) retro-style kitchen towels that match your décor. Snap curtain clip rings on them and slide them onto the tension rod.
                                        Sophie

"What was that?" Mars asked. He flew to the picture window with the rest of us behind him.

"There's a fire at my house!" Mars exclaimed.

Bernie craned his neck. "Oh. You mean at Natasha's house."

"It's still half mine." Mars scrambled past us and ran to the front door.

At that moment the lights went out. Sirens wailed in the distance. I locked the kitchen door, made sure the stove was off, and ran out the front door, taking the time to lock it behind me. The dogs yelped and whined at being left behind. Mars, Bernie, and Nina were already halfway down the block.

I could hear Natasha screaming. I wasn't much of a runner, but I sped along the sidewalk as fast as I could. Wong stepped out of a squad car near me and began to yell, "Step away! Back up, folks. We could have live electrical wires down. You do not want to be electrocuted. Back away from the vehicle."

The car was barely visible in the ball of flame.

"Go, go, go!" Wong instructed.

Everyone who lived on the street had emerged from their homes. Firetrucks arrived and soon firefighters joined Wong in shooing everyone back to a safe distance.

Wanda, Natasha, Charlene, and Griselda huddled in a tight little mass. I ran back to my house and fetched warm blankets for them. When I returned, Natasha was sobbing on Mars's shoulder.

In the light of the fire I could see his face. While he had a heart of gold, I was willing to bet Natasha wouldn't win him back. He had had enough of her daily dramas.

I handed Wanda a blanket. "At least the house isn't on fire."

"There's no electricity, though," said Charlene.

"Everyone on the block is out, maybe even more," Nina quickly pointed out.

Mars had released Natasha and asked, "What happened?"

"We heard a blast, the house shook, and the next thing

we knew a car was on fire outside on the street," said Griselda.

We already knew that much. I looked around and could see neighbors who had quickly donned coats and ventured outside with flashlights to see what was going on. Fire-trucks blocked the street and in the glow of headlights, I could see police officers diverting traffic.

Wong joined our little group to ask questions of Natasha, who ignored her queries.

"Should we gather our valuables? Photo albums and such?" she asked in a squeaky voice.

"Looks like they have it under control. You may have soot on the exterior walls, but I don't think there's any risk of it spreading to your house," said Wong. "Do you know whose car that is?"

"My car is in my garage," said Natasha. "And I think I saw Charlene's and Griselda's cars parked in the alley behind my house. Mom? Where did you park?"

"Natasha, honey, if that were my car, I would not be standing here quietly. I can see my car. It's fine," said Wanda.

"I hope no one is inside of it," said Bernie.

The horror of that thought silenced us for a moment.

"It exploded," said Charlene. "Like in a spy thriller."

Wong grinned. "It's probably nothing quite that exotic. The neighborhood will smell a little rotten for a day or so. Everyone will work through the night to restore power and tow the car out of here. You should be back to normal in a few hours."

Bernie took off to check on The Laughing Hound, but the rest of us continued to gawk at the burning car.

The blaze waned until the car was only a stinky dark hulk on the street. Flashlights floated over it occasionally, revealing a charred exterior.

Two hours had passed since we ate our dinner. Nina

and Mars cleaned up the kitchen, while I took the dogs out for their evening stroll. The street was eerie without any lights. Inside homes, an occasional flashlight or battery-driven lantern glimmered, but instead of being reassuring, they managed to cast odd shadows and left me feeling uneasy.

The dogs must have noticed, but their noses guided them. We strolled away from the burned-out hulk where authorities still gathered, dealing with the aftermath of restoring electricity, determining the cause of the explosion, and hauling the car away. Their distant voices added to the creepy atmosphere. I wasn't inclined to walk long even though I'd brought a flashlight. I found myself flicking it in the direction of every little noise. I wasn't certain how far the power outage extended, so while I really would have liked to turn around and go home, I headed for the area where the DIY Festival was being held to check on it.

The houses, including Lark's, loomed dark. I thought about how the town must have looked in the 1800s at night. One of the homes we passed had gas lamps on each side of the front door. What a difference it made. The house looked charming.

I spied one of the festival security guards.

"Any problems?" I asked.

"Aww, a few kids who have no business being out anyway. We shooed them away. Most of these folks must have read the advice we sent out. They've set up cameras and alarms so we'll know if anyone is messing with their stuff."

"You're keeping an eye on the penny bar, right?"

"You bet. And that lady with all the gold gave us a nice bonus. In all the years I've been doing hired security gigs, that has never happened!"

I had to give Greer credit. "That was nice of her."

"No kidding. The only way anyone is getting in there is over my dead body."

I wished he hadn't said that. But I bid him a good night and asked him to call me if any trouble arose. With a little luck, the power would be back soon.

Thankfully, the power had been restored when I rose the next morning. I lingered under the warm water of the shower, then blew my hair dry and stepped into a coral dress cut in a princess style. It was comfortable and slenderizing. I pinned my hair up in a loose coil and added earrings with bright rosy stones set in silver dangling off of them.

When I arrived in the kitchen, Mars had let the dogs out and made my tea. I felt totally pampered and could smell something delicious baking in the oven.

He pulled out a tray of cinnamon rolls.

"I know you didn't bake these. Where did you get them?"

At that moment, Bernie entered the kitchen with Daisy and Muppet. "Oh good! They're ready." He took sugary icing out of the fridge and poured it over them. It melted on top of the hot rolls, but we ate them anyway, savoring the warmth and heady cinnamon.

"From The Laughing Hound?" I asked.

Bernie nodded. "I went down there last night to make sure everything was okay. Our power went out briefly but came back on right away, so nothing was interrupted."

"Are you planning to work from here today?" I asked Mars. "Or should I wake up Nina?"

"Nina, the child we never had," Mars joked. "Better get her up. I have a meeting later this morning. When will her husband be back?"

From the doorway to the foyer, Nina stumbled into the kitchen. She wore a plush lavender bathrobe and fuzzy slippers with dog faces on them. "I'm having no luck at all. His plane had to take a detour due to mechanical problems. He spent the night in Salt Lake City and has to be in El Paso tomorrow. He wants to know if he should continue to fly east or go on to El Paso."

She held her hands over her face. "I love you guys and I'm so glad to have friends who look out for me, but I must be putting a crimp in your style. What's that they say about fish and guests? Three days before they stink? Maybe I should check into a hotel. Or just assume that no one is coming back to look for me and that I can go home."

Mars, Bernie, and I all said, "No!" at the same time.

"Don't be silly. I love having you here," I said.

"And you're not cramping my style a bit," Mars reassured her.

"We want you to be safe, Nina," said Bernie. "Should we go to your house for some fresh clothes? I've got a couple of hours before I have to be back at the restaurant."

She sniffled and wiped her nose with a tissue. "You're too good to me. I feel so ridiculous needing a chaperone like a child who would get into mischief left to her own devices."

"All the more reason to figure out who killed Lark and Dulci," I said. "No one will be comfortable about you going home unless he has been captured."

She nodded and reached for a cinnamon roll.

That simple gesture seemed to say it all. I went upstairs to brush my teeth. When I returned, I said, "I'm perfectly happy for you to spend the day at the DIY Festival with me. Call me and I'll come get you."

As I walked along the street toward the tents, I thought it was sort of silly to imagine that I could protect Nina. I was fairly sure that I couldn't. On the other hand, it would be harder to attack two people. And the fact that the killer appeared to have waited until Lark and Dulci were alone gave me some confidence that the mere presence of a second person might deter him.

I spied Emery standing in front of Lark's house. He looked like he hadn't slept since Dulci died. His face was haggard, he hadn't shaved, and he looked scruffy. He flagged me down. "Do you know where Lark's daughter or son live?"

"I'm sorry, I don't. But Paisley will probably be here any minute to open her tent."

No sooner had I spoken than we heard loud voices.

"Because I don't want to." Paisley came into view, followed by Frank a few steps behind her. "It's not your decision to make. It's mine!"

She unhooked bungee cords securing the walls of the tent and rolled the sides up.

Emery whispered to me, "Is that her?"

"Yes. I'd be happy to introduce you."

Frank glowered at Paisley and didn't help her with the tent. "I know about this stuff, Paisley. Your mom was a calculating witch. She did this on purpose but now that she's gone, you can undo it. All you have to do is sign the papers."

Paisley ignored him and moved pieces of furniture around to showcase them better.

"Why won't you listen to me?" Frank grumbled.

"I said no. Now stop badgering me," she said.

Emery whispered, "Maybe this isn't a good time."

But Paisley had seen us.

"Paisley?" I waved at her and encouraged Emery to come with me.

When I introduced them, Paisley caught Emery in a hug. The two of them cried and sat down in a couple of her rocking chairs. Through their tears they began to compare notes. The same autopsy results. The same time of day. The same ladder next to them.

"Did Dulci leave a sign?" asked Paisley. "Mom drew something in the dirt."

"I don't think Dulci could have drawn anything," said Emery. "She was on the brick terrace. What did your mother draw? That could be a clue."

"A circle with a dot inside it."

"A circumpunct?"

Chapter 25

Dear Sophie,
I saved my childhood furniture imagining that my
child would use it. It's darling white French provincial–
style furniture with gold accents. I have a seven-
year-old son. Help!
                    Footballs and Dinosaurs in France, Idaho

Dear Footballs and Dinosaurs,
Take heart. Paint the furniture a boyish color, like
navy or gray. Once the gold accents are gone, the
furniture will look completely different.

                                            Sophie

Paisley gasped. "That means something to you?"
    "It's an ancient symbol. "As I recall it means the sun.
Or in some religions it is the beginning of creation and
eternity."
    "Eternity?" Paisley said in surprise. "Mom knew she
was dying and left us a message that she wasn't really
gone? That she would be with us in eternity?" Paisley
sobbed.

Frank showed no sympathy. He said dully, "Oh, fine. Imagine that was Lark waving bye-bye. She's still manipulating you from beyond the grave with her little surprise in the will. The woman was nuts and a control freak. There, I said it. For years I have reeled in my thoughts about her. She didn't want you to marry me and now she's reaching out from her grave to punish you."

Emery stared at Frank in shock. "I must say I think you are being extremely unkind. Can't you see that your wife is in pain about the loss of her mother?"

Frank's hand curled into a fist. "Who *are* you?"

"Dr. Emery Chapman. The husband of Dulci Chapman, who was murdered in exactly the same manner as your mother-in-law."

Frank stammered, "I . . . I'm sorry. I didn't know. That explains why the detective came prowling around again."

"It was in the newspaper," Emery pointed out.

"Yeah," Frank said, nodding. "We've been a little busy. I can't say we're reading the news much these days. I heard about it, but it never occurred to me there would be a connection."

I thought this might be a good time to get in a few questions. "Emery, do you or Dulci have a coin collection?"

"No. I like sports memorabilia. Oh, wait! Dulci collected those quarters with the states on them for our grandchildren."

Paisley blew her nose and nodded. "My mom did, too."

I would have to check, but as I recalled the coins were still in circulation. Could they be worth much? Had one been made with a mistake, making it super valuable?

"What about jewelry? I know Lark had some special items. How about Dulci?"

Emery's eyes narrowed as he gazed at me. "You think they were killed in plain old robberies?"

"Was anything missing from your house?" I asked.

Emery's expression changed to one of surprise. "I don't know. I was so shocked and devastated that it didn't occur to me to look for anything. You saw her, Sophie. Did they take her diamond or her wedding ring?"

I understood how he had felt. I hadn't been close to Dulci but my own horror in finding her dead had been so overwhelming that I hadn't noticed her rings. "I'm sorry, Emery. I didn't pay any attention to that. Wolf would know. I think she wore a coin necklace."

"That was one of her favorites. I gave it to Dulci for her fiftieth birthday," he said. "Ridiculously expensive but the coin is real gold and you only turn fifty once. She was thrilled with it."

"Did she wear it in Portugal?" I asked.

He shook his head. "She didn't like to travel with good jewelry, except for her wedding rings."

So much for that theory. I was fairly certain that Dulci had been wearing her coin necklace when I found her. If the goal had been robbery, it would have been gone.

Paisley reached for his hand and clutched it. "What did they do?" she asked in a soft voice. "What could the two of them possibly have done that would have angered someone enough to kill them?"

Emery held her hand as if it gave him solace. "Was Lark's house ransacked?"

Paisley drew a sharp breath. "No. But her luggage was strewn on the floor of her closet and the laundry room was in disarray. That wasn't like Mom at all."

Frank's phone rang. He glanced at it and walked away to take the call.

I whispered to Paisley, "Is the family heirloom really gone or did you hide it from Frank?"

"I wish I had been smart enough to hide it from him. The very day she died, when he took the kids home, I should have gone through the house and hidden things, but I was, I don't know, in a state of shock? I'm just now beginning to think more clearly. I don't have it. I swear. Mom's murderer could have taken it, or it could have been Frank, or Bennett. They weren't anything I would wear—"

"They?" I asked.

"There were three pieces, all in the same box. You could tell they were old because of the way they had been made. There was a ring set with a huge stone, and two brooches containing large emeralds meant to look like clovers. I think my grandfather's father may have made them."

"You're sure they're gone now?" I asked. "Could your mother have hidden them somewhere?"

"Anything is possible. I didn't even know about them until almost a year ago. I was helping Mom set the table for Christmas Eve dinner. She had stashed the box in a nook, like a little hiding place, behind a drawer. It fell over and I couldn't get the drawer to shut, so I pulled it out and there was the box. I didn't recognize it so I opened the box. And there were these three amazing pieces inside."

"You asked her about them?"

"That's when she told me they were very valuable heirlooms that she had inherited from her father when he died," said Paisley.

"Did you ever mention them to anyone outside of the family?" I asked.

"I don't think so. But that doesn't mean Frank or Bennett didn't blab about them." Paisley waved at someone.

I turned to see her uncle Cal.

"Paisley, darlin'." He reached out for her. "How are you holding up, sweetheart?"

She let go of him and wiped her tear-stained face. "Uncle Cal, you can't even imagine how awful everything has been. So many problems and I keep wanting to turn to Mom and ask her advice, but she's gone." Her voice went up in pitch on the word *gone*.

He gathered her in his arms again and patted her back. "You can always come to your uncle Cal, darlin'."

She pulled away. "Do you know anything about a valuable family heirloom? A couple of brooches and a ring?"

"First I've heard of them. But you know your grandfather was a jeweler. I imagine he had some very fine pieces."

"I can't find them anywhere. Oh! Where are my manners? Dr. Emery Chapman, this is my father's brother, Cal Bickford."

The two men shook hands.

"The Realtor, I believe?" asked Emery. "I have heard of you."

"I always like to hear that. My best clients come from word of mouth. I was very sorry to hear of your wife's passing," said Cal.

"Thank you. It was such a shock. Paisley and I were just comparing the similarities in Lark's death and that of my wife."

"Oh?"

At that point, I excused myself and returned to focusing on the festival.

At noon Nina showed up with Humphrey. Her hair was a mess, and she looked like someone had put her through the ringer. "Are you okay?" I asked.

"No. Bernie very kindly accompanied me over to my house this morning and what did we find? Someone broke in."

"I thought you had those things put on your doors so no one could get in," I said.

"I did. I need sustenance. Can we go to lunch?"

"Sure." I was getting hungry myself.

Nina decided on a little shop with outdoor tables. It was a beautiful day for sitting outside in the sun. The skies were a clear blue and there wasn't even a hint of humidity in the air. She ordered a cheeseburger with the works, but I went with spiced shrimp and coleslaw, while Humphrey ordered hush puppies and fried catfish. When they brought our iced teas, sweetened for Nina and Humphrey and plain for me, she told me what had happened.

"Somebody broke through a window and climbed in. Wolf said whoever it was knew exactly what he was doing because he came prepared with gloves and knocked all the little shards down so he wouldn't cut himself. The police came to fingerprint again but we all knew they wouldn't find a thing. Bernie had to go to work but Humphrey had the day off, so he came to be my bodyguard." She smiled at him.

The only adult in the world who might be less helpful than me in a dangerous situation was Humphrey. I thought fondly of the time he had jumped on someone and ridden piggyback in an attempt to subdue him. "What did he take?" I asked.

"That's the stupidest thing! As far as I can tell, he didn't take anything. He rummaged through closets and drawers. The house is a wreck."

Humphrey nodded. "It will take her days to straighten it all out."

"What about the coin collection?" I asked.

"It's still there. My husband keeps it in a hidden safe. Whoever broke in didn't find it. All the coins are still there."

"But that doesn't make sense. Why bother to break in?"

"Wolf says they're usually looking for drugs like bottles of prescription pills. We disappointed the burglar there. Aspirin and melatonin are about all we have. But if it was someone after that kind of thing, wouldn't he have taken some booze with him? Nabbed a necklace or a bracelet?"

Our food was delivered, and Nina wasted no time biting into one of the tallest cheeseburgers I had ever seen. I peeled my shrimp and noshed on one.

"So good," Nina said. "I needed that after this morning. Here's the thing. I've been thinking about this. The burglar didn't find what he wanted. What if he was looking for me?"

For all of thirty seconds I lost my appetite. As the horror of what she'd said subsided, logic returned. "Why would he want you?" She started to say something, but I held up my finger to stop her. "And if he was the one Muppet barked at, then why would he dare to break a window, making noise that Muppet and neighbors might hear?"

"And why trash the house?" asked Humphrey.

"Might I remind you that the Colonel next door doesn't have very good hearing. If he had gone to bed, he would have taken his hearing aids out and wouldn't have heard a thing. Not even his dog, Winston, or Muppet barking. And here's the other thing. You keep asking me what happened in Portugal."

Finally! Maybe we could get to the root of the situation.

"Something did occur to me, but it didn't happen in Portugal. It happened right here in the airport. Clearly, you know my husband flies a lot for his job. So when we had to wait for our plane, because everyone has to arrive so early now, my husband strode right into one of those areas for frequent fliers. It's an upgrade when you accumulate a lot of miles. And the woman working behind the bar said, 'Hi, Dr. Norwood. Where are you off to today?'"

She took another bite of that enormous burger. I rued my decision to eat coleslaw. It probably had more mayonnaise and maybe even the same number of calories as half her juicy burger.

"Mmm," Nina murmured. "So good! So we took our drinks to a table near the bar and that was when Lark came in. And the woman working behind the bar said, 'Good afternoon, Mrs. Bickford, what can I get you today?'"

I ate my shrimp, which were loaded with Old Bay spice and delicious. I waited for her to continue.

"Don't you see?" she asked.

"No," I said.

"That makes me feel better. I didn't either," said Humphrey.

"That's why it took so long to come to me. It didn't strike me as anything unusual. But then I wondered why would people at the airport know Lark by name? That woman certainly didn't know who I was."

Maybe Nina was onto something. "You're saying that Lark traveled a lot, like your husband."

"Exactly. Do you know why?"

"No," I said.

"I don't, either. She was basically a stay-at-home mom who volunteered all over town and threw those fabulous dinner parties. So what was she doing traveling so much?" asked Nina.

It was a good question. "Paisley said she traveled a lot even when Paisley and Bennett were young. Some lady, a Mrs. Gurtz, used to stay with them. I met her briefly. She seemed very nice."

Nina finished the last morsel of her burger. "Let's find this lady and ask. And we should track down Bennett. Maybe he knows something Paisley doesn't."

We were waiting for our check when Natasha pulled up a chair. She sat down and sighed. To most people, she would have looked chic with her flawless makeup and shining hair cut in the latest shoulder-length style. She wore a thick oatmeal-colored sweater with dramatic sleeves, a matching knit oatmeal skirt, and shiny patent leather oatmeal high heels that would have caused me to fall in two steps. I would have looked like an oatmeal snowman in that outfit. It was made to be worn by some-one like Natasha.

But I could tell she was feeling lower than a snail. Tears welled up in her eyes. "I've done it. Cal Bickford has a pocket listing for my house."

"Pocket listing? What's that?" asked Nina.

"The house is for sale, but it won't be offered to the general public yet. Hence the word *pocket*. Cal has several interested buyers. He's showing the house this afternoon."

Chapter 26

Dear Sophie,
My mother-in-law gave me extra rolls of wallpaper
that she didn't need. It's beautiful, but not enough
for a whole room. What else can I do with it?
  Not Enough Wallpaper in High Rolls Mountain
                          Park, New Mexico

Dear Not Enough Wallpaper,
I love the look of wallpaper on the wall behind
shelves. Or on the back wall of an old hutch that
needs to be covered up. If it's a bright or light
color, you might line the back of a dark closet or
cabinet with it.
                          Sophie

Natasha looked off in the distance like she was dis-
traught. Most of the time when she did things like
that, I thought it was intentionally dramatic, but this time
she truly was upset. "I'm sorry, Natasha."

"It's still your fault. You never should have paid Mars

for his half of the house. You set a poor precedent," she blathered.

I wasn't going to argue with her. I had done what was right, whether she liked it or not. "In the future," I said snidely, "I shall try to take you into consideration in any decisions I make."

Nina spewed tea, which, fortunately, landed mostly on her empty plate.

"Good grief, Nina," Natasha said angrily. "Did you intend to stain my outfit?"

"Oh, Natasha," said Nina sweetly, "every time I feel the tiniest bit sorry for you, you manage to set me straight again. So where are you going to live?"

"I don't know!" Natasha wailed. "I'm going to be homeless."

"You can always move in with your mom," I said wickedly.

For a moment, I thought Natasha might faint. "I would sooner bunk in your dreadful house, Sophie."

And just like that, I knew she would be all right.

"Natasha, you have two jobs. If you cut back a little bit on expenses, you could probably afford payments on Mars's half of the house."

"There's nowhere to trim the budget. I can't dress in the sort of off-the-rack clothes that you wear. I have an image to uphold."

I paid the check, glad she had said that. I no longer felt bad for her.

Humphrey shot me a look. "I thought TV stars made a lot of money."

Natasha gazed at him as though she'd just realized he was there. "That's so sweet of you. If only we did make as much as people imagine we do."

Nina and I left Natasha and Humphrey at the table and

headed back to the festival. Most of the kinks had been ironed out in the first couple of days, now it was really just a matter of babysitting. Nina stayed with me and I felt she was quite safe. We were surrounded by vendors and shoppers, no one would dare accost Nina in front of so many people.

For the first time since the festival had commenced, I had time to browse and look at all the amazingly clever projects. Inspired by the painted furniture, I bought some chalk paint, intending to tackle the little table in my basement. If I ruined it, I guessed I could always paint it a solid color. But the MacKenzie-Childs style of bright colors and dots mixed with checkerboards called to me. I was looking forward to trying my hand at it.

Nina bought a summery wreath for her front door and an adorable bird feeder. But all the while, I was wondering why Lark had traveled so much.

When we reached Paisley's tent, chaos ensued. Wolf was in a deep discussion with Paisley and Frank. Carmela, Frank's mom, had just arrived with the children. Paisley smiled as they rushed her and clung to her legs. With Wolf looking on, Paisley took the time to kiss each of them, a quick process, since most of them seemed eager to run off and play. Only Tommy remained behind, somber and wide-eyed. He carried a book with him.

I thought we probably shouldn't interfere since Wolf was likely there on business, so I was fully prepared to focus on the other vendors, but Paisley called Nina's name. I crossed over to Paisley with her.

"Nina, did Mom say anything to you about doing business in Portugal?" asked Paisley.

"Business?" Nina said incredulously. "She was on vacation."

"Not a word?" asked Wolf. "Maybe she didn't have wine with lunch because she had an afternoon appointment?"

Nina snickered. "Absolutely not. We drank plenty of wine and port."

"My mother loved to travel. Some people are homebodies and the mere thought of leaving town gives them the heebie-jeebies, but Mom traveled all over the world. It's what she did," said Paisley, shrugging.

"Without your father?" asked Wolf.

"She traveled less when we were little kids. But she often went without Dad. He couldn't always get away on the spur of the moment because he had to work."

Wolf squinted at her. "In the past couple of years, she has been to Paris, London, Miami, San Francisco, Hong Kong, Geneva, Kuwait, New York, and Tokyo. Are you saying she flew all the way to these places for a couple of days just for fun?"

Carmela had been silent, but she stepped forward and pulled a sheet of paper from her purse. "Maybe I can clear this up." She held out the paper to Paisley and asked, "Do you recognize these?"

Everyone craned their necks to see. The image wasn't clear, as though it had been printed on an old machine. Underneath the image were the words, *Portuguese Crown Jewels*. I looked closer and made out an ornate necklace encrusted with diamonds, two rings with ridiculously large single stones, and two brooches set with green stones that looked like clover.

Paisley gasped. "Where did you get this?"

"From the Internet. You can find anything there. You can't keep secrets anymore, Paisley," said Carmela with a schadenfreude grin that worried me. I took a closer look at her. Petite, but chubby, with dark eyes that glinted with mischievous delight.

"I don't understand," said Paisley. "Why would Mother have crown jewels?"

"Are those the ones that were stolen from a Dutch museum a few years ago?" asked Nina.

Wolf watched carefully, letting the little drama play out.

"You bet they are," said Carmela with far too much satisfaction. "What was your mother doing with priceless stolen jewels, Miss Fancy Pants?"

Miss Fancy Pants? This woman did not like her daughter-in-law. I couldn't believe she would call Paisley something like that in front of us!

"I can't imagine, unless my grandfather made replacements. He was very good at that sort of thing. A lot of people asked him for Princess Diana's engagement ring. You know, the one with the twelve-carat sapphire surrounded by diamonds? I know for a fact that he made the same ring with tanzanite for a lady. It was worth a small fortune!"

"Or maybe," said Carmela, who was beginning to remind me of the Wicked Witch of the West, "your mother traveled so much because she was a jewel thief."

Paisley stared at her in shock. "I do not know why you dislike my family so much, but that's the most awful thing you could say. How dare you? Ask anyone in Old Town. My mother was very respected. By everyone." Paisley held her chin high at an odd but defiant angle.

Carmela persisted. "Your classy mother with her fine china and expensive crystal was nothing more than a thief. She looked down on us like we were scum, but the truth is that she was nothing but a porch climber."

The words *porch climber* raised goose bumps all over

me. Could Carmela have murdered Lark? I had thought the ladder was supposed to mislead everyone into thinking she had fallen. But was it more than that? A sign? A message that Lark and Dulci were porch climbers? Thieves and swindlers? Had Carmela known Dulci? What could I ask that might elicit that information but wouldn't sound like I had lost my marbles?

I never got a chance.

"My mother was not a criminal!" Paisley said in a loud and defiant voice.

Tommy screamed at Carmela, "I hate you! Why are you so mean? I never want to see you again!" He took off running, fled through the gate, and disappeared into his other grandmother's backyard.

"Now look what you've done," Frank spat at Paisley. "You've been poisoning him against my family." Shaking his head, he said to Carmela, "I'm going to get him right now. He *will* apologize to you."

As Frank walked away, Paisley ran after him. "Leave Tommy alone! He's just a little boy and he's been through a lot in the last few days."

Frank walked determinedly toward the gate.

Wolf exhaled and hastily strode after them, leaving Nina and me alone with Carmela.

She laughed. "All you people in Old Town think you're so special. The only difference between you and me is that you steal the big stuff and you don't get caught because you have crooked friends in high places. A little money greases the way and, whoosh, it's a done deal."

"I beg your pardon," exclaimed Nina. "You don't even know us."

Carmela eyed us with disdain. "I know your kind. That's all I need to know." Her voice was bitter.

"Do you happen to be acquainted with Dulci Chapman?" I asked as pleasantly as I could.

"Hah! There's another snotty woman." She laughed so hard she couldn't speak. "Did you know she thinks she can change a bad kid into a good one by letting him color pictures?" She burst into another round of uncontrollable laughter. "What a nitwit. I don't know where folks get these crazy ideas."

Wolf returned with Frank. I was glad to see that poor little Tommy hadn't been dragged back to tell this horrid woman he was sorry.

"I warned you against marrying Paisley," Carmela said to Frank. Shaking her head, she said, "Who names a child *Paisley* anyway? They were a bad lot, through and through. Good riddance to that witch. She was a terrible influence on the grandchildren. You know why Tommy hates me? It's because Lark let him do whatever he wanted. They know when I'm around there's discipline. Those children know better than to misbehave on my watch."

At that very moment, a horrified scream drew our attention. The vendors and visitors all gazed at the Eames children.

Oscar had not only painted the faces of two of his brothers bright yellow and royal blue, but he also had up-ended an entire paint can on his own head and giggled as fluorescent green paint dripped over his hair and down his face and clothes. I was glad *I* didn't have to wash him.

Wolf, Nina, and I stepped away to let the adult Eameses deal with Oscar's latest mischief. When we were safely out of range of the paint Oscar was flinging at people, I asked Wolf, "Carmela is wrong, isn't she? Lark wasn't some kind of jewelry thief."

"Mmm. She may or may not have been a thief, but I

have to be highly suspicious of her travel record. It's sort of hard to imagine why she would have gone to Paris twice last December, both times for only two days. If she had some kind of business that would account for her travel, or if she had a sick relation and only went to one place, that might be understandable. But this does cast doubt. I need to find out more about what she was doing, but so far, no one knows."

"Maybe she did some kind of work for an airline?" Nina suggested.

"We'll be checking that out, of course. I have to be honest, I don't know what to make of it. I thought maybe she had a lover, but she'd been doing this for years, even when her husband was alive," said Wolf. "The only thing the trips have in common is that they're very short. Most often just for a night or two. The tour of Portugal is the only extended trip that I've found so far."

"Have you checked to see if Dulci did the same sort of traveling?" I asked.

Wolf nodded. "Emery says they took an annual vacation, sometimes went to see relatives. Completely normal as far as I can tell. I asked to see her passport and it verifies what he told me."

"Unless she had a second passport," mused Nina.

"That would be worrisome," agreed Wolf. "No, I have a feeling that Lark was up to something that she kept secret. Not even Humphrey knows."

"Okay, wait a minute," I said. "How was she paying for all these flights? Surely, you've checked her bank account. All that flying must have been expensive. Was she getting paid to fly?"

"She was getting an erratic income, not a regular paycheck. At this point it's not entirely clear where it came from."

"You mean like laundered money?" I winced.

"I don't know," said Wolf.

I spied Tommy sitting by himself on a step and looking forlorn. He clutched his book to his chest and leaned forward with his legs tucked under him. I excused myself for a moment and walked over to him.

"What are you reading?" I sat down next to him.

"Grandma gave me this book and used to read it with me. Mom says Grandma is in heaven watching over me. I've been carrying it around, so she'll know I miss her."

"Your grandma was very special to you, wasn't she?"

He swallowed hard and nodded. "I hope they catch the person who murdered her. And I hope it was Carmela and that she'll go to prison for a long time and I'll never have to see her again."

Ouch! "You know she's your grandmother, too," I said gently.

"No, she's not. I have disowned her. Do you know what that is? It's when you don't recognize a person as related to you. She always says mean things about my mom and my grandma. I don't ever want to see her again."

I had a feeling that Carmela's hatred toward Paisley and her family had probably begun a long time ago, before Tommy was born. What a shame that Carmela hadn't hidden her true feelings from her grandchildren.

Tommy leaned against me and I stroked his hair. "In a few days, everything will have calmed down and be better again." I glanced at the title of the book. *Sean and the Mystery of the Symbols*. Cute, I thought. Dan Brown for kids. On a whim, I asked, "Tommy, what does a circle with a dot in it mean?"

"Gold."

"You're sure about that?" I asked.

"Well, it can mean the sun, too, but Grandma and I decided that a sun should have rays coming out of it. Doesn't that sound more like the sun?" he asked.

"It does!" I said. But I was thinking that his grandmother, Lark, was no dummy. She had used a symbol that Tommy would understand. Now if only the stupid adults could figure out what she was telling us. *Gold.*

Chapter 27

Dear Natasha,
My new husband brought the most ghastly old fur-
niture with him when we moved into our new
house. This stuff belongs in the garbage! How do I
get rid of it without blowing up my marriage?
                    Allergic to Musty Junk in Old Town
                              Alexandria, Virginia

Dear Allergic to Musty Junk,
This requires stealth. One piece at a time must dis-
appear with a new piece in its place so he won't no-
tice. For instance, replace the torn, dirty recliner
with a comfy new chair! Under no circumstances
should he see his furniture waiting for the garbage
pickup.

                                            Natasha

That night Bernie brought a pizza, my personal favorite, white pizza with veggies, artichokes, and salami slices. It seemed like forever since I had eaten pizza and I could hardly wait to sit down to eat and relax, though given that the killer was still on the loose, it was questionable how much any of us would be able to truly unwind. I fed Mochie, Daisy, and Muppet, who settled down with full tummies, Mochie lying on his side to lazily wash his paws.

Nina whipped up rum runners, which were the perfect complement for the pizzas. In fact, they were so good that I thought I might serve them at a summer party.

Humphrey knocked on the door just as we sat down to eat. He carried a bakery box. I dared to hope it contained a dessert. "I heard Mars had a date and thought I'd better come over to protect Nina."

"Aww." Nina blew him a kiss.

"A date?" I asked. "Not with Natasha?"

I could see Bernie and Nina exchanging glances as though they were uncomfortable telling me the truth. "It's okay. You can tell me who he's dating."

"Greer Shacklesworth," said Bernie, before biting into a slice of pizza.

"The second time in two days. He must like her," I observed.

"She's very pretty," said Humphrey. "Even if she *is* a snob."

"Really?" asked Nina. "She always looks like she just rode a horse on an estate in Middleburg and drove into town for lunch."

Bernie laughed. "A most apt description, Nina. That's all show, you know. It's amazing how easy it is to fool people."

"What do you mean?" asked Humphrey.

"There is no horse or estate, and she lives in a condo north of Old Town," said Bernie.

"And just how do you know where she lives, Bernie?" Nina snickered.

"You need not bother jumping to salacious conclusions. The Laughing Hound delivers. I know where everyone lives. On a more interesting topic, is it true that Lark was fencing jewelry?" Bernie bit into another slice of pizza.

Nina and I exchanged a look.

"That got around fast," I said. "Who needs TV when you can have a beer at The Laughing Hound and catch up on everything?"

"There's some truth to that," said Bernie. "I won't deny it."

Nina and I filled Bernie in. "The symbol Lark drew when she was dying means gold. There's valuable jewelry missing from Lark's house, and she traveled extensively around the world, on very short visits."

I glanced at Humphrey to see if he would contradict anything I had said.

Humphrey summed it up. "It seems clear that Lark was killed because someone wanted the jewelry. If only I had gone back. I could have prevented her death."

Bernie, Nina, and I chimed, "No!"

"Humphrey, old man," said Bernie, "had you done that, you would also be dead right now." He sipped his martini and fixed his narrowed eyes on Humphrey. "Lark was a very secretive woman. Wasn't she?"

Humphrey reacted as though he'd been slapped, jerking his head back and viewing Bernie in horror.

"Don't get me wrong," Bernie continued. "Lark was always kind and gracious to me. But she hid her relationship with you. And now it seems, she hid something else. Something that took her all over the world for brief stints."

Humphrey shuddered. "I knew about the trips. Not in the beginning, though. She would say she was busy, had a club meeting or would be visiting relatives. I had no reason to doubt her. And then one day she slipped up. I hadn't seen her in three days. I guess I arrived shortly after she returned from a trip. She had this heavy green coat. Loden, I think she called it."

Bernie nodded. "Very European."

"She had tossed it over a chair, I thought I would hang it up to be helpful. Something made a crinkly noise in the pocket and I pulled out an airline ticket. She had flown to Florence, Italy. There was no way she could deny it. It contained her name, the dates, and the destination."

Humphrey's chest heaved as he took a deep breath. "When I confronted her about it, she said, 'I'm getting sloppy.' Then she took the ticket from me and shredded it."

"Maybe she's a spy," breathed Nina. "That would change everything!"

"That was what I thought," said Humphrey. "I pressed her on it a little, but she would only wink at me, giggle, and change the subject."

Bernie shook his head. "If Lark had been with a federal agency like the CIA or FBI, they would have been all over her murder. Wolf would have been informed and he would not be walking around town following up leads and asking questions. No way."

Humphrey looked glum but nodded. "I figured if that was the case, I'd have had a visit from them already. Sophie would have, too."

"Then what was Lark involved in?" asked Nina. "Moving high-class stolen jewelry? Paisley recognized the pieces from that picture immediately."

"I've traveled all over the world," said Bernie. "People have asked me to do a lot of things for them. Some really weird. But no one has ever approached me with stolen jewels. Not even my mother, and she loves jewelry. How could someone like Lark have obtained crown jewels? I can't even wrap my head around how much they're worth."

"Her father," I said. "Maybe he wasn't the fine jeweler her children thought. Maybe she received stolen jewels and brought them to him to pry out of the settings and create new rings to sell. That way, they would no longer be identifiable."

Nina picked a slice of salami off the pizza and munched it. "What was it that Paisley's mother-in-law said? Something about how Lark wasn't any better than them?"

"Did she imply that they were jewel thieves?" asked Bernie.

"Not overtly. But what if that was what she meant? Didn't Wolf say her husband had been in trouble with the law?"

"Yes, I think he did," I said. "But a brawl in a bar is way different from fencing stolen goods. Especially crown jewels."

"I don't know about you," said Humphrey. "But I need chocolate." He opened the box and lifted out a chocolate cheesecake.

Nina squealed. "It's been forever since I had cheesecake. Bring it on!"

Someone tapped at the door. Mars peeked in. I unlocked the door and swung it open. "You're home early."

He shrugged off his coat and slung it into the den where he'd been sleeping. "Wow! I'll have some of that."

"So how was the date?" asked Nina.

"Fine," he said.

I detected a definite lack of enthusiasm. "You don't look very happy."

He smiled. "I'm happy I made it home in time for dessert."

"Ouch! You don't like Greer?" I asked, getting up to make tea and decaf coffee.

"She's attractive." He sounded like he was searching for something nice to say about Greer.

Bernie snickered. "You can tell us, Mars."

"She's kind of dull. She was fine but uninteresting. You know, I think maybe I'm too old for dating. I kept imagining that the conversation here would be much more intriguing," said Mars.

At which point, Nina breathlessly told Mars about her broken window, and why we thought Lark was fencing stolen jewelry but wasn't a spy.

Mars silently took it all in and then roared. "You see what I mean? It's hard to top all that. Greer never had a chance."

While we savored the chocolate cheesecake, I asked Bernie, "Where does Bennett Bickford live?"

"There's a newish group of red brick condos on Duke Street. No lawns, one of those places where you can lock the door and be gone for a while without worrying about the grass or the mail."

"I think I know which one you're talking about," I said. "That makes sense since he's on the road so much. Thanks."

Mars looked at me. "How are we supposed to figure out who would have killed Lark for the Portuguese crown jewels?"

"What I want to know," said Nina, "is why did that person kill Dulci and come after me?"

None of us had an answer to that.

Mars located the sheet of paper where he had made notes, and I poured hot tea and decaf coffee for everyone.

"Fact," said Mars, "Lark drew a symbol for gold when she lay dying. And it's a fact that the time and manner of Dulci's death were so similar to Lark's death that it was very likely the same killer."

"It's also a fact that the crown jewels have gone missing," added Nina.

"Frank's mother loathes the Bickfords and made fun of Dulci for being an art therapist," I added.

"That's right! Did you think it sounded like Carmela might have had a problem child who went to see Dulci?"

"It did," I said.

"What did she call him? *The bad kid*. Dulci and art therapy couldn't turn a bad kid into a good kid," Nina recalled aloud.

Bernie blinked rapidly. "Are you suggesting that Carmela or someone in Frank's family murdered Lark because they didn't like her and then also murdered Dulci because they didn't like her, either? Those would be some really sick people."

Nina raised her palm in a gesture to stop. "Once again, I am left out of the equation. I didn't even know Frank's mother."

I was looking forward to the end of the DIY Festival. There wasn't all that much for me to do there now. I rose early anyway and let the dogs out while I made myself a nice hot mug of tea. I glanced at the time. If I showered and dressed quickly, I could pay Bennett a visit before the festival woke up and commenced again.

An hour later, Mochie sat in the bay window doing his post-breakfast grooming while Muppet and Daisy had jumped into bed with Mars. I had showered, dried my hair, and dressed in a beige linen skirt and a coral sweater set. It was very preppy, but convenient. When the sweater was too warm, I could tie it over my shoulders. Simple hoop earrings looked fine, and then I ruined the look with a pair of Keds, which were a necessity for walking around all day. I grabbed my purse and slipped out the door without waking the dogs.

It was a little hike to Bennett's condo from my house, but I figured the exercise would do me good and maybe even work off enough calories for me not to feel guilty about a bagel with salmon or a chocolate croissant for breakfast later on. The red brick building was a curious construction, more wide than tall. I walked up the steps, opened a door, and strode into a lobby. "Mr. Bickford?" I said to the gentleman at the desk.

"Back that way on the right."

I thanked him and followed his instructions. I hoped it wasn't too early. I didn't mean to catch him in his jammies. The door was unremarkable, simple and plain. I pressed the buzzer.

"Yes?" came a male voice over a speaker.

"It's Sophie Winston, your mom's friend?"

Chapter 28

Dear Sophie,
I love collecting itty-bitty things. Like tiny stone dogs and cats. And little glass birds and squirrels. But they kind of all merge and they're really hard to dust. How can I display them?
Collector in Littleton, Colorado

Dear Collector,
Find a wooden box that's about twelve inches tall and eighteen inches wide. Make two shelves to fit inside it and add screw eyes and a wire on the back for hanging. Use strong glue to attach a decorative frame on the front and place your little treasures inside.
Sophie

I heard a buzzing noise and tried the doorknob. The door swung open and Bennett, dressed in a Columbia sweatshirt and training shorts, smiled at me. "What can I do for you, Sophie?"

"I'm sorry to intrude. Do you have a few minutes?"

He showed me into a large room with an ornate fireplace. I was pretty sure the condos weren't very old, but the molding on the fireplace was impressive. It was the kind of thing I usually saw in very old homes. A giant bay window lined with cushions jutted outward, overlooking other fancy homes. The décor was nice, but simple, which I understood was the trend. I sat down on a plush sofa, thinking he must be a fairly good gambler if he could afford to buy a condo in this building. "I understand that Lark traveled a lot."

"That's right."

"I thought maybe you could shed some light on that."

He gazed at me, seemingly perplexed. "I'm not sure what you want to know. Mom liked to travel."

"It's sort of unusual for someone to travel often but only for a couple of days, even when it required a very long flight."

"Is it? I do the same sort of thing."

He did, didn't he? "Was Lark also a professional gambler?" I asked.

"No. Mom liked a scratch-off lottery ticket now and then, but she was never into gambling in general."

I felt like he was giving me the runaround. "Bennett, the night after your mother was murdered, someone tried to break into my best friend's house. She was lucky. She made it out alive. Then Dulci Chapman was murdered under circumstances much like your mother's. I'm trying to figure out why."

He nodded. "You want to save your friend."

"Yes. In addition, Paisley tells us a valuable family heirloom was stolen, except it turns out that the alleged heirloom looks a lot like stolen crown jewels. I was hoping you knew something about that."

"You must know by now that my mother's father was a

phenomenal jeweler. He was commissioned to make jewelry for movie stars and royalty. He made it all by hand, one piece at a time. Consequently, it's not out of the question that he left my mom some remarkable jewelry when he died. While he was often entrusted with crown jewels, he would never have taken on the repair or reconstruction of anything that had been stolen. Having said that, I trust you know that easily identifiable jewelry can be very difficult to track. It goes underground. The stones are usually recut. Sadly, some of the largest stones are broken down into smaller stones because the mere size would be too obvious. And then they slither from the black market back into the hands of the wealthy."

I stared at him. "Why do you know all this?"

"Because my grandfather was an amazing jeweler. I played in his salon when I was very young, and I remember meeting famous people who came to him. He was a gentleman." Bennett smiled as he spoke of his grandfather. "Jewelry never held much interest for me. When I graduated from Columbia, my grandfather gave me a gold watch." He turned his arm so I could see an Audemars Piguet on a caramel-colored leather strap. "It's the only jewelry I need. A few days before he died, he told me he had hoped to meet my wife in his lifetime. But since he hadn't had that opportunity, he hoped she would appreciate the diamond engagement ring he had been saving for me to give her. It's in my safe deposit box."

So that part was true. "Why do you think Lark was murdered?"

He rubbed his hands together. "I don't know. I've met Humphrey. Frankly, I think Mom could have overpowered him. I don't know if the timing was coincidental. That has weighed on me. Did the killer not know she had returned from her vacation? Or was he waiting for her to return?"

"Carmela Eames said unkind things about your mom

yesterday. I gather there was no love lost between the two families?" I asked.

Bennett licked his lips and thought. He was a measured guy, not prone to blurting something out or showing his feelings. He reminded me of Wolf in that way. Which, now that I thought about it, was exactly the kind of trait needed to be a gambler. "Mom was always the thoughtful hostess, always putting her best face forward, always gracious."

He nodded and sucked in a breath. "That was my mom. She included Frank's family at holidays. She made a fuss over each of them. But Frank's family is often"—he paused as if searching for the right word—"emotionally overwrought. My parents were quiet people. Friendly, for sure, but they didn't raise their voices much. Our home was fairly tranquil. They read or listened to classical music. The Eameses are the opposite. They shout, even when they're not angry. They're loud and boisterous and often wildly incorrect about things. I have always viewed it as two very different kinds of people coming together. I know Mom wished Paisley had married someone else. But it wasn't because of his family. Mom and Dad didn't like Frank's woefully misinformed beliefs. He was always telling us how we were being used and manipulated by the government. How the system was set up wrong and everyone was against him. How he knew better and if my parents would just listen to him, they could avoid paying taxes. He doesn't espouse a political viewpoint so much as it's plain old evasion. The world is against him at every turn. It worried them a lot."

"Could Frank have killed Lark?" I asked.

"He's on my short list." Bennett grimaced. "But then, I imagine I'm on everyone's short list as well."

I was wondering if I should ask whether he murdered her. He saved me the trouble.

"I didn't kill Mom. I'd sooner have hurt myself than ever harm her. She was a wonderful person and a kind mother. I never imagined her dying like this."

I felt terrible for questioning him. He might be a suspect, but the one thing I had taken from our chat was that he had loved his mom. I didn't think he had killed her. I thanked him for talking with me and headed for the door. As he closed it behind me, I realized with a start that someone was watching me. I sucked in a deep breath and was about to turn around and beg to be let in, when a man emerged from the shadows.

It was Wolf. I sagged with relief. "What are you doing here?" I demanded. "You nearly gave me a heart attack."

He smiled. "I did *not* expect to see you here."

"Are you spying on Bennett?" I asked.

"Sophie, your love life is none of my business—"

I cut him off. "Love life?" I shrieked. "You think I'm some kind of cougar who chases younger men?"

"The guy in front told me a lady friend was visiting Bennett."

I walked right up to Wolf and even though I would dearly have liked to have punched him, I thought better of it. "For your information, I was trying to verify information about Lark and her traveling."

"And what did you learn?"

Reluctantly, I admitted, "Nothing new. Everything Paisley told us was correct."

"In the future, I would appreciate it if you allowed me to do my job," he said.

I was about to throw back a nasty line at him, when I realized that wouldn't do me any good. In a calm voice I said, "I'm trying to protect Nina."

"I know you are. But stay out of the way of my investigation."

I looked him straight in those big brown eyes. Both of us knew that wasn't going to happen.

"Listen, Soph. It's beginning to look like there may be some nasty players involved. Lark's travels have opened some unexpected lines of inquiry. I don't want you to get hurt. Keep your head down."

I walked away wondering about those nasty players. Did that mean lovely Lark had been involved in something illegal like Carmela had said?

I hustled over to King Street and treated myself to coffee and a croissant. As I walked toward the tents, I recognized wreaths and birdhouses bought at the festival decorating the homes and businesses in Old Town.

When I passed Natasha's tent, Wanda hollered my name. "C'mon in here, darlin'," she said.

Griselda and Charlene huddled with Natasha, whose eyes looked like they were rimmed red from crying. She'd put on her makeup and was elegantly dressed, but she'd mismatched the buttons on her blouse. "What's going on?" I asked.

Her voice shaking, Natasha said, "Cal is showing the house this morning."

"To that nice Dr. Chryssos," said Griselda.

It was good news. But probably not from Natasha's viewpoint, after all, Chryssos could probably afford the house. "Look at it this way, Natasha. Somewhere in Old Town is a house that's crying out for your special touch," I said.

Her face brightened. But only for a moment. "I'd rather stay in my house, where everything is already perfect. The thought of dealing with something like your kitchen just horrifies me!"

She always knew just how to get my goat. I rushed out of her tent and straight into Greer. Oh no. Not another problem.

She smiled at me, looking long and lean in jeans and a loose blouse that was tucked into one spot at her waist. It wouldn't have hurt her to button the blouse up a little higher. The large gold bracelet hung on her wrist again, but now I was fairly certain it wasn't solid gold. "Sophie," she said breathily, "could you ask Paisley to keep her little monsters out of my tent? I don't want to stir up any bad feelings or I'd say something myself. You know how sensitive people are about their spawn. It's really for their own safety. Some of the chemicals I use could be very dangerous if they dipped their fingers or, heaven forbid, put it in their mouths. I've watched them. They would do that in a heartbeat!"

"Yes. Of course. We want them to be safe."

"Thank you."

I hurried toward Lark's house, passing Greer's tent along the way. *Gold*. Could Lark have meant to point a finger at Greer? I stopped and looked at her tent for a moment. Greer's name had never come up. Did Greer have some connection to Lark that we didn't know about? It was something to consider at the very least.

I moved on and found Paisley sitting in her tent slumped forward, gazing at her hands.

"Paisley?" I said gently. "Are you all right?"

She turned sad eyes toward me. "I didn't think things could get worse than Mom being murdered."

Chapter 29

Dear Sophie,
I'm itching to put up a gallery wall, but my friend did one and it's awful! Any advice?
                    Afraid in Deadwood, South Dakota

Dear Afraid,
It's easiest if everything is the same size and in identical frames. If not, then look for an imaginary line to follow on your wall. It might be the height of the windows or the trim. The line can also be vertical. Lay out your pictures on the floor or a bed to see how they fit together, starting at the imaginary line. Move them around until you like the way they look and hang them!
                                        Sophie

Paisley raised exhausted eyes to me. Blue bags sagged underneath them. "Everything is falling apart. Do you think my mom was a fence for stolen jewelry like they're saying?"

I tried to imagine how I would feel to learn something like that about my mother. It was impossible. I wouldn't have believed it. "I don't know what to think. Paisley, if your mom said the word *gold* to you, what would you think she meant?"

"Jewelry?" She shrugged. "I don't understand."

"Neither do I. I think that's what she managed to draw in the mulch. By the way, Greer asked me to caution you about the boys coming to her tent. She uses caustic chemicals and doesn't want them to get hurt."

Paisley nodded. "Sophie, could I talk to you about something personal?"

"Sure. I'm sorry I didn't bring another latte." I pulled up a chair and sat down beside her. People were already browsing through the display tents.

"That's okay. I haven't got much appetite these days." She gazed at the ground. "Frank didn't come home last night."

"I'm so sorry, Paisley." I wrapped an arm around her and gave her a soft squeeze.

When I let go, she looked at me, her chin trembling. "And I'm glad." She burst into tears.

"That's the strangest glad I've ever seen."

Paisley wiped her face with the back of her hands. "We had a terrible fight about Tommy. He's such a great kid. He's smart and helpful and so sweet. But his outburst yesterday at Carmela caused such a commotion. The whole Eames family was in an uproar. I actually thought about packing up the kids and taking them to a motel somewhere. But then Frank turned on me. He wants to contest my mom's will. He's so upset that we can't have the money now. But I don't want to contest it. I'm fine with that Humphrey guy. Better than fine. Frank can't waste my inheritance on that crazy business of his. I understand now. I get it! Mom was protecting me from Frank. He didn't come home. And now, I don't want him to. I'm so torn. He's my husband and the father of my children!"

I tried to be encouraging. "You have been through a lot this week. So have Tommy and Frank. Maybe life will look different when everything settles down."

"Could you stay here and watch for customers for a few minutes? Mrs. Gurtz is looking after the children in the backyard."

"Sure. No problem." I figured I was in a prominent enough place. If a vendor needed me, I was in plain view.

"Thank you so much!" Paisley handed me her phone and showed me how to make a sale. Then she kissed me on the cheek and took off running.

I was thankful that I didn't hear any screams coming from behind the house. Maybe they were behaving.

A tiny woman wearing a weather green sunhat admired an expensive armoire that Paisley had painted with gorgeous peonies. "Excuse me," she said. "Do you know if Paisley will be dropping the price at the end of the festival? I've been coming by every day because I just have to have this. Each day I'm afraid someone will have bought it."

"Gosh, I'm sorry but I don't know if she has plans to lower the price. She should be back soon."

At that exact moment, a redhead browsed through with a man, whom I presumed was her husband. "Honey, wouldn't this armoire be perfect in our foyer? It's just the right size."

The man smiled at me. "Do you have a measuring tape?"

The tiny woman said in a sweet little voice, "Isn't it gorgeous? I just bought it."

"That's a pity," said the redhead. "You really ought to put a SOLD sign on it."

I tried to overlook her huffiness. I grabbed one of Paisley's cards and hurried over to her. In a whisper I said, "Paisley would be happy to make one for you in customized colors that suit your décor."

"Really?" said the woman. "Thank you. That might be even better."

In a stroke of luck, the couple remained to browse and seemed to be considering some other items, thus making it impossible for the tiny woman to back out. She handed me her credit card. I hoped I knew what I was doing when I swiped it through Paisley's phone with the little square antenna on it.

Luckily, it went through fine. I handed her the phone to sign.

"I'll send my son around later today to pick it up. Is that all right?" she asked.

"That would be great." I breathed a sigh of relief. It would give Paisley an opportunity to wrap it appropriately. I tore a little piece of paper off a notepad and used a Sharpie to write SOLD on it. I didn't see any tape and didn't want to take a chance with it marring the paint anyway, so I stuck it in between the armoire doors, where it, thankfully, stayed put.

It took Paisley over an hour to return. She arrived in a hurry, carrying two bags marked with the logo of a nearby grocery store. "I'll be right back," she called to me as she let herself through the gate.

She returned in minutes. "I am so grateful. Thanks for minding the shop. I still can't reach Frank, which really upsets me. He was supposed to get groceries today. He must be very angry because he's not answering his phone—" Paisley stopped abruptly. "That's how it happened with mom." She shook her head nervously. "No. I'm being ridiculous. And so is he by running off. He's probably at his mom's house being babied while I have to take care of everything, as usual."

I had a very bad feeling that wasn't the case. Carmela bustled toward us, looking peeved. "Where is he? Did you turn him against me? Or did you hide his phone?"

Paisley's face flushed. "You don't know where he is, either?"

"Whaddya mean, either?"

"He left our house last night and never came home. I thought he was at your house."

"He'd have been safer there, that's for sure. What did you do to him?" Carmela grabbed Paisley's arm and twisted it behind her back. "Tell me!"

"Whoa!" I said. "Let Paisley go right now. There's no need to attack her."

"You mind your own business, why doncha? Now, where is he?" She jerked Paisley's arm higher.

Paisley howled in pain. "I don't know!"

I whipped out my phone and dialed Wolf's direct number. When he answered, I said, "We need help right now at Paisley's tent."

"On my way," he said.

"Carmela, please." I moved closer, hoping I wouldn't get slugged. "Let her go."

"Okay." Carmela released Paisley and shoved her forward, causing her to fall on the ground.

I walked over to help Paisley get up. I offered her my arms and assisted her off the ground. Thankfully, I saw Wolf running toward us. But when I was looking at Wolf, Carmela hauled off and punched me right in the face.

"Ugh!" I went down like a lead balloon, thankfully landing on my well-padded posterior. "What is wrong with you?"

"I can't find my son, that's what!"

"Ma'am," Wolf said, flashing his identification, "what's going on here?" He reached out a hand and helped me to my feet, but never took his eyes off Carmela.

"Oh swell, a cop," said Carmela. She raised her palms. "I haven't done anything. They won't tell me where my son is." And then tears streamed. She sniffled and pulled a tissue out of her purse. "I can't find him anywhere. They were the last to see him."

She bowed her head and continued the act, but I caught a glimpse of her looking at me out of the corner of her eye. I swear she was laughing.

"Nice show," said Wolf. "I saw you punch Sophie."

Carmela raised her head. "Oh! You're on a first-name basis with the snotty one."

"I am not snotty. And I'm going to have a black eye."

"Maybe the officer here is the one who hit you."

"Ma'am, do you *want* to add more charges to assault?" asked Wolf, clearly irritated with her.

"Police brutality against senior citizens," she whimpered. "You should arrest Paisley for hurting my boy and hiding him."

"Where is Frank?" asked Wolf.

Paisley rubbed her shoulder. "I wish I knew. He stormed out of the house last night and won't answer his phone."

"I'm telling you, sir," said Carmela, playing the beleaguered mom. "She did something to him." And she added, "Just like she did to her mom."

Chapter 30

Dear Natasha,
How do I get the dead smell out of the china cabi-
net my husband inherited?
            Holding My Nose in China Grove, Texas

Dear Holding My Nose,
Sunshine usually makes a big difference. Take the
china cabinet out to the road where they pick up
your trash. Leave it there until it is gone.
                            Natasha

It was the most terrible thing she could have said. Paisley broke into real tears and Carmela actually had the gall to snicker as though she was pleased to have upset Paisley.

Wolf said something into his radio. I hugged Paisley.

"Was anyone with you last night when he left?" asked Wolf.

Paisley lifted her head from my shoulder. "Six little boys."

"Shoot!" spat Carmela. "They'll lie for their mommy. Are they even old enough to testify? They're just babies.

And the oldest one, Tommy, is a liar who has been turned against me by his mom."

Wong ran around the corner toward the tent. "Yes, sir?" she asked, panting heavily.

"Go in the house and look around for Frank Eames. Take Sophie with you."

"I'll go," said Carmela.

"You and Paisley will stay right here," said Wolf in no uncertain terms.

Wong eyed me. As soon as we were through the gate and out of earshot, Wong asked, "Is that a bruise on your face? Sophie, you have a black eye. What's going on?"

"Frank's mother slugged me. Frank walked out on Paisley and the kids last night and no one knows where he is. He's not answering his phone. Paisley has no idea. His mom is accusing Paisley of doing something terrible to Frank."

Mrs. Gurtz sat in a rocking chair on the porch with Oscar on her lap. He attentively listened to her as she read a book to him. Tommy was showing his other brothers how to play croquet. They laughed and ran around in crazy circles. It was a lovely peaceful scene among a riot of colorful blooms. I was sorry Lark wasn't there to enjoy it.

A large, battered designer purse had been deposited next to the rocking chair. Up close there was no mistaking the lines that had been etched into Mrs. Gurtz's face. She wore a slash of rosy lipstick, but no other makeup, and smiled at me cheerily. It was like an old Mary Poppins had arrived to take care of everything.

Mrs. Gurtz glanced at us and raised her eyebrows but never missed a beat reading the book. We walked in through the kitchen door.

"You take the main floor and I'll check upstairs," said Wong.

I felt very confident that I wouldn't find Frank hanging out on the main floor. The children had probably run through most of the house this morning and would have noticed their dad. I took my time wandering through the elegant dining room. A chandelier caught the light and sparkled overhead. The china cabinet had been emptied into boxes that sat on the floor, probably from Frank's ill-fated attempt to sell everything the day after his mother-in-law died. The living room was still in excellent shape. The foyer was elegant as I remembered it. I made my way through a butler's pantry. I had always wanted one, but Lark's was a mess. Dishes and glasses were haphazardly piled on the floor, a few of the glasses already broken. The cabinets hung open as though people had pawed through them. In search of the crown jewels, perhaps? The laundry room off the kitchen was a mess as well. Someone had removed the clothes from the laundry hamper and piled them on the floor. Once again, the cabinets were ajar. Lark's beautiful home looked like it had been ransacked.

I spied a door in the laundry room that I hadn't noticed before. The dank smell of basement wafted up to me when I opened it. I reached for the light switch. *Click, click.* I tried again with no results. The light must have burned out. I glanced around the laundry room for a flashlight and found one in a pile of household items near an empty cabinet. I flicked it on and returned to the basement stairs. Halfway down, I found Frank.

Chapter 31

Dear Sophie,
I love painted furniture. But I have no artistic skill
whatsoever. Is there an easier way?
                    Hopeless in Artesia, California

Dear Hopeless,
There is an easier way! Use decoupage to attach a
picture that you like or use stencils!
                                        Sophie

"Wong!" I called. I raced to the bottom of the main staircase and yelled for her. When I heard her hurried footsteps upstairs, I raced back to the laundry room.

Wong caught up to me. Wordlessly, I pointed the glow of the flashlight at the bottom of the basement stairs where Frank lay crumpled.

"Is he dead?" she asked.

"I don't know. I didn't go all the way down. I thought it would be better if you checked so I won't mess up a potential crime scene."

Wong pulled out her radio and requested an ambulance. "Should I call Wolf?" I asked.

"Let me check on him first. Paisley and Frank's mom are going to freak."

I waited at the top of the stairs as Wong crept slowly down. She shone her flashlight around, stepped over Frank, and disappeared. I guessed she was making sure no one was hiding in the basement.

From where I stood, it appeared to be a finished basement with wall-to-wall carpeting in a peachy cream shade. The walls were a vertical-grooved cream paneling, probably covering up ancient bricks or stones.

Wong returned and knelt beside Frank. I could see her checking for a pulse. She ran up the stairs. "He's alive. Stay right here. Don't let anyone in except the EMTs. I'm going outside to tell Wolf. One of us will be back in a flash. Got it?"

I heaved a breath of relief. "Got it!" I affirmed. I certainly didn't want any of the children seeing their dad like this.

In her absence, Dr. Chryssos arrived. "Sophie! How lovely to see you again." He leaned toward me with a grin. "We really have to stop meeting like this."

I smiled at his old joke.

He stepped back. "Is that a black eye?"

"Probably." I hadn't taken the time to look at myself in a mirror. But my cheek felt hot when I touched it.

"I bet Lark has some freezer bags somewhere," he said.

I followed him into the kitchen. "I don't think he's dead," I blurted.

"That's good news!" He chuckled. "A condition I rarely encounter. Hmm, someone must have gotten their information wrong or I wouldn't have been called."

He poured crushed ice into the bag and folded a fresh kitchen towel around it. "Who punched you?"

"Frank's mother."

Dr. Chryssos shook his head. "Keep that pressed against your face. If you have any vision problems, I want you to go to your doctor right away. I'll just check on him since I'm here." He walked down the stairs.

The sound of the ambulance siren was music to my ears. With so many people and tents on the street, they pulled up in the alley behind Lark's house. I could hear the boys outside, greeting the EMTs by their names. I flew to the kitchen door and asked Mrs. Gurtz to keep the children out of the house.

She flashed me a horrified look, but clearly understood and immediately organized a game around the side of the house. All of them went with her, except for Tommy.

The EMTs walked by him into the house. I showed them to the basement door and watched them walk down.

I felt someone behind me and turned, expecting Wolf. I found Tommy looking at me wide-eyed, his chest lifting and falling rapidly. "Is somebody dead?"

"No." I patted him on the shoulder to reassure him. "Go on with Mrs. Gurtz."

He didn't budge. "What happened to your eye?"

"Someone hit me."

"The person who's dead?"

"No one is dead, Tommy."

"A lot of people lie to me because I'm a kid. Are you lying to me now?" he asked.

"You are so smart," I told him. "I am not lying to you. That's what Officer Wong told me."

"Who is it?" he asked.

He was clever enough to know it was most likely some-one to whom he was related. But I thought his mother or a professional should tell him the news about his dad. It wasn't my place. So I lied. "I'm not certain. Now, shoo!" I turned him around toward the door and marched him out with my hands lightly on his little shoulders. "Go on." I stayed there and watched to be sure he didn't follow me back inside.

Wolf finally came around the side of the house. I pointed him in the right direction. "Have you told Paisley and Carmela?"

"They know Frank has been located. Wong may have to handcuff both of them. Carmela is ready to brawl."

It didn't take long for the EMTs to bring Frank up the stairs on a stretcher. He was securely bound in place so he wouldn't shift, and they had placed a neck collar on him. I hoped he hadn't broken his neck. His eyes were partly open but didn't seem to register anything. I hoped for the best. He might be a jerk, but he didn't deserve to die.

Dr. Chryssos ran up the stairs. "Looks like a bad fall. If I had to guess, I'd say he broke his neck. We'll know as soon as they get X-rays. I'm not sure how long he's been lying there, but I'd guess it happened during the night."

"Any chance you can tell whether it was a chance fall, or he was pushed?" asked Wolf.

"I couldn't do a thorough exam on him. Impossible to tell. But the fact that the lightbulb was shattered doesn't bode well," said Dr. Chryssos.

He and I followed Wolf to the front door where Wolf gave Wong the signal to allow Paisley and Carmela to come into the house. The two of them ran, Paisley besting Carmela by a significant margin.

"The EMTs are transporting Frank to the hospital," Wolf told them. "You can see him on the stretcher out back as they load him into the ambulance."

Carmela was breathless and stomped through the house, half bent over. I hoped we wouldn't have to send her in the ambulance as well. Her condition didn't prevent her from waggling a finger at Wolf. "You are out! When

I'm through with you, you won't have a job. And don't think I can't put a curse on you."

To think I had been concerned about her!

She was out of earshot when Dr. Chryssos said sarcastically, "Charming. And she curses people, too!" He shook his head. But then he looked at me and said, "I'm told you're not seeing anyone at the moment."

Wolf's head snapped toward him. "Don't be so sure."

"That was completely unnecessary," I muttered at Wolf.

"Oh!" said Dr. Chryssos. "Have I been misinformed?"

I hurried to answer before Wolf could say something snide. "You have not. Wolf is just irritated because I had a chat with Bennett Bickford this morning."

"I have no idea what time she arrived there," Wolf teased.

"Bennett? Isn't he a little young for you?" asked Dr. Chryssos.

"I also talk to Tommy, who is ten," I said, and strode out the front door.

Dr. Chryssos caught up to me. "Would you care to have dinner tonight?"

"I would like that," I said. "What time?"

"Seven? At The Laughing Hound? I know the manager. I'm sure he'll accommodate me with a late reservation."

"Sounds great. I'll meet you there." I didn't bother telling him I knew the manager, too.

Dr. Chryssos went on his way, and I phoned Francie and Nina to see if they were available to cover for Paisley at her tent.

While I was on the phone, Tommy wandered out to the tent and waited politely while I finished my phone call. "Will my dad be okay?" he asked.

I sat down in a chair to face him eye to eye. "I hope so. He took a very bad fall down the stairs. He's at the hospital now and the doctors will do their very best to help him get better."

"Who pushed him?" asked Tommy.

"Why would you think someone pushed him?" I asked.

"Because they don't like him."

"Who doesn't like him?"

Tommy shrugged. "I don't know who they are. I've heard people talking is all."

I opened my arms for a hug, and he laid his head on my shoulder. After a minute, I said, "I bet Mrs. Gurtz could use some help with your brothers."

He pulled back and nodded. "Mom says we have to be nice to her because she's old."

"That's probably true."

"And her daughter has a disease and can't help her earn money, so she's poor."

"That's very sad. Another reason to be nice, huh?"

"Her grandson steals from them."

"Ohh. That's not nice at all!" I made a mental note to be careful what I said around Tommy. He clearly paid attention when the adults were talking.

"But I like Mrs. Gurtz no matter what. I better go help her." Tommy ran to the gate and let himself through. I watched until he disappeared in the rear of the house.

Poor Mrs. Gurtz. Taking care of Paisley's brood would have worn me to a frazzle. I was impressed that she could handle them.

Nina and Francie showed up fifteen minutes later, armed with a cooler of drinks and goodies to munch on. They fussed over my eye and Francie handed me a cold can to hold against my eye.

"What happened to Mars?" I asked.

"He had a meeting," said Nina. "We thought we'd be okay with so many people around."

"Francie, do you know a Mrs. Gurtz?" I asked.

"Sure! At one time she was the most popular cleaning woman in Old Town. Don't tell me she died."

"As a matter of fact, she's in the backyard caring for the Eames boys."

Nina perked up. "I can always use a good housekeeper."

"Lordy, Nina, she might be older than me," said Francie. She whispered when she said, "I don't think she can do in-depth cleaning anymore. I hear a lot of her clients keep her on because they know she needs the money. Her husband had a good job, but the man did not believe in saving. He was a live-in-the-moment kind of guy. Then he died and her daughter got sick. I forget what she has, but most days she can barely get out of bed, so it's up to Mrs. Gurtz to support her, too."

"I heard something about a grandson?"

"Last I heard he was out west somewhere. Mrs. Gurtz put together every last penny she could find to bail him out of jail for theft and that crumb bucket ran off. Never showed for his court date. She lost every cent. Good riddance, I say!"

"She seems very nice, but her life is so hard," I observed.

"That's how it is sometimes," said Francie. "The people with the biggest troubles keep them to themselves and smile so pleasantly that you'd never suspect the problems that plague their daily existence."

I left Nina and Francie and walked the festival area, taking care of minor matters. News about Frank had spread fast and I found myself answering questions. Most people asked if he was all right. I had no good answer for that. But the second most commonly asked question worried me—was it true that he had murdered Lark?

If he had, who would have thrown him down the stairs? The possibilities were frightening. Paisley or Bennett led the pack. Surely not little Tommy. Could Humphrey have done something like that to avenge Lark's death? I didn't know of a reason for Frank to have murdered Dulci, but Emery would certainly have been able to knock Frank down the basement stairs.

I hoped that when he came around Frank would be able to tell the doctors who had pushed him. It was certainly possible that he had fallen, but Dr. Chryssos had made an astute observation about the broken lightbulb. I had to remember to call him Peter tonight!

The day was passing quickly. So many of the vendors asked me about next year's festival that I went home at one o'clock and posted an online vendor application form for the following year offering a discount to those who signed up early. I hadn't planned to run the festival the next year but, except for the early hours, it was sort of like a vacation for me since I was close to home. I let Daisy and Muppet out for a few minutes, then shared a lunch snack of leftovers with them. I checked my eye before I left. Holding ice against it had grown old fast. It looked awful. And there was no amount of makeup that could hide it. My vision was fine though. I was grateful for that. I located sunglasses that weren't quite large enough to cover the spreading bruise and slid them on. I gave each dog a cookie, locked the door, and went back to work.

As I walked to the tents, I looked up at the beautiful blue sky and the sun. The heat and mugginess of summer would appear soon, but the timing of the festival couldn't have been better. Not a single day of rain.

But the lovely day led me to think about poor Frank, who wasn't enjoying it. I phoned Wolf to find out if he had an update on Frank's condition.

"He broke his neck when he fell and is now in surgery," said Wolf. "They're hoping it didn't impact his spinal cord."

"How are the two Mrs. Eameses getting along? Did the tragedy bring them together?"

Wolf snorted. "I think we can be very glad that we're not part of that family. We had to put them in separate waiting rooms. Hospital security is keeping an eye on them."

I thanked him and asked him to stay in touch with updates.

I had reached the vendor area and slowed my pace because of the crowds. Francie and Nina looked comfortable in Paisley's tent but much of the furniture was gone.

"What happened here?" I asked.

"We're news central on Frank Eames," said Francie. "Everybody is coming by to ask how he is."

"And while they're here they see Paisley's beautiful furniture and buy pieces. And a couple of people have picked up pieces they bought earlier," said Nina. "People know this is their last chance to buy until next year."

I noticed that the gorgeous armoire was gone.

Nina gestured toward a chair. "The crime scene investigators are in the house. What do you think happened to Frank?"

I sat down and tried to organize my thoughts. "Paisley said Frank left the house last night and never came home. He could have gone somewhere else, I don't know about that, but he clearly came to Lark's house. When I looked around this morning, I thought the main floor looked like it had been ransacked."

"He was searching for the crown jewels," said Nina.

"Or he encountered someone else who was looking for them," suggested Francie.

"It seems obvious that two people were there. He might have even taken someone with him. Whoever left him there must have thought he was dead. Frank was lucky in that respect," I said.

"So that means the second person was already there, a

friend who went with him, or arrived later and found him looking for the crown jewels," Nina summarized.

"I wonder if Frank had found the jewels and a fight ensued over them," said Francie. "That would account for the fall down the stairs."

My voice came out rather grim when I said, "Someone bothered to break the lightbulb at the top of the stairs. That means someone planned to push him down."

Chapter 32

Dear Sophie,
I'm afraid to look under my sink. Isn't there a way
to straighten out all that stuff?
* Must Be More Organized in Lime Sink, Alabama*

Dear Must Be More Organized,
Take everything out of the cabinet under your sink
and clean it. Throw out what you don't need or
use. Mount a tension rod across the space and hang
all the spray bottles by their handles. Find two
plastic containers that can slide into the sides of
your cabinet. Fill them with all the other cleaning
items. Don't forget to put a lock on it if you have
small children.

Sophie

Francie and Nina stared at me in horror.
"I can't even imagine anyone being so desperate for those jewels. They've been underground for years. No wonder Lark didn't tell anyone about them and lied to her own daughter. She probably knew the kind of people who

would do anything to get their hands on them," said Francie.

"She might have been the kind of person who knew how to get her hands on them," grumbled Nina.

"Do you really think that?" I asked. "I would have trouble being a fence for stolen goods."

Francie laughed. She pointed her finger at the houses across the street that loomed over the tents. "I would bet that Lark wasn't the only respectable person in Old Town who owned stolen jewels, artifacts, or paintings. The upside to that, of course, is that they're generally well cared for. I think we might be surprised to find just how many billionaires have private collections full of priceless objects that have gone missing."

"You don't think very well of your neighbors," said Nina.

Francie cackled, and I got up to stroll through the tents in case anyone needed anything.

Unfortunately, most people had heard about my black eye. Carmela had landed her punch well. I didn't bring up her name, though, except when I stopped by the tent of Bud Linkous. The older antiques dealer had been around for a long time.

"What did you do to deserve that shiner?" he asked.

"Wasn't fast enough," I replied. "Carmela Eames nailed me."

He sighed. "Sorry to hear that. I hoped when Al Eames died it would change the dynamics in the family."

"What do you know about them? Do you think they could have murdered Lark?"

"I don't know." He scratched his weathered face. "Well, seeing it's you who wants to know, I'll tell you the truth. But I don't want you blabbing about where you heard it. The Eameses are a mean bunch."

"Can I send Wolf your way if I think it's necessary?" I asked.

"Yeah. Pity about you and Wolf. He's a good man. But Al Eames was not, and neither was his father. The reason I followed his death closely is because he came into my shop the day he died. Now, I knew from experience that whatever he was selling had been obtained by illegal means. And I don't sell stolen goods." He waved a hand at his antiques. "Never have. I'm not going to help anybody who needs money laundered, either. I run a clean business. So when Al came in, I told him right off the bat that I was not interested. And he said to me, 'You will be this time.' And he pulls out jewelry. I don't sell much in the way of jewelry. I'm not a jeweler. But I can tell from the way it's made that these are old. Really old. Maybe a couple hundred years old. 'Where'd you get these?' I asked him. And he had the nerve to say, 'Doesn't matter. What'll you give me for them?'"

He stopped for a moment when a lady came in to browse. "I can take one hundred off that table if you're interested."

She smiled at him. "I'll think about it."

When she left, he continued, "I told Al I wouldn't give him a red cent and he'd best get on out of my store. And then he asks me if I'll buy them if he takes the stones out of the settings. Well, that's a sure sign they were stolen. I told him I was not getting involved. And then on the news that night, I heard a man was killed in a hit-and-run accident in Bethesda, Maryland. I didn't give it much thought. Bethesda has all those crazy one-way streets. But the next morning in the paper, I saw that it was Albert Eames who was killed. And I knew then and there the people he stole that jewelry from were onto him."

"What did the jewelry look like?"

"Real old. A ring with a big stone in it, and two brooches that looked like clovers."

"You may be hearing from Wolf." I gave him a kiss on his wrinkled old cheek and left the tent so that lady could come back and strike a bargain with him.

I walked along, surprised by the fact that Frank's father had been in possession of the crown jewels. I stopped in the middle of the crowd milling through the tents.

Al Eames must have gone from Bud's shop to Lark's house. He left the jewelry with her. Because he couldn't unload it? Or so her father would remove the stones? Had the person who killed Al figured out that Lark had them? But then why didn't they break into her house sooner? Why wait a year?

Something was missing. There was no perfect murder. Every time a person walked into a house, he left a little something there. DNA, fingerprints, lint, fur from pets. What was I overlooking? Had Lark realized Al was murdered because he stole the jewels? It seemed like too many people knew about them. We knew for sure that Frank had been looking for them. That accounted for the mess in the house as he rummaged through everything. But who was the other person? Carmela wouldn't have harmed her own son. Bennett? Paisley?

And then an awful thought occurred to me. What if Lark had sold them before she left on her trip?

I moved out of the way and flicked on my phone, looking for the photo I had taken of the mulch on the day Lark died. Could it be anything else? A G, perhaps? The longer I looked at it, the more convinced I was that it was a circumpunct. What was she trying to tell us? The sun or gold?

"Hello," came a familiar voice. I tore my gaze from the photo. Mars stood in front of me.

"Ouch!" he said, looking at my face.

"It's all the rage in makeup," I quipped.

"Doesn't suit you. What happened?"

I told him about Carmela.

"Are you going out with Greer again?" I asked.

"Don't think so," he whispered. "Why?"

"I'm wondering if she knew Lark. Or had any dealings with her."

"Because she dips things in gold?" he asked.

"Of course. What else could *gold* mean? If you were dying and you wanted to leave a message but only had the strength and ability to draw a sign, why would you draw a circle with a dot in it?"

"I would not have." He met my annoyed gaze. "Okay, I get your point. Why would someone murder Lark?" He ticked items off on his fingers as he spoke. "Jewelry, as already established. Her wealth. Her house. There must be one hundred reasons, including that someone envied her or didn't like her."

"We're not getting anywhere," I said. "Just find out if Greer knew Lark."

"I'm not sitting through another boring dinner with her."

"Then bring her some coffee," I said.

He stuck a pretend dagger in his chest. "I shall take one for the team. But you come rescue me if I can't get away."

"Will do." I tried to hide a grin as I watched him walk off.

I gave him a little time to buy the coffees. I was beginning to think that Lark had drawn the sign for gold because the crown jewels were probably set in gold. How would you draw a jewel? Gold would be more understandable. You would think that an elegant woman who fenced jewelry wouldn't be friends with people like Al and Carmela. Obviously, they hadn't liked her. Or at least Carmela hadn't.

Had Carmela known that Al was going to take the crown jewels to Lark? Had she demanded them back after Al's death? Could it be Carmela who had murdered Lark? But why would she murder Dulci? The strangest thoughts were running through my head. Was there a fence of well-to-do housewives in Old Town? Had Lark confided to Dulci about the jewels? Or could the killer have reason to believe that Lark had given Dulci the crown jewels to sell to someone?

No. I was getting too far afield.

I checked the time on my plain old inexpensive watch and walked toward Greer's land of gold. Sure enough, she was flirting with Mars, a coffee in her hand. Good job, Mars!

"There you are," I called. "Have you put your phone on *silent* again? Bernie's been looking for you," I fibbed.

Mars pulled his phone from his pocket. "I was in a conference earlier and turned it off." He looked at Greer. "This is interesting stuff. It's really impressive. I'd better go see what Bernie needs."

"Thanks for the coffee." Greer flicked a wave toward him.

I walked away with Mars. "Well?"

"She knew Dulci, but not very well. Emery bought some of her coin jewelry. I had to listen to a painfully long explanation of how she dips them into the gold without leaving any marks on them."

I glanced back at Greer as casually as I could. She was still watching us, but she wasn't smiling.

"Did she say anything about Lark's death?"

"The regular stuff. So sad for the family. Nothing very interesting."

"Do you think she could have murdered Dulci or Lark?"

With a straight face, Mars said, "She could have bored them to death."

"Not funny. She's like that girl in the movie *Goldfinger*,

who was covered in gold. Lark left us the symbol for gold. If anyone should be a suspect, it's her!"

"I'm not sure she's interesting enough to be lurking in the night murdering people."

Mars took off and I found a quiet spot to put in a call to Wolf.

"Hi, Soph," he said over the phone.

"Any updates on Frank?"

"He's out of surgery. They won't know much for a while."

"You know Bud Linkous, the antiques dealer, right?"

"Sure. Nice guy."

"He doesn't want this to get around, but he confirms that on the day that Frank's father died in a hit-and-run accident, he had come to Bud to sell him the crown jewels."

Wolf was silent. "If Lark was a high-end stolen jewelry reseller, then why would he go to Bud first? Why wouldn't he go straight to Lark?"

I didn't have an answer for that. "Family feud? Carmela hates Paisley and her family."

"It would blow me away if this turned out to be some sort of rival jewelry fencing fight," said Wolf. "I think that would be a first for Old Town. Thanks, I'll check in with Bud. Anything else?"

"Not really. I'm convinced that Lark left us the symbol for gold. I sent Mars to ask Greer Shacklesworth if she knew Dulci or Lark. She's the only person I can think of who jumps to mind from the word *gold*."

"I haven't got anything linking her to the murders. Call me if you turn up anything."

At five o'clock I called it quits and went home. The Laughing Hound was elegant in some ways and casual in others. I studied my closet for the right thing to wear to dinner.

I finally chose a simple black sheath with a V-neck. Appropriate for all occasions, it would never be out of place. And then I had to tackle my black eye.

Carmela had done a number on my left eye. Horrible shades of black, blue, and red surrounded my entire eye. Even my cheek was tender and pink. I did the best I could with my concealer, but it clearly wasn't meant for use over an extended area. Nevertheless, I used it liberally and hoped it wouldn't cake up during dinner. Then I used much more eye makeup than normal, which made me look like a Goth hooker. I washed it all off and started again using a lighter hand. Thankfully, my eye wasn't bloodshot.

Giving up on my face, I selected a pair of black sandals with moderate heels that would allow me to navigate the brick sidewalks without twisting an ankle. A chunky faux gold bracelet went on my wrist. But the dress needed something else. Remembering Dulci's pendant, I pawed around in my jewelry until I found a similar gold coin pendant and hung it on a choker-length stiff wire. It fell perfectly in the V of the neckline. I supposed it could be a real coin but thought it unlikely. A simple pair of hoop earrings worked well with it.

I twisted my hair back in a loose chignon and was ready to go. I found a little black clutch purse and transferred the essentials.

Mochie, Daisy, and Muppet had watched me dress. "What do you think?" I asked.

Mochie yawned. Daisy and Muppet wagged their tails. They all followed me down the stairs where I found Nina and Mars in my kitchen.

"Wow!" said Mars. "You look great! Except for your eye."

"Where are you going?" whined Nina as if she wished she were going with me.

"Just The Laughing Hound. Nothing terribly exciting."

"A date?" asked Mars.

My instinct was to be coy. But then I thought about his date with Greer. Even if he now found her boring, he had gone on a date and we had been divorced for years. There was no reason not to admit the truth. "Yes, with Peter Chryssos."

Nina gasped. "I knew you two would hit it off! Lark, Dulci, and I might have mentioned you to him a time or two during our trip." She gave me a knowing look.

But Mars frowned at Nina. "That's right. I forgot that he was on your tour. Lark and Dulci would both have opened their doors to him had he knocked, even early in the morning."

Chapter 33

Dear Natasha,
My daughter and I live in a small house. She loves to collect things and has tons of stuffed animals. How can I organize her belongings and get them out of piles?
     Mom Tripping over Everything in Tripoli, Iowa

Dear Mom Tripping over Everything,
Nail a long shelf on one or two walls of your daughter's room, about two-thirds of the way up from the floor. Paint the wall underneath a fun color and keep the top part white. Now you can place items on the shelf, and you can even screw in cup hooks for hanging pictures!
     Natasha

"No, no, no," I said. "I see where you're going with this. We don't have a reason in the world to think Peter is involved in Lark's and Dulci's deaths."

"Nina," said Mars, "if Dr. Chryssos knocked on your door, would you open it and let him in?"

She looked at me sheepishly. "Yes, of course."

"That doesn't prove anything," I argued. "She would also open the door if you knocked on it in the middle of the night. So there."

Mars's mouth shifted back and forth. "I don't like this."

"Besides, whatever happened in Portugal, I wasn't there. The killer isn't after me." I said it with confidence. I really didn't think I was a target.

"You're right," said Mars, way too cheerfully. "He falls in the same category as Greer. Have fun tonight."

"Thank you, Mars." I was surprised by his attitude. "I appreciate that."

I fed Mochie and the dogs. "What are you two doing for dinner tonight?"

"We'll just root around in the fridge and nosh on left-overs. That okay with you, Nina?" asked Mars.

"All right. It's boring, though. Couldn't we order in from somewhere?" she asked.

"I'm off. See you two later. Should I bring you dessert?"

"Yes!" Nina shouted as I walked out the door.

I locked it behind me in case they forgot and headed toward The Laughing Hound.

The hostess directed me to the outdoor terrace. Dr. Chryssos waited for me, seated at a table in the center of the terrace directly under hanging Edison lights that crisscrossed the outdoor dining area.

Dr. Chryssos—Peter—and I both ordered pork tenderloin with mango and peach salsa. He ordered a bottle of white wine and we toasted to summertime. I tasted the wine, and nearly choked. In a dim recess of the terrace, near a door that I happened to know led to the kitchen, Nina, Mars, and Bernie lifted their own glasses in a toast in my direction.

Peter had his back to them, thankfully. All I had to do

was avoid looking their way. He leaned toward me, so close that for a few seconds I thought he might kiss me.

"I like your necklace. Very nice. Do you collect coins?" he asked.

"I don't. But some make very nice jewelry."

"I couldn't agree with you more. The sort of thing Greer makes. You need one with a real gold coin."

I smiled. "Maybe after I pay off my house. I'm sure they're very expensive. How did you know that my necklace isn't real gold?" I asked.

Peter's eyes met mine. "I'm afraid coin collecting is one of my hobbies. Some people like paintings, some like racehorses, I find coins fascinating. I believe you're wearing a Morgan silver dollar."

My hand flew to my necklace. "I thought it was gold."

"Your pendant is gold," he conceded, "but I recognize the silver dollar. It was probably plated with gold. I can see how it might be confusing to the unwary. Both the early gold Liberty dollar and Morgan silver dollar have Lady Liberty on the facing in the same direction with stars around the edge. But they're slightly different sizes and Lady Liberty's head is different, and, except for the date, I don't believe there's any writing on the front of the Liberty gold coin."

"You really know your stuff," I said.

"I enjoy it. There's so much history and politics involved in coins."

Our main course arrived, interrupting our conversation. Trying to sound very casual, I asked, "Is there a coin collecting club in Old Town?"

"Not that I'm aware of. I believe there's one for the Washington, DC, area, but I haven't joined yet."

"I've heard Emery might collect coins," I said, knowing full well that Emery had denied it.

"Does he? I wasn't aware of that. I know he's very keen on sports collectibles."

Maybe it was true that Emery didn't have an interest in coins.

Our conversation quickly turned to the murders. Not exactly romantic, but, after all, he was a pathologist. The details were his business. I tried to stay clear of anything that might violate the HIPAA laws so I wouldn't make him uncomfortable. "Have you heard how Frank is doing and can you tell me?"

Peter looked at me in surprise. "I haven't heard a thing. The mango in the salsa is so refreshing."

"It's delicious. Thank you for inviting me to dine with you tonight. Do you have any personal theories about the murders?" I asked.

"They were similar in some ways, which would lead one to suspect the same killer. I have a feeling that Frank may have been in the wrong place at the wrong time. While the attack on him could have been perpetrated by the same person who murdered Lark and Dulci, there was no attempt to garrote him. He was whacked over the head and pushed down the stairs. Rather sloppy actually, since he survived."

I tried not to pay attention to Nina, who was trying to discreetly signal me from across the terrace. The sun had gone down, and fortunately, I could barely see them across the terrace in their corner. When my phone rang in my clutch, I knew exactly who was calling. Really! Couldn't the three of them just act like adults?

"I'm so sorry. I should have turned my phone off." I reached into my purse, pulled out my phone, and flicked the little switch that would make it dead as a doornail. I slid it into my purse.

That event generated a conversation about technology and how it hindered and helped.

"I'm often on call, so I keep my phone nearby and turned on. But sometimes, on my days off, I place it on my desk and ignore it all day long. It's really quite liberating."

"Nina says you're recently divorced."

He sighed. "Might as well get that albatross out of the way. I'm sorry to say it's a dreadfully boring story. Not even original. We had a housekeeper, and a lawn man, and a very big house in Potomac, Maryland. No children. My wife entertained herself by playing golf and ran off with the golf pro at our club."

"I'm sorry," I said. "That must have been hard on you."

"It was initially. I felt quite the dunce. But it's in the past. The separation dragged out far too long, but the divorce finally came through and I'm all the better for it. I'm relieved to put that chapter behind me. I moved to Virginia, bought a nice town house here in Old Town—"

"Oh! That's right. You were looking at Natasha's house. How did that go?"

"I wasn't looking for another place. I'm happy where I am now. But Cal called up and said he wanted to show it to me. He thought he could get me a deal."

I would have been upset by that, but Natasha probably pushed Cal and he picked up on her desperation. "Did you like the house?"

"Great location! It looks wonderful from the outside. The interior isn't really my style, but more important than that, it's just too big for me. I would rattle around in there."

"That's too bad. It sounds like you like your current home."

"It has Old Town charm and character. I've been doing some research into the previous owners. It probably sounds sappy, but I like having that tie to history."

"It doesn't sound sappy at all. I think most of the people who live here enjoy that feeling. I often think about what went on two hundred years ago when I'm out walking my dog in the evening."

"How about we get dessert to go and we take it back to my house so I can show it to you?"

"I'd like that," I said.

"Chocolate cake okay?" he asked.

"Fine!"

"I'm glad you said that because it's my favorite." Peter grinned at me. "I never can pass up a good chocolate cake and The Laughing Hound serves a fantastic one."

From the way he was looking at me, I had a feeling the lights right over our head, while charming in the distance, probably weren't doing much to improve the look of my eye.

"You, uh . . ." He patted his cheek just under and to the side of his eye.

I hated to imagine. When I felt my face, I realized that my makeup had become an oil slick. Excusing myself, I hurried off to the ladies' room.

It was worse than I thought. I dampened a disposable hand towel and wiped a glob of makeup off. I hadn't thought to bring any with me. Now I had a big streak of red and blue showing in between more slimy makeup. I washed it all off. Maybe it was better to be a natural horror than a fake one.

The door to the ladies' room slammed open and Nina rushed in. "Dr. Chryssos is gold!" she hissed at me. She banged all the stall doors.

"What are you doing?"

"Making sure he isn't in here."

I tilted my head. "I don't understand."

"That's because you won't answer your phone," Nina fussed.

"I turned it off. I was having dinner and you knew it. It would have been rude of me to take calls."

"He is gold," she said, looking straight into my eyes.

"Are you saying he's a catch?"

"Chryssos means 'gold' in Greek!"

Chapter 34

Dear Natasha,
Can I paint an old piano?
                    Music Lover in Nashville, Tennessee

Dear Music Lover,
No. I can't imagine why you would want to. I
don't recommend it.

                                    Natasha

I was stunned. Chills ran through me. "Do you think Lark knew that?"

"Possibly. If she was traveling the world to pass off stolen jewelry, I imagine she would have known the word for gold in a whole bunch of languages," said Nina. "Or he could have told her."

She might be right about that. "Motive. What was his motive?"

"The crown jewels," Nina said, sounding exasperated with me.

"She didn't tell anyone she had them. Even Paisley found out by accident. Why would she tell him?"

"Maybe they got cozy. They were spending a lot of time together. Maybe she felt she could confide in him."

"What about Dulci? No," I murmured. "It has to be a coincidence."

"We think you should wrap up your date."

I grinned. "Oh, that's just so cute. But I'm not thirteen."

"I wouldn't be so sassy if I were you. He could be dangerous, Sophie. We'll follow you home from a discreet distance."

"I appreciate your offer, but we're going to his house for dessert."

"No!" she hissed. "Tell him something came up and you have to go home."

I debated. Maybe he would understand. Once Wolf caught the real killer, I could tell him the story of finding out his name meant *gold* during our date and we would have a good laugh about it. Part of me wanted to go back to my date and see his house. But now Nina had planted a seed of doubt in my mind.

The door opened slightly. "Any ladies in here?" asked Mars.

"Not a one," Nina assured him.

He barged inside. "Your eye looks awful."

I knew it did. And the harsh light of the bathroom didn't help. "Thank you so much," I said in mock graciousness.

"What's taking so long? Go out there and end your date. Tell him Francie fell and it's an emergency."

"I was just about to do that." I put on lipstick, which really didn't help my appearance, and floated by the two of them, out into the bar. I walked through it toward our table, but the hostess caught up to me.

"Sophie!" she trilled. "Dr. Chryssos said to tell you he stepped outside."

"Thank you," I said, turning left to the front door. I

walked out, still arguing with myself about whether I was overreacting about Peter's name meaning *gold*. The street-lights and the charming lanterns outside The Laughing Hound offered enough light to see the sidewalks and street clearly. But there was no sign of Peter. Had he grown weary of waiting or thought I was ditching him? I looked up and down the block but didn't see him.

And then I heard a grunt and the sound of scuffling. "Peter?" I walked cautiously in that direction. A small unlit alley ran to the right. As my eyes adjusted to the darkness, I realized that two men were tussling. The larger man appeared to have the upper hand.

"Help!" I screamed. "Stop that! Someone call the police!"

The larger man looked around and I realized that my dark dress must have helped me blend with the night. But my big mouth had given me away. He dropped the other man and sped at me.

"Help!" I screamed.

He slugged me so hard in the face that I fell to the ground. The sound of his footsteps fading into the night as he ran away was like heavenly music.

I scrambled to my knees and crawled over to the other person who lay far too still. I rolled him over on his back. Even in the darkness, I recognized the face of Dr. Peter Chryssos. His eyes were open but unseeing. I tapped his cheeks gently, but he didn't come around.

I pulled my phone from my clutch and turned it back on. My shaking fingers fumbled, hitting the wrong things. I couldn't waste time. I didn't want to leave him, but I had to summon help. I jumped to my feet and ran back to the restaurant. I flung open the door and shouted to the hostess, Bernie, Mars, and Nina, "Call 911! Call 911!"

I ran back out and flew down the street to the tiny alley.

I placed my phone on the ground, the light from it glaring garishly in the dark. "Peter," I said softly, waiting for him to groan. "Peter!" His eyes were still open, but he wasn't blinking. I slid my fingers onto his neck, silently praying for a pulse. As sirens wailed in the distance and the clamor of voices behind me grew, I realized that Peter was gone.

Chapter 35

Dear Sophie,
My new wife doesn't like my favorite furniture. It's
beginning to disappear from our house. How do I
stop this?
        Horrified in Old Town, Alexandria, Virginia

Dear Horrified,
First you need to help your wife understand the
emotional connection you have to your furniture.
Then I suggest painting it cream or white. It's
amazing how quickly old furniture can look new
after a couple of coats of paint. If it's a ratty re-
cliner that bothers her, have it reupholstered.
        Sophie

I was still on my knees bent over Peter when I heard Nina and Mars talking to me and asking questions. "Is he alive?"

I picked up Peter's hand and held it. Not that it would help anything. It certainly wouldn't bring him back, but if his spirit lingered, I didn't want him to feel alone. I squeezed his hand, hoping against hope that he might squeeze back.

He didn't.

Sirens blared behind me and headlights exposed the harsh reality.

Hands plucked at me, helping me to my feet, and I backed away to make room for the EMTs, knowing what they would discover.

Someone, the police, I expected, arrived with more lights. I heard one of the EMTs say the medical examiner should be called. I felt an arm around me, Nina's probably, and we staggered to the sidewalk where people clustered, looking on.

I insisted on staying until Wolf came. I was the only person, at least that I knew of, who had seen what happened. Mars, Nina, and Bernie nodded solemnly. It was the right thing to do.

Wolf arrived shortly. After checking on Peter, he walked over to me. "I understand you were with Dr. Chryssos when he was attacked?"

I explained that I had been in the ladies' room and couldn't find him on the street in front of the restaurant. "But I heard grunting sounds and saw a larger man attacking him. When I yelled, the big man punched me and took off running."

"That explains the other black eye."

Two? I had two black eyes at once? I'd have gladly suffered them if it meant Peter could have survived.

"Did you notice anyone watching you in the restaurant?" asked Wolf.

"As a matter of fact, I did. Mars, Nina, and Bernie were watching us like we were zoo animals."

Wolf's mouth twitched like he was trying to hide a grin. "Other than the three of them?"

"No. But now that you mention it, I bet we were visible

from the street. We ate outside and lights were hanging right over our table."

"Wolf," said Mars. "It turns out that Chryssos means *gold* in Greek."

Wolf's only reaction was to think about it. "Thanks for telling me. Sophie, you go home and get some rest."

"He's definitely . . ." said Nina.

"Yes, he is," Wolf replied.

Bernie returned to the restaurant, and the rest of us walked home quietly.

The dogs were overjoyed to see us. "Sophie," said Mars, "I know how much you like to walk the dogs, but until they catch this guy, I think you shouldn't go anywhere by yourself."

I tended to agree. Nina brought me a pack of frozen peas for my face, which I gladly pressed on the right side.

"You need to change clothes," said Nina. "What's that on your dress?"

I leaned forward. Something very dark brown and sticky clung to my knee and my dress. I scooped a little bit up and sniffed it. "Chocolate cake. We were going to have dessert at Peter's house."

I trudged upstairs and took a shower, returning in a fluffy white bathrobe. It would probably soon be too hot, but at the moment, it felt warm and comforting.

Nina brought me a cup of hot English breakfast tea. "Any normal person would want Scotch after what you went through tonight."

I smiled. "I guess the big elephant in the room is whether or not Peter's death had anything to do with Dulci's and Lark's deaths."

"He *was* on the trip," Nina pointed out.

Mars was gazing out the window when he said, "What if Peter murdered Lark and Dulci?"

"Or was the one who pushed Frank down the stairs?" suggested Nina.

I thought back to the cheerful guy who tended to my black eye in Lark's kitchen. "Peter was a victim. Why are you turning him into a killer?"

Nina poured Scotch for herself and Mars. The three of us settled at the kitchen banquet in a somber mood.

"It doesn't fit together," said Mars. "I think we can agree that there was something in Lark's house that everyone was after. Most likely the crown jewels."

"Which, if they're the real thing, are probably worth millions," said Nina. "I was doing some research on it today."

"I think we're dealing with two people." Mars sipped his drink.

Nina groaned.

"Two people who are working together?" I asked.

"Probably not. Think about it. Frank and someone else were in Lark's house searching last night. There are only two possibilities. Frank found the jewels and the other guy threw him down the stairs and stole them. Or the other guy was searching the house for the jewels, realized that Frank would rat on him, and tried to kill him."

"Then he might be the same person who murdered Lark," I said.

"Could be. But why kill Dr. Chryssos?" Mars doodled on a pad of paper.

"Because he knew something?" suggested Nina.

"Or because someone thinks Lark gave Dr. Chryssos the crown jewels," mused Mars.

"That doesn't make any sense," I said. "It's useless speculation."

Mars sat back. "Here's something that isn't speculation. The car that was set on fire last night. What do you bet someone set it to draw attention away from Lark's house?"

Someone rapped on the door wildly, causing all of us to jump.

The outdoor light gleamed on Natasha. Mars opened the door for her.

She barged in. "Is it true that Dr. Chryssos is dead?"

"I'm afraid so," I said.

She sagged into a chair, flinging her arms out dramatically and letting them sag. "I'm cursed. I must be. No one else has these problems. He wanted to buy the house. Cal said he *loved* it! Cal wanted to meet him tonight so he could write up his offer but no, Dr. Chryssos had something more important to do. What could be more important than buying a house?"

Mars, Nina, and I looked at one another.

"It could only happen to me," Natasha moaned. "What did he die of?"

"Murder," said Nina.

Natasha sat up straight, her arms no longer limp. "What's going on in this town?" She frowned. "Lark and Dulci were so much like me. Brilliant hostesses. Our dinner party invitations are coveted. Aren't they, Mars?"

"Okay," he murmured.

"What if I'm next?" Natasha asked.

"You didn't go to Portugal," said Nina. "The trip seems to be a common thread that we can't figure out."

"Thank goodness for that! You had me worried for a moment," said Natasha.

"How are your mom and Griselda getting along?" I asked.

Natasha slapped her palm against her forehead. "I was correct not to tell Mom about Dad's other wife. They're inseparable. They cried when they met. They laugh together, they can't stop talking about natural remedies and cures. It's like I have two mothers now. All I wanted was a mom who wore sweater sets and pearls and didn't know or care which weeds are poisonous. And now I have two who scatter herbs in the moonlight," she wailed.

We couldn't help ourselves. Maybe it was the pent-up worry or the stress of Peter's death, but Mars, Nina, and I laughed so hard that we couldn't stop.

"Well that's not very nice," Natasha sputtered. "I pour my heart out to you and—"

"Lighten up, Natasha. It is kind of funny," Mars choked.

Natasha tilted her head and studied me. "What happened to you, Sophie? Your face is a mess."

I didn't go into details. I certainly wasn't going to volunteer that I had been on a date with the very man who should have been signing a contract to buy her house. "Believe it or not, I had a worse day than you, Natasha."

She left in a huff.

I was beat, but I knew I couldn't sleep, I was far too riled up.

Nina, in a sweet attempt to distract us, pulled out her phone and started to show Mars and me photos of her trip to Portugal. I stared mindlessly at the sea, at the churches, at the spires, and the ornate designs on a cathedral that Nina claimed were secret messages. I could tell one was a snail. It had been hard enough to figure out the meaning of the circumpunct. I couldn't imagine what a snail might mean. *Slow*?

"These are from the day I got lost. See the tile store? Aren't the tiles amazing?"

Mars and I politely agreed that they were.

"And this is the cathedral with the secret messages again," she said. "It has this amazing . . ."

I tuned out as she droned on flipping through photos. Why were other people's travel photos usually boring?

And then something caught my eye. "Wait! Go back."

She flicked backward through the pictures.

"There. Right there." I pointed at a photo of the cathedral.

"That was the day I got lost. I wound around and arrived back at the Lisbon Cathedral."

I pointed at a woman going into the cathedral.

Nina gasped and enlarged the image.

There was no question about it. The woman wearing a black lace mantilla who was going into the building was definitely Lark Bickford.

Chapter 36

Dear Sophie,
I am so inspired by the black and white diamonds in MacKenzie-Childs furniture. I'd like to try it myself. What's the best way to get that harlequin effect?
 Coveting Clever Design in Checkerboard, Montana

Dear Coveting Clever Design,
Paint a base color first, usually the lighter color. Use masking tape and lay it out carefully. Then paint with the darker color.

Sophie

"So what?" asked Mars.

"Wasn't Lark on the tour bus the day you went out alone?" I asked Nina.

"I thought she was."

"She wanted to go to the cathedral by herself," said Mars. "I don't see how that matters."

I thought back. "Peter Chryssos said she told him she

went to the cathedral to light candles for family members. Why wouldn't she have told you that?"

"She was snubbing me?" laughed Nina.

"Or maybe she went somewhere else and didn't want you to know."

The next morning, I felt like a sumo wrestler had battered me. Every muscle in my body screamed when I moved. I had no choice, though. It was the final day of the festival. The vendors would be packing up and the tents would be down before dark. I had to be there.

I took a long hot shower, hoping the heat would help loosen me up. I felt better until I saw my face in the mirror. After the embarrassment of having my thick makeup slide down my face last night, I decided the only good solution was the biggest sunglasses that I could find. I searched my closet for huge dark Jackie O–style glasses. They were perfect. Maybe it was a good sign and the day would go better than I expected.

I checked my phone for the temperature. Sweater weather was over. The stunning sun in the blue sky would be heating us up today. I slipped on a hot pink blouse and stepped into a white skirt.

The gold pendant that was really a silver coin dipped in gold still sat on my dresser where I had left it last night. I knew it was silly, but Peter had liked it so I wore it again in his memory. I layered on a rope necklace that was longer and liked the effect. Round hoop earrings and black flats completed my outfit.

I tiptoed downstairs, wondering where Mochie and the dogs were. I found them in the kitchen, where Mars handed me a mug of tea with sugar and milk. Nina was there, too, and said, "We thought we'd get breakfast at Big Daddy's. Is that okay with you?"

"Poor Mars," I said. "You feel like you have to guard both of us."

"Bernie's going to meet us, and Humphrey, too."

How awful. I was so grateful to them, but I really didn't like them giving up their lives and things they had to do, just to follow Nina and me around. "You don't think Nina and I would be okay together? There will be crowds of people."

"After last night? Not a chance."

We fed Mochie and the dogs, rinsed out our mugs, and made sure the door was locked behind us.

As I had expected, the festival buzzed in spite of the early hour. People were frantically buying one-of-a-kind items that they might not be able to find again.

Toby, who had pitched in to help Frank, sat in a chair at Paisley's tent.

"Any word on Frank?" I asked.

"He's not good. Paisley asked me to go ahead and close down the tent. She's at the hospital and the kids are with Mrs. Gurtz. I'm waiting for Cal and Bennett to give me a hand moving the furniture inside the house."

"Into Lark's house?" I asked, surprised that was where they were putting everything.

"Paisley thought that was best for the time being. We would need Frank's truck to move everything and she doesn't even know where he left the truck."

I could just imagine how hectic Paisley's life must be with Frank in the hospital. Finding his truck was probably the last thing on her mind.

A couple of vendors drew me away with questions. As soon as I finished with them, Mars, Nina, and I headed to Big Daddy's Bakery. We bought coffee, ham croissants, and chocolate croissants, and ate our unhealthy but delicious breakfast near the fountain in Market Square.

I bit into a salty ham croissant and watched people as they walked by. One of them had killed three people and maybe a fourth if Frank didn't recover. It wasn't fair of me to cast doubt on the whole community, though. Whoever it was had been someone they knew. Someone, I reminded myself, for whom Lark and Dulci were willing to open their doors.

Whitney, the travel agent, spied Nina and rushed over to chat. She carried a pricy new Prada purse in a summery coral shade.

"I see you got that new purse you wanted," I said. "It's lovely."

"Thanks. I adore the color. But I was horrified to hear about sweet Peter Chryssos." She tilted her head and lowered her sunglasses. "Do you have a black eye?"

Nina chortled, "Two, if you can believe that."

"Thank you, Nina," I murmured, not removing my glasses.

Whitney's watch chimed and she glanced at it. "I've got to run. I have an appointment. Take care of those black eyes, Sophie." Whitney hurried away.

I watched her go, thinking about her handbag.

"Soph? Sophie!" Mars interrupted my thoughts.

I looked over at him. He had a pen posed over a pad of paper. "I thought we could review the facts. Only facts, not supposition."

I smiled. Some things never changed. Mars was a bottom-line guy.

"It all began with Lark's death," said Nina.

"No," I said softly. "It began with Lark when she visited the cathedral by herself."

I could see the doubtful look Mars and Nina exchanged.

"For Pete's sake, Sophie. She went to pray," exclaimed Nina, sounding exasperated.

"Show me that photo again, please."

Nina huffed, but she pulled up the picture on her phone and enlarged it.

Lark's head was bent forward and the mantilla hung down, almost concealing her face. She had dressed all in black. At first glance, she looked like any other woman going to church.

"I'm surprised she's wearing the mantilla," said Nina. "We went in a lot of churches but none of us covered our heads with anything. The tour guide said we didn't have to. But I recognize her black shrug and skirt."

"I think she's trying to blend in," I said.

Mars clucked. "That's conjecture."

"Look at her carefully." I restored the size of the photo to normal. "If she had not been murdered, do you think we would have noticed that this was Lark?"

Mars's mouth twitched to the side. "I'm not convinced, but why would she care about blending in?"

"Because she was buying or selling stolen jewelry," I said.

"Just to humor you, I will list Lark's visit to the cathedral, however, I don't think it had anything to do with her murder."

"That works for me, and I think you should also list that when they were leaving the hotel for the airport, someone distracted them by throwing a doll."

"How could that have anything to do with the murders?" asked Nina.

"I don't know but bear with me. You, Nina, were selected for a thorough customs exam that caused you to lose your shoes while everyone else waltzed through. Then, on arrival here, Whitney's purse was stolen while she collected her luggage."

Mars's eyes widened. "Are you saying that Lark actually went to the cathedral to pick up or pay for some jewelry? Then when the baby was thrown, someone delivered it to Lark's purse?"

Nina perked up. "Customs was tipped off and they thought it was in my bag? We were all given a blue bag with the travel agency's logo on it," said Nina. "Is that why I was pulled and searched so thoroughly?"

"Maybe. It would explain why Whitney's bag was stolen. Whatever it was, they had lost it," I theorized.

"And that's why they killed Lark?" asked Mars. "Because she didn't have the thing they were looking for? When they didn't find it at Lark's house, they went to Nina's and to Dulci's."

"Gold," I said. "It must be something gold."

"There are serious problems with your scenario," said Mars. "Why wouldn't they have handed the priceless gold thing to Lark when she went to the cathedral? And it doesn't explain why Peter Chryssos was killed."

Just like that, Mars managed to blow enough big holes in my poorly cobbled together theory to collapse it entirely. "He was on the trip, though," I pointed out, not quite ready to concede defeat.

"Maybe Peter knew something. Or maybe he found the item!" Nina suggested.

"There you are!" Bernie joined us. "How are your eyes, Sophie?"

I briefly lowered my sunglasses. All three of them recoiled. "Give me a break. There's nothing I can do about it."

With that, I threw away my coffee cup, and asked, "Everyone ready to follow me around?"

Two men were already removing the demonstration tent from Market Square. The live demonstrations were officially over.

We headed back to the tents. As we passed Greer's tent, she called out, "Mars!"

I heard him groan behind me. "Hi, Greer," he said.

She waved at him eagerly. I knew he wouldn't be thrilled about it, but I entered her tent and said, "Good morning. How did the festival go for you?"

"Great! I think I've found some new customers. And I sold out of a number of things. I'll be busy making new stock over the next couple of months."

Trying to sound casual, I asked, "Was Dr. Chryssos one of your customers?"

She glanced at my coin necklace. "He bought a few gifts from me. He loved my marble coasters." She pointed to round coasters made of marble and dressed up with geometric lines of gold across them. "I was so sorry to hear what happened to him. He was a nice man."

I nodded sympathetically but I was looking at the coin necklace she wore. "That's lovely."

"Thank you. An old boyfriend gave it to me." Greer touched it.

Nina leaned closer for a better look. "Is it pure gold?"

"Of course," said Greer as though that were a silly question.

I looked at it with a critical eye. It was similar in color to mine and had the Liberty Head looking in the same direction. "I think Dulci had one like that."

"She has a beautiful coin necklace. It's a different coin than mine, though."

I fervently wished I could bring Peter in to look at Greer's necklace. I thought the head was smaller than the one on my coin. What had he said? Something about writing. There was no writing on the real gold coin, only stars and maybe a date. Sure enough, stars circled the entire perimeter with the year 1895 at the bottom.

"It's all so interesting," I said.

Greer laughed. "A little bit of gold can perk up almost anything. Do you like that, Mars?"

He looked up with the expression of a child caught in the act of taking a cookie. In his hand he held a gold key ring with a monogram on the oval fob. The ornate letters were beautifully engraved ECE. "Very nice," he said awkwardly.

"What's your middle initial?" she asked.

Mars paled. "T."

"Thomas?" she guessed with a smile.

Mars shot me a look. His name was a little pompous. But she was going to prod him like a kindergartner until he confessed.

"Tate," he said.

"Marshall Tate Winston? Gosh, that sounds impressive."

"If only he had lived up to it," Bernie quipped.

We all chuckled good-heartedly.

Greer looked past me. "Mars, I'll be packing everything up this afternoon. How about dinner tonight?"

Mars didn't even flinch. "I'm sorry. I promised Sophie and Nina that I would have dinner with them."

"Oh. Maybe another time?" asked Greer.

"Sure. Soph, didn't you need to help Paisley?" he asked quickly.

"I'm glad the festival went so well for you, Greer," I said, walking away. As soon as we were out of earshot, I phoned Wolf.

Chapter 37

Dear Sophie,
My son's wife, whom I dearly love (can you hear the sarcasm?), wants to throw out an antique china cabinet that has been in my family for two generations because (get this) it offends her delicate little nostrils. How do I get rid of the smell?
Loving Mother-in-Law in China Grove, Texas

Dear Loving Mother-in-Law,
There are several great cleaners on the market, but first try placing newspaper inside with activated charcoal on it. Leave it for several days. If that doesn't work, try wiping it down with vodka. Just don't strip the varnish.

Sophie

When Wolf answered the phone, I asked, "When Dulci died, was she wearing a necklace?" The four of us walked while I talked.

"I'll have to check. What's up?"

"Just a hunch. She owned an expensive gold coin necklace. I think she might have been wearing it when I found her. Can you get me a photograph of it?"

"I can do that. But I'm not following you. If someone killed her for it, they would have taken it."

"Yeah. Maybe. Text the photo to me when you have a chance. Any word on Frank's condition?"

"I'm waiting for an update."

I thanked him and ended the call. "No news yet."

Mars, Bernie, and Nina took shelter from the sun under Paisley's tent. Cal and Toby carried furniture into Lark's house. Not much was left in the tent. A few other vendors were offering scandalously low prices and crowds of people hurried to get bargains. One of the vendors hailed me and a line of them quickly formed with questions for me. Most of them were easily answered and small problems were resolved on the spot.

After the last vendor went on her way, I joined Mars under Paisley's tent, which was now empty. "Where are Nina and Bernie?"

"They went to get drinks."

Cal, Toby, and Bennett joined us, looking worn out. Cal wiped his hands on a towel. "It appears the summer humidity has arrived."

"It's nice of you to help Paisley," I said.

"It's what you do for family. Now that her mom is gone, I feel like I should look after her," said Cal.

"Hey!" cried Bennett. "I'm not dead yet, you know. She still has a brother."

Nina and Bernie arrived with cold sodas in cans. Bennett, Cal, and Toby helped themselves. Cal stood with his back to me, looking at Lark's house.

"The location can't be beat," he said. "And that side yard is something you don't find too often in Old Town. I think she'll sell fast." He reached into his pocket and pulled out a pen and papers, handing them to Bennett. "You can sign now, Bennett, and I'll go over to the hospital to get Paisley's signature."

"A listing agreement?" asked Bennett. "I don't think we're ready for that."

"What's the problem?" asked Cal.

"No problem. It's just too soon." He folded the contract and tucked it into the back pocket of his jeans.

Cal frowned at him. "I thought Paisley needed the money. That's what Frank said."

"I'll talk to her about it," Bennett assured him. "She's overwhelmed right now between Mom's death and Frank in the hospital. I think selling the house would be too much. Cleaning it out and all will take time. There's really no need to rush. If Paisley needs some cash, I can help her."

Cal slapped him on the back. "You're a good man, Bennett."

Was he? He claimed he didn't know about the crown jewels. Yet Lark had confided in him about the spendthrift trust in her will. I guessed those weren't conflicting things. Lark clearly would have opened her door to him, but would Dulci? Did he even know Dulci? Not many people would blame him for tossing Frank down the stairs if they knew how he treated Paisley. I stared at him. He wasn't a small man, but would he have looked like a large man next to Peter Chryssos? I didn't think so. Toby wasn't very large, either, but Cal had some heft to him and exceeded Bennett in height.

I scolded myself. Was I going to walk through the streets of Old Town judging men and their guilt by their height and girth? I sipped my ginger ale, glad for the cool liquid in the growing heat.

Cal pointed at me. "I have a buyer for your house, Sophie."

I gazed at him in surprise. "My house is not for sale."

"It could be a quick deal," he said.

"I think it would be a very long deal because I'm not selling."

"I've been in this business long enough to know everyone has a price," Cal said pleasantly.

"In that case, I will be the first exception."

"Who is the interested party?" asked Mars.

"What kind of businessman would I be if I told you that? Sophie could go straight to her and I would be cut out of my commission!"

"It's a woman," said Bernie.

Cal raised his eyebrows. "There are a lot of women in Old Town.

I adjusted my sunglasses and Bennett promptly asked, "What happened to your eye?"

"Eyes," corrected Nina.

I wished the sunglasses had horse blinders on the sides so no one could see my eyes at all. "I seem to be getting punched a lot lately."

Cal stepped forward and looked at me closer. "Now how did that happen?"

"Frank's mother, Carmela, for starters." Sensing that Cal might be prone to gossip, I tried to change the subject. "Is it true that Frank's father fenced stolen goods?"

I watched their expressions. Toby seemed excited. Bennett smacked his lips and said nothing. Cal nodded somberly and said, "His dad and his uncle. I understand they were small-time crooks. Lark told me once that they had a shed full of stolen toasters and TVs."

"That's very sad." I couldn't imagine growing up that way. No wonder Frank had strange ideas.

Cal continued, "They tell me a rival is suspected of the hit-and-run that killed his father. The uncle died not long after that. Not exactly the crowd to run with."

Cal stretched out his arms to someone and Natasha waltzed into the tent. "This looks like the place to be!"

She air-kissed Cal on both cheeks. "Have you shown the house today?"

"Not yet. Such a pity that Dr. Chryssos died. He was on the verge of signing a contract."

What a liar! He was totally misleading Natasha. I supposed it didn't matter since Peter couldn't buy it now. But it irked me.

"Do you want to look at Lark's house while you're here?" Cal asked Natasha.

"It's not for sale yet," Bennett said firmly.

"It will be, son. She might as well look," said Cal, sounding like an authoritative uncle. "Mars? Would you care for a tour?"

"Is the air-conditioning on? I'll do anything to get out of this heat."

Natasha and Cal entered the house. I collected the empty soda cans and carried them inside, followed by Bernie. I tossed them into the trash can, noticing a paper towel with something brown on it inside.

Bernie's voice came from the laundry room. "Wow. I really should put in a first-floor laundry room. We have to go down into the dungeon to do laundry."

Upstairs I could hear murmuring, presumably from Cal and Natasha.

"Sophie?" Bernie came into the kitchen. "What's that?"

What, indeed. I had pulled the paper towel out of the trash gingerly with the tips of my thumb and forefinger. There was no doubt in my mind that the brown smear on the paper towel was chocolate cake.

Chapter 38

Dear Natasha,
I live in a studio apartment. It's tiny but it's all I can afford right now. How do I arrange it when there's so little space and my bedroom is my closet and my living room?
                              Living in a Box in New York City

Dear Living in a Box,
Create zones. A sleeping zone, an eating zone, a desk zone, and a dressing zone. It will feel much larger when all your clothes are in one area and dishes, etc., are in another.
                                        Natasha

"Would you know the smell of the chocolate cake from The Laughing Hound?" I asked in a whisper.

Bernie bent to sniff it. "Could be chocolate cake from anywhere. But it looks fresh."

"Good point."

Bernie's eyes met mine. "You're thinking the person who killed Peter Chryssos came back here."

"Which means it's someone who has a key to the house," I hissed.

He motioned for me to follow him. He headed for the laundry room and pointed at the washing machine. Trying to be very quiet, he opened it, but it was empty. He tried the dryer, but it was empty, too.

It sounded like Cal and Natasha were now in the dining room, not far from us. I stepped back into one of the piles of clothes on the floor and a corner of something black peeked out from the very bottom.

Moving faster than I'd have thought he could, Bernie whipped the garment out and held it up. It was a man's jacket, size XL with a hood. One of the sleeves had been torn and chocolate icing clung to the bottom.

Bernie stashed it back under the other clothes and said in a loud voice, "Is this a good brand of washing machine?"

It was perfect timing. Cal and Natasha walked in. "The house isn't really my style. But I could change a lot of it. The kitchen would have to be redone," Natasha said.

"The kitchen is beautiful!" I protested.

Cal held up his forefinger and said, "Sophie, you can buy this house. Just say the word."

I wanted to say a few words to him. Only a few people could have keys to Lark's house, and one of them was Cal. The only other people I could think of were Paisley, Bennett, and Humphrey. I could strike two of them without another thought. That left Cal and Bennett. One of them had waited for Peter last night, then ran back here to change clothes, assuming no one would be the wiser. Either Cal had slipped up in his eagerness to show the house to Natasha, or Bennett was sweating bullets.

I desperately needed to call Wolf. At that moment, my phone jingled, nearly scaring me out of my wits. I glanced at it. Someone at the police department had sent Wolf and me a photo of Dulci's necklace. I had to lift my sunglasses a hair to see it properly. I knew instantly that it was a fake. It looked exactly like the one I was wearing. It was a Morgan silver dollar with *E·PLURIBUS·UNUM* printed around the upper edge. Unless she had two very similar necklaces, the person who killed her took the one that was a genuine gold coin.

"Something important?" asked Cal reaching for the phone.

Instead of letting him have it, I flashed it toward him and Natasha, then flicked the photo closed. "It's just a necklace that I'd like to have. Nothing important."

"It looked like a gold coin." Cal stepped toward me. My heart beat like crazy. "It is." I touched my necklace and forced a smile. "This one is a fake. Well, not fake, it's a silver dollar dipped in gold to look like it's gold. The other necklace is a genuine gold coin."

Cal seized my arm. "Let me see it!"

"Hey!" Bernie protested. "Let her go."

Cal towered over me, and I knew he was the person who punched me the night before. He was dangerous. Obviously, he thought nothing of killing Peter Chryssos.

"Show me the coin!" he demanded.

I opened my phone and found the picture.

He released my arm and took the phone. Meanwhile, I was thinking that Mars and Bennett were outside. If we didn't show up fairly soon, they would come looking for us. There were three of us in the laundry room and one of him. But Natasha didn't know what was going on.

I tried to catch her gaze, but she was far too interested in the gold necklace. "But that's just like the one you're wearing," said eagle-eyed Natasha.

"Exactly! Why would I want another one?" I tried to sound light and cheerful, but I was wondering how we could take Cal down. I didn't think he was armed. He was wearing jeans and a T-shirt. There wasn't much room to hide a weapon.

He handed me back the phone. "I didn't know that you're a coin collector," he said, sounding much calmer.

"I'm not. This necklace is the only coin that I own. But there's just something so special about a real gold coin."

Cal's eyes grew dark and his face was menacing. "Chryssos. He told you. And now you're toying with me."

I played along, wondering how to text Wolf without Cal seeing me. "Told me what?"

"About the coin!" he roared.

I backed into Bernie, who whispered in my ear, "I'll take the top. Go!"

I dove for Cal's legs. He was stronger than I had anticipated. *The backs of the knees,* I thought. I wrangled my way behind him, intending to hit the backs of his knees, but it sounded like Bernie was struggling. I pulled myself up to the counter, and jumped on Cal's back, holding on to his neck. It was like riding a bucking bronco.

"Natasha!" I screamed. "Either get Mars or call Wolf."

I could hear her running through the house yelling, "Mars. Mars!"

Bernie and I had Cal in a position where he couldn't fight off both of us. He tried backing up and putting pressure on me, but he hadn't considered my size or the countertop. I pulled open the drawer where I had found twine and bungee cords a few days ago. While he used both hands to fight off Bernie, I took out a bungee cord, wrapped it around his neck, and pulled it tight.

He stopped fighting Bernie and reached toward his throat trying to loosen the cord around his neck. I tossed a couple of bungee cords to Bernie, who fastened Cal's feet together at the ankles.

Mars and Bennett ran into the laundry room. In seconds, they had secured his arms behind him by wrapping the twine around his wrists several times. It wasn't perfect, but it would probably hold until the police arrived. I loosened the bungee cord on his neck.

Nina was on the phone with the police.

Cal flung a few unsavory words at us.

"Are you okay, Bernie?" I asked.

"I have a feeling I'm going to match you tomorrow."

"Match me?" I didn't understand.

"Your eyes."

My sunglasses had fallen off during the tussle.

Mars handed them to me.

"Thanks." I turned my attention back to Cal. "Why did you kill Peter Chryssos?" I demanded.

Cal started to laugh. He choked and coughed but kept laughing. "You really don't know?"

Since talking about the coin had upset him, I took a wild stab. "Because of the coin?"

"Of course it was because of the coin. He was pressuring me. Everyone else thought he was such a great guy. Well, let me tell you, he was a cold, calculating, greedy swine."

"Which coin was it?" I asked, trying to sound like I knew what I was talking about.

"The 1907 Saint-Gaudens Double Eagle. It's worth millions."

"Lark picked it up for you in Lisbon?" I asked.

Cal blinked at me. "Are you kidding? Lark was a Goody-Two shoes. That coin was hot! Everybody wanted it. It had been stolen from a private collection. The owner deserved to lose it. He bought it when it was stolen from someone else. Nobody knows who the rightful owner is anymore. Chryssos had to have it, but we had to get it here without anyone knowing."

I took a chance. "Then why did you kill Lark?"

"It was an accident. I swear."

"That injury on the back of her head didn't look like an accident to me."

"I meant to knock her out. Just long enough to find the coin. But she fell down the stairs and I couldn't revive her."

"Stairs?" I was shocked. "You carried her from the foyer to the back porch? That's why you placed a ladder next to her? You hoped people would think she had fallen off it?"

"I never meant to kill her. You have to believe me."

"I'm confused," I said. "You said Lark was a Goody-Two shoes and wouldn't have brought you the coin."

"She didn't know she had it. The plan was to slip the coin into her bag in Portugal. Then she would innocently carry it back here without realizing it. But somewhere along the way, it got lost. Chryssos had already paid a deposit of one million dollars for it and then we couldn't find the stupid thing."

"So you came to my house next? I would have let you search in my bags if you had asked. Lark would have, too," cried Nina.

Cal looked miserable. "Chryssos was some kind of angry. He'd lost a million dollars. He was crazy. Completely crazy. He seemed like a good guy, but he was out of his mind about that coin."

"That's why you murdered him? To shut him up?" asked Mars.

"With Chryssos gone, it didn't matter anymore where that coin landed. For all I know, somebody dropped it in a sewer grate or a trash can and it will never be found again."

"Why did you take Dulci's gold necklace?" I asked.

"I didn't," said Cal. "That wasn't me. Dulci was dead when I got there. I went through her stuff, but I never touched her. I saw you open the gate, so I left by the front door. I figure Emery knocked her off."

I didn't believe him. Everything else he had said fit what had happened, though.

"But you did take the crown jewels?" I asked.

Cal stared at me like I had lost my mind. "I don't know anything about crown jewels."

Either he was very good at faking innocence or he didn't know about them.

"Did you set the car on fire?" asked Mars.

Cal's eyes shifted. "Yeah. I needed a diversion to go through the houses looking for the coin. You can't imagine the pressure Chryssos put on me. If I didn't find it, I would be the dead one."

I had forgotten about Bennett. He stood in the corner, watching his uncle and listening. His uncle had murdered his mother. It had to make her death a thousand times worse.

"Then you're the one who broke the light and knocked Frank down the basement stairs. Why did you hurt Frank?" Nina asked.

"He caught me in the house. He came over to search for those jewels and I was afraid he would find the coin."

Wolf finally arrived. Unbeknownst to me, Nina had called Wolf and kept him on the line. He had heard everything Cal said.

In short order, Cal was handcuffed and taken out to a squad car. We watched in the dark as it drove away. I searched for Bennett and wrapped my arms around him. "I'm so sorry."

Chapter 39

Dear Sophie,
I am in love with hallway organizers. We desper-
ately need one for coats and clutter, but our entry
isn't wide enough for a seat. Suggestions?
        Clutter Be Gone in Hallandale Beach, Florida

Dear Clutter Be Gone,
Cut a beadboard four to five feet wide and about
six feet tall. Paint, and mount on your wall. Cut a
one-by-four the same width, paint and place at the
height you want to hang coats. Add hooks. Over-
top of the one-by-four, add a shelf or even an open
cabinet in the same color for other clutter. Jazz it
up by adding a large mirror on the opposite wall to
make the area feel brighter and wider.
                                        Sophie

Bennett drove to the hospital to break the news to
Paisley. The rest of us walked to my house in the dark.
Daisy and Muppet danced in circles on our arrival.

Mochie jumped on a chair and demanded attention and ear scratches.

We took all the leftovers out of the fridge and the chocolate mayonnaise cupcakes out of the freezer. It was an odd giddy dinner. Nina mixed rum runners for everyone. They were strong but delicious and after our ordeal, most welcome. Our conversation rambled through how strong Cal was, whether he was lying about not killing Dulci, where the priceless Double Eagle coin and the crown jewels might really be, and how relieved we all were that Cal was now safely in police custody.

For the first time in days, my friends slept in their own beds in their own homes.

The summer sun didn't wake me in the morning. Mochie did. He patted my cheek with his paw. It was adorable. Every bone in my body aching, I rolled over and glanced at the clock. It was noon!

I forced myself out of bed and into the bathroom where I regretted looking in the mirror. A hot shower eased the achiness in my muscles. I pulled on skorts and a sleeveless white shirt. My face was hopeless. At least I didn't have to wear sunglasses around my own home.

I fed Mochie, let Daisy out, and made myself a huge mug of steaming hot English breakfast tea. I carried it outside and joined Daisy in the backyard. She came to me, wagging her tail, but I could tell she missed romping with her little friend Muppet.

I sat in the shade surrounded by pink, orange, red, and lavender blooms. I didn't even mind the warm air. I was just glad we had managed to subdue Cal last night.

Daisy's ears perked and she ran to the side of the house. She returned with Nina and Muppet. Muppet ran wildly through the yard with Daisy following her. Nina plunked

coffee, bagels, cream cheese, sliced salmon, and her favorite, pimiento cheese spread, on the table. "I'm starved,"
she said, plopping into a chair.

"You look gloomy. Did you search your bags for the
coin last night?"

"Of course! Alas, I am not a millionairess."

"Then what's wrong?"

"Someone wants to adopt Muppet. She's coming to see
her this afternoon."

"Oh, Nina! It's so hard to be a foster parent. I don't
know how you can give up any of the sweet fosters."

As if she understood, Muppet ran toward us, all wiggles
and waggles. She looked up at Nina with adoring brown
eyes.

"You've had a lot of foster dogs. You've been through
this before."

"I know," she said, tears welling in her eyes. "But Muppet is the only one who saved my life."

Given what happened to Lark and Dulci, that was undoubtedly true. "Call the rescue and tell them it's a failed
foster."

"I haven't talked to my husband about it."

"Didn't you say he owed you after your miserable trip?"
I asked.

"He does!" Nina picked up her phone and called the
rescue organization.

I couldn't hear everything the woman said on the other
end of the conversation, but I did hear when she said,
"You're a perfect match and you can still foster other animals."

Nina was beaming when she hung up the phone. "All I
have to do is swing by this afternoon to sign the docu-
ments."

"How will your husband take the news?"

"I think he'll agree that we should give Muppet a wonderful life. Even though she's tiny, I'll sleep better knowing she's on the alert."

I slathered a bagel half with cream cheese and placed a slice of smoked salmon on it. "Thanks for bringing breakfast."

"Thanks for letting me stay with you! What a week! Why would Cal confess to murdering Lark and Chryssos but deny that he killed Dulci?" Nina scooped pimiento cheese out of the container and smoothed it over her bagel.

"I don't know. Because he's afraid of Emery?"

A scream broke the peace in my backyard. Natasha's mother, Wanda, ran toward me with Natasha right behind her carrying an old-fashioned doctor's satchel. "Why didn't you call me?" cried Wanda.

Natasha handed over the satchel.

Wanda opened her bag. "You poor thing. We heard about it this morning." She dipped her fingers into a mash and spread it on my face. "Now this is just comfrey root. It will make you feel better."

"Have you had breakfast?" asked Nina. "I brought plenty. I even have salmon."

"I don't mind if I do. Did Natasha tell you the good news?" asked Wanda.

Natasha appeared pained.

"Griselda and I found a perfect little store. It's a second-floor walkup on King Street with all these wonderful old beams in the ceiling. One of the walls is brick! It's just fabulous! And we're getting a great price on it."

Natasha groaned. "Tell them why."

"The landlord is quite smitten with me." Wanda grinned. "He's single, too. Natasha, I don't know why you're so upset. This way Griselda and I can help you pay for the house."

"You're moving up here?" I asked.

"Isn't it wonderful?"

Natasha looked less than thrilled. "Griselda and Charlene are moving out of the garage apartment and into my house. I'm going to rent the apartment, and with all of us chipping in, we should be able to swing the payments."

"Does that mean you made a deal with Mars?" I asked Natasha.

"Yes. He called this morning and we worked it out. Alex is drawing up the papers."

"Now I'm taking off the comfrey," said Wanda, gently wiping my face, "and putting on arnica. That'll help the blue color fade away faster."

"Wanda, it will be so nice having you in the neighborhood," said Nina.

"Thank you, darlin'. You girls just let me know if you need anything."

"Mom, they're grown women."

"You'll always be girls to me."

After breakfast, Nina and I walked the dogs in the direction of Lark's house. I wanted to be sure all the tents had been removed and that no trash had been left from the festival.

The street and sidewalks looked remarkably clean. We stopped in front of Lark's house. It was peaceful and still. No one would ever suspect what had gone on there.

"Do you suppose we'll ever find out what happened to the crown jewels and the coin?" asked Nina.

"I'd say it's highly doubtful. Someone took the crown jewels. They've probably been sold. They were lost for so long and now they're gone again. It's kind of mind-boggling to think how many ancient valuables are in someone's private stash. Or even lost in trash around the world."

"Or right under our feet," said Nina. We both looked down at the brick sidewalk.

We strolled on to the river. The sun glinted on the rippling surface and Wolf stood at the railing, looking down into the water.

"Did you get any sleep last night?" I asked.

"Not much. Even when I went home, I couldn't get Cal out of my mind. He destroyed his brother's family, all for money. I don't know if they'll ever recover."

"Any news on Frank?"

"He has finally taken a turn for the better. I was able to talk to him and he confirmed that it was Cal who coaxed him to the stairs, pointed out the broken lightbulb, and then pushed him down. Of course, Frank was in the process of turning the place upside down looking for the crown jewels and Cal was afraid he would find the priceless coin."

"Do you think Lark fell down the stairs like he claimed?" I asked.

"That's consistent with the finding of the autopsy."

"I don't remember you telling me that before," I said.

Wolf grinned. "I don't tell you everything."

"How about Dulci?" I asked.

"Cal still denies having anything to do with her death." Wolf turned to face me. "In the chaos last night, I forgot to ask why you wanted that photo of Dulci's necklace. Was it what you expected?"

"Sort of. Emery told me he bought Dulci a necklace with a solid gold coin in it for her fiftieth birthday. But the one in the photo, the one she was wearing when she was taken to the morgue, was like my necklace. It's pretty, but it's a silver dollar dipped in gold. The coin is only worth about thirty dollars."

"Then where is the solid gold one?" asked Nina.

"I'm thinking one of two things happened. Emery bought her a thirty-dollar necklace and passed it off as solid gold or her killer swiped it." I patted Daisy, who was watching birds.

"I hope Emery was fooling her," said Wolf. "Otherwise, her killer came prepared to swap the necklaces, thinking no one would be the wiser."

Chapter 40

Dear Natasha,
I want to put up a picture gallery on my wall. I think they're so cool. But no matter how hard I try, it's just not pretty. What am I doing wrong?
    Loves Pictures of Family in Fort Pickens, Florida

Dear Loves Pictures of Family,
Photo walls are out. I'm not sure they were ever in. If you must display all those photos, hang two five-foot-long shelves on a blank wall, one over the other. Set your framed photos on the shelves. Do not add any more shelves! Only two!
                                    Natasha

That afternoon, I spent a little bit of time taking care of business, making phone calls, and scheduling appointments.

Then I retrieved the old side table from the basement, hauled it outside, and cleaned it up. Armed with plenty of old rags, I painted a soft turquoise chalk paint on the legs.

As I worked, my mind kept going back to Dulci. Had someone other than Cal killed her for her necklace? But what about the ladder? Was that a coincidence? Or had someone meant for it to look like Lark's death? The latter, I thought, remembering Dulci's high heels. I supposed she could have intended to kick them off and climb the ladder in bare feet, but that seemed unlikely.

Anyone could have seen her in the necklace and followed her home. But the timing and the blow to the head were so like Lark's death.

I pawed through the bag of paints I had bought and came to a dead stop on a tiny jar of gold paint. What was it that Greer had said? A little bit of gold made a big difference. She and Dr. Chryssos had shared a love of everything gold. That was for sure.

But if Chryssos had enough money to ante up a million dollars for a single coin, then surely he wouldn't have killed Dulci over a necklace that would have been worth a thousand dollars, if that.

"Soph? Where are you?"

It was Mars's voice. Daisy romped to him as he rounded the corner. "Trying to be Paisley?" he asked.

"Not quite. Do you remember this old table?"

"That takes me back. Way back. It's handy but never was very attractive."

I laughed. "I figured it was a good place to start because I couldn't make it worse."

Mars sat down on the grass beside me. Daisy immediately took advantage of the situation and nuzzled his face.

Mars, about to be bowled over by Daisy, held out his left hand. Something dangled from his fingers.

I took it from him. It was a gold key ring with a monogrammed fob. "M—W—T," I read aloud, laughing. "She's after you, Mars."

"I don't find it amusing. And I don't want her dipping

things in gold and bringing them to me. I have to stop this."

"On the bright side, your monogram is very pretty. What was the one she had in the store? Maybe another boyfriend gave it back to her," I teased.

"Two Es," he said.

"And a C." Mars's eyes met mine. "Emery Chapman. What's his middle name?" Holding Daisy at bay, which was no small feat, Mars Googled him. "Dr. Emery Edward Chapman," he read. "Maybe we should pay him a visit."

I changed into a dress with abstract swirls of summery pinks and peaches, and a pair of flat white sandals. I didn't have to bother with makeup, except for a little lipstick. I put on my Jackie O sunglasses and was ready to go. We left Daisy inside with Mochie where she would be cool, locked the door, and walked over to Emery's house.

Mars banged the knocker and Emery opened the door.

"Come in, come in! Could I offer you something? I was just making some decaf coffee. I must be getting old. Can't drink the real stuff after noon."

"Sounds great. Can I help?" I asked.

"It's all done. I'll just be a minute."

Mars and I sat down in the room with the French doors that looked out on the brick terrace where Dulci had lain.

Emery bustled in with a tray and set it on an ottoman coffee table. He had thought of everything. Coffee cups and saucers, beige cloth napkins, spoons, milk and cream, and a platter of blondies. He retrieved the coffeepot and poured it. "Thank you for coming. It's too quiet around here."

Mars accepted a coffee cup and poured in a dollop of cream. "When are you going back to work?"

"In a week or so."

Mars pulled the key ring out of his pocket and held it out to Emery without saying anything.

Emery paused. He stared at it, making no effort to take it into his hands. "I'm sorry."

"For what?" asked Mars.

"That she's obsessing about you now. On the other hand, I'm glad she moved on."

"Does Wolf know about Greer?" I asked.

"Know what?" Emery kept cool.

"That she was obsessed with you?"

"Uh, no. I don't believe I mentioned that. It was over."

What, exactly, was over? "Emery, did you have an affair with her?"

He rubbed his forehead. "It was very short-lived. I loved Dulci with all my heart. I slept with Greer once after a party when Dulci was out of town. It was a mistake. A huge mistake. I didn't want it to go on. I explained that to her, but Greer is persistent. She just wouldn't let go."

Dulci had wanted to speak to me about something. I bet it was about Greer. Had her own husband murdered her to be with his girlfriend? I tensed up and asked gently, "Did Greer threaten to tell Dulci? How did Dulci find out?"

"I think Greer was spying on me. She turned up everywhere. I finally told Dulci that Greer seemed fixated on me."

"And you never thought she might kill Dulci?" asked Mars, sounding incredulous.

"No! What would make me think that? I figured she would lose interest and move on to someone else"—he gestured toward Mars—"and now she has. In fact, that was the reason for our three-week vacation in Portugal. We needed to get away from her and I thought it would help her if we were gone. She would have to focus on someone else."

"Emery, that coin necklace you bought Dulci, do you have any pictures of her wearing it?"

He pulled out his phone and flicked through photos. "Here, she wore it to a New Year's party."

I lifted my sunglasses and enlarged the picture so I could see the coin better. "Did she have another coin necklace or was this the only one?"

"That was the only one."

"I'm not a coin expert. But I suspect that Dulci's murderer replaced her necklace with a fake. Not even a very good fake, because I can tell the difference."

Emery stared at me in what I thought was genuine shock. "The forbidden fruit," he murmured. "Greer went after the things she coveted." He bowed his head and rubbed his forehead with one hand. "What have I done?" he whispered.

Chapter 41

Dear Sophie,
My family is meeting our future in-laws for the first
time and we're having a sit-down dinner in my
backyard. I would love to do a solid strip of flow-
ers down the center of the very long table. It's a
fortune at a florist. Can I do that myself?
        Lots of Flowers in Bloom Junction, Ohio

Dear Lots of Flowers,
Make a long, waterproof piece to hold the flowers.
You can buy cheap plastic containers and attach
them in a line with floral tape. Fill with floral foam
and tape it down. Now add water and your flow-
ers. Pack them in so it looks very full and remem-
ber to keep them low to encourage conversation.
                                Sophie

In the twilight of early evening, Emery wiped his eyes and
looked up. His eyes widened in horror.
    Mars and I looked toward the French doors. Greer stood

just outside in a wispy white dress, the gold coin necklace around her neck, and stared in at us, her face grim.

She tried a door handle. It opened readily and she stepped inside. "You shouldn't have told them, Emery. I had everything under control. No one suspected. No one would ever have known. I positioned Dulci just like Lark. I even hit her over the head like Lark's killer and placed the ladder beside her. Then, although it was torture, I stayed away from you. I even pretended to have a crush on Mars. I played my role perfectly. But now you have created a problem."

I looked at her hands to see if she was armed. Her hands hung by her sides. That dress probably didn't hide a weapon unless it had deep pockets that I couldn't see. I wished my phone weren't in my purse.

"How did you get into the house that morning?" I asked.

"Like I did just now. The door was unlocked."

I eyed Emery's iPhone. How could I grab it without alerting her? "Would you care for some coffee?" I asked, scooting forward toward the ottoman.

Greer looked at me like I was the crazy one. "No, thanks."

I picked up the plate of blondies in my right hand and cupped the iPhone in my left hand at the same time, hoping her eyes were on the luscious blondies. "Blondie?" I asked Greer.

At the same time, I squeezed the buttons on both sides of the phone, praying it wouldn't make a noise when it called 911. We needed to tackle her. As long as she didn't have a knife or a gun, we could do that. I was sore, but I could distract her.

She wasn't that far away from me. I was lousy at throwing things, but the closer I was, the better my chances. And if nothing else, she would be distracted. Pretending to offer Greer blondies, I moved toward her, smiling with the plate extended in my hand, just like I was offering hors d'oeuvres. And then I turned the plate up and smashed it into her face.

Mars tackled her. Greer fought like a lion.

I managed to grab one of her hands. "Emery, bring me something to tie her with!"

He ran to a landline phone, unplugged both ends of the telephone cord, and brought it over. We managed to tie her hands, which helped subdue her until the police arrived.

It was another long night. Wolf questioned us so late that I was beginning to be sorry I had wasted the blondies on Greer.

Wolf gave us a ride home. It was after midnight when I unlocked my kitchen door and apologized to poor Daisy and Mochie for leaving them in the dark without their dinner. They acted like they loved me anyway.

I let Daisy out while I fixed their dinners and made myself a ham sandwich.

Our tummies full, we went to bed.

Three weeks later, Paisley invited us to a barbecue at Lark's house. Lark's white wicker garden furniture and the white cloth on the table were perfect backdrops for the pink, red, and coral flowers blooming in her yard and the red gingham cushions on the chairs. The children ran around in circles, seemingly not even noticing that their father wasn't there.

Mrs. Gurtz sat in a rocking chair on the porch, while Bennett manned the grill and Paisley ran back and forth to the kitchen. We heard a scream and crowded into the kitchen asking if everything was all right.

Paisley's hands were shaking. "I . . . I had the news on. Let me rewind it."

The anchor came on. "In worldwide news, Portugal has announced that part of the crown jewels stolen years ago have been returned. They were left in a donation box in the Lisbon Cathedral five weeks ago. Authorities have been examining them and can now confirm that they are indeed part of the missing crown jewels of Portugal."

"That was Mom," Paisley whispered.

Mrs. Gurtz smiled. "Those things worried Lark silly. She was afraid someone might steal them. She finally decided the church would know what to do with them. Looks like she was right."

"You knew about them?" asked Paisley.

"Sure. Your rotten father-in-law came slinking by here to ask your grandad to pop the jewels out of those settings. Said he couldn't find anyone to buy them."

Paisley asked with a tremor in her voice, "Mom bought them?"

"Of course not. But she and your granddad and I talked about what would be the right thing to do. Lark found pictures of them on her computer and knew how special they were. We figured them for millions. Then your father-in-law died and your mom and granddad held their breath, terrified that someone would come around looking for them. But no one ever did. And now they're back home, where they belong."

Nina poked me. "That's what she was up to in the picture. She was taking the crown jewels to the church."

"Clearly she was not a stolen jewelry fence after all."

Mrs. Gurtz overheard me and laughed until I thought she might cry. "Stolen jewelry? Lark was one of the most highly regarded jewel couriers in the world."

"What?" Paisley asked as she and Bennett came closer.

"No way. We would have known about it," said Bennett.

Mrs. Gurtz laughed again. "Little mouths tell everything. You two were darling, but she knew the safest thing was not to let anyone know. Her father started her in the business when she was quite young. He knew he could trust her. And it built up from there. I found out quite by accident. Lark swore me to secrecy for her safety. I can keep my tongue!"

We pigged out on barbecued ribs, potato salad, three bean salad, and a giant strawberry sheet cake with strawberry icing.

When I had a minute alone with Paisley, I asked, "How is Frank?"

"Crazy as a loon. The DIY Festival changed my life. Remember the morning I came to you because I was afraid Frank had killed Mom for her money?"

"Of course."

"I had a lot of time to sit in that tent and think. And I had to ask myself if I was seriously afraid that my husband could have murdered my mother, then why was I with him? He was always yelling, especially at Tommy. I could see the fear in my child's eyes and realized that Frank's belittling Tommy was changing him from a bright, inquisitive boy into a shadow. I was on the verge of telling Frank we were through when he left the house and Cal threw him down the stairs. Those were miserable days. I cared about Frank and felt so guilty for planning to split up. I realized I didn't want him to die. I just didn't want to be married to him anymore."

I had no idea what to say. I'm sorry? I wasn't sorry, although I knew handling six small children on her own would be difficult. "Thank goodness you have Mrs. Gurtz."

Paisley drew a deep breath. "She's over eighty years old. I don't know how much longer she can do this, but she desperately needs the money and I need the help. Did you hear that the boys and I are moving into this house? I've managed to fit bunk beds into two of the bedrooms upstairs. I'm taking the smallest one. It will work and Humphrey"—she waved at him across the room—"approved it. I'm putting the kids in regular school. They think Tommy might be ready for seventh grade! We thought that all along but I'm going to start him off with his own age group. I think that will be an easier adjustment for him."

I went home that night feeling better about Paisley than I had in a long time. Everything would work out for her.

Two months later, I was working at a nursing convention at the Washington Marriott Wardman Park Hotel when a buzz arose in the massive convention hall.

"What happened?" I asked someone standing near me.

The nurse smiled and flicked out her phone. "An old lady bought a purse at the thrift shop in Old Town and found a gold coin in it that is worth millions! They think it slipped through the lining and that's why the owner didn't notice it. No one has claimed it, so it's going to auction and will bring a fortune!" I glanced at her phone. With a big smile on her face, Mrs. Gurtz proudly held up the coin.

Recipes

Freezer Chocolate Chip Cookies

Makes approximately 40 cookies.

Preheat oven to 325. Line cookie sheet with parchment paper.

12 Tablespoons unsalted butter (1½ sticks), softened, preferably Plugrá or Kerrygold
¾ cup light brown sugar
½ cup granulated sugar
1 large egg, room temperature
2 teaspoons vanilla
2 cups flour
½ teaspoon pink salt
½ teaspoon baking powder
1½ cups semi-sweet chocolate chips
Flaky sea salt, optional

Cream the butter with the sugars until they are well incorporated. Add the egg and beat it in. Add the vanilla and beat. Mix the flour, salt, and baking soda in a bowl. With the mixer running on low add a little bit of the flour mixture at a time. When no flour is visible, mix in the semi-sweet chocolate chips.

Roll the dough into loose balls a little bit bigger than an inch in diameter. Place them on the baking sheet about 3 inches apart because they will spread. If you want to salt them, sprinkle them now. Bake for 10 minutes.

To store in the freezer, line a cookie tin with wax paper. Lay the cookies on the wax paper in a single row. Add more wax paper and lay cookies on it in a single row. Repeat until full. Top with a sheet of wax paper and fit the lid on tightly. Place in the freezer. To serve, remove the quantity of cookies you need (even if it's only one for you!). Set it on a plate and let thaw for 30–45 minutes. Enjoy!

Bourbon Chocolate Chip Blondies

This recipe makes a thin, chewy blondie.

8 x 8 pan

6 Tablespoons butter
⅔ cup flour
½ teaspoon baking powder
½ teaspoon salt
¾ cup dark brown sugar
1 large egg
2-3 Tablespoons Bourbon
1 teaspoon vanilla
¼ cup semisweet chocolate chips
Flaky sea salt, optional

Preheat the oven to 350. Grease and flour an 8 x 8 pan and line with one piece of parchment paper cut to fit the sides, but long enough to act as handles and two sides for removing the blondies.

Melt the butter and set aside.

Mix together the flour, baking powder, and salt and set aside.

Beat the eggs with the dark brown sugar until thick and lighter in color. Beat in the bourbon. With the mixer on low, alternate adding the flour mixture and the butter. Give one quick mix to combine and pour half of it into the pan. Sprinkle the chocolate chips in a single layer and pour the remaining batter over them, spreading it out over the top. If adding flaky salt, dust the top with a pinch or two.

Bake 20 minutes. (Do not bake longer or else they won't be chewy!) Using the edge of the parchment paper as handles, lift out of the pan and cool on a baking rack. They can be eaten warm or cold.

Pork Tenderloin with Mango Peach Salsa

1 pork tenderloin
Pepper
Garlic powder
Salt
1–2 Tablespoons olive oil

Preheat oven to 400.

Sprinkle both sides of the meat with pepper, garlic powder, and salt and rub it on meat.

Heat the olive oil in an ovenproof pan large enough to hold the entire tenderloin. Brown the meat on each side for 2-3 minutes. Place pan in oven and roast for at least 20 minutes. *The amount of time your roast needs will vary with the size. It's best to check the internal temperature of the meat. Pork should be 145 degrees. Let the meat rest for at least five to ten minutes before cutting.*

Serve with Mango Peach Salsa.

Mango Peach Salsa

1 peach, diced
2 ripe mangos, diced
½ Vidalia onion, diced
1 teaspoon lemon juice

Toss the peach, mangos, onion, and lemon juice together and serve on the side. Serves 3–4.

Oven Roasted Potatoes with Bacon

1 pound of gold or red potatoes
1–2 Tablespoons olive oil
1 teaspoon garlic powder
1 teaspoon paprika
¾ teaspoon sea salt
pepper to taste
4 ounces bacon

1 large rimmed baking sheet or pan

Preheat oven to 400. Scrub the potatoes, dry them, and cut into small cubes no bigger than ¾ of an inch. Pour the oil into the pan and coat the bottom of the pan. Add the potatoes to the pan and toss to coat with the oil. Sprinkle with garlic powder, paprika, salt, and pepper. Turn potatoes again to coat.

Cut one slice of bacon in thin (¼ inch) slices. Sprinkle over potatoes and turn again to mix. Shake the pan to spread the potatoes. They should be in one layer.

Roast for 10 minutes. Turn the potatoes, shake the pan, and make sure they're in one layer again. Roast another 10 minutes. (If you have cut the potatoes larger, they will require a longer cooking time.) Meanwhile, place a piece of a paper towel on a microwave-safe plate. Place the remaining bacon on the paper towel and cover with another paper towel. Microwave for 3 minutes.

When the potatoes are done, crumble the microwaved bacon over the potatoes and scrape the bottom of the pan with a spatula to mix the potatoes with the rest of the bacon. Serve.

Sugar Snap Peas

I love these to nibble on. Look for them fresh in the cooler or the vegetable section of your grocery store. They're literally a snap to prepare.

Water
Ice
Salt (optional)
1 package sugar snap peas

Bring the water to a boil. In the meantime, prepare a large bowl of ice water. Add the salt to the water (optional). Pour in the sugar snap peas. Cook about one minute. Scoop them out of the boiling water and pop them into the ice water. Serve.

Chocolate Mayonnaise Cupcakes

Makes 24 cupcakes.

I hope you'll love this recipe as much as I do. It's officially my go-to recipe for chocolate cupcakes now. You can frost them with your favorite frosting, of course, but fair warning—the chocolate frosting recipe that follows is so creamy it might become your favorite frosting!

3 cups all-purpose flour
⅔ cup unsweetened cocoa powder
1½ teaspoons baking soda
¼ teaspoon baking powder
1⅔ cups sugar
3 large eggs
1 cup mayonnaise
1 teaspoon vanilla extract
1½ cups water

Preheat the oven to 350. Place cupcake papers in wells in cupcake pan.

Mix flour, cocoa powder, baking soda, baking powder, salt, and sugar in a medium bowl.

In a mixer, beat together the eggs and sugar until light and fluffy. Add the mayonnaise and vanilla and beat. Alternate between adding the water and the flour mixture. Divide the batter among the cupcake papers, filling three-quarters full.

Bake 18 minutes. Frost with Chocolate Frosting.

Chocolate Frosting

This recipe has to be made in a double boiler. It's worth the hassle!

4 ounces unsweetened chocolate
4 large egg yolks
⅔ cup granulated sugar
⅛ teaspoon salt
½ cup heavy cream
1¼ cups softened unsalted butter

Melt the chocolate in the top of a double boiler over hot water. Meanwhile beat the egg yolks with the sugar. Mix in the salt and heavy cream. Pour it slowly into the chocolate and stir constantly. Bring it briefly to 160 degrees, (you may need to turn the heat down a bit afterward) and continue stirring until thick. Remove from heat and cool. Cream the butter thoroughly. Add the cool chocolate mixture one spoon at a time until it is all mixed in. If it is too soft, chill in the refrigerator until ready to use.

Pear Upside-Down Skillet Cake

2 pears
Lemon
¼ cup canola or olive oil (not one with intense flavor)
1 large egg
⅔ cup sugar
¾ teaspoon baking powder
¼ teaspoon baking soda
½ teaspoon cardamom
1 teaspoon vanilla
1 cup flour
⅓ cup milk
4 Tablespoons (½ stick) butter
⅓ cup light brown sugar
crème fraîche or lightly sweetened whipped cream

Preheat oven to 350.

Peel, core, and slice the pears. Toss with a squeeze or two of lemon so they don't turn brown.

Place the oil, egg, sugar, baking powder, baking soda, cardamom, and vanilla in a mixing bowl and beat or whisk together. Alternate adding flour and milk until everything is blended. Set aside.

On the stovetop, melt the butter with the light brown sugar in a skillet. Position the pear slices on top of the mixture, crowding them in. Pour the batter over the pears and slide the skillet into the oven. Bake 25–30 minutes, or until a cake tester comes out clean. Flip over onto a serving platter.

Serve warm with crème fraîche or lightly sweetened whipped cream.

Berry Pecan Coffee Cake

9 x 9 baking pan

1½ cups flour
1 teaspoon baking powder
1 teaspoon baking soda
¾ teaspoon salt
1 teaspoon cinnamon
1 stick (8 tablespoons) butter (room temperature)
1 cup dark brown sugar, packed
½ cup regular sugar
2 large eggs (room temperature)
1 cup applesauce
1 cup blueberries

Topping

½ cup pecans
3 Tablespoons butter
2 Tablespoons dark brown sugar

Take butter and eggs out of fridge to bring them to room temperature.

Preheat oven to 350. Place pecans on a baking sheet and toast 5–6 minutes or until fragrant. Set aside.

Lightly grease the pan and line with one piece of parchment paper cut to fit the sides, but long enough to act as handles and two sides for removing the cake.

Use a fork to mix together the flour, baking powder, baking soda, salt, and cinnamon in a bowl. Set aside.

Cream the butter with the sugars. Add the eggs and beat. Add the applesauce alternating with the flour mixture and beat until smooth. Fold in the blueberries.

Chop the pecans with the brown sugar and butter. Sprinkle over the top in lumps. It will sink while it bakes.

Bake 35-40 minutes or until center is set and a cake tester comes out clean.

Nina's Rum Runners

4 ounces light rum
4 ounces dark rum
4 ounces banana liqueur
4 ounces blackberry liqueur
4 ounces orange juice
4 ounces pineapple juice

Mix all ingredients in a blender with one cup of ice. Blend on high. Serve in tall glasses.

Read on for a sneak preview of the next
Domestic Diva mystery . . .

THE DIVA SAYS CHEESECAKE!

In a delicious new Domestic Diva Mystery from *New York Times* bestselling author Krista Davis, entertaining guru Sophie Winston is faced with a midsummer nightmare when a celebration in Old Town Alexandria, Virginia, is the appetizer for murder . . .

Old Town's midsummer festivities are getting a tasty addition this year. To coincide with a public performance of Shakespeare's *A Midsummer Night's Dream*, Bobbie Sue Bodoin, the Queen of Cheesecake, has hired Sophie to organize a dinner with a dessert buffet on the waterfront. Bobbie Sue's homegrown company is thriving, and since her baking dish overfloweth, she wants to reward her employees.

Bobbie Sue has only one menu demand: no cheesecake! But her specialty isn't the only thing missing from the evening—Tate, Bobbie Sue's husband, is too, much to her annoyance. Next morning, however, Tate's dead body is discovered. Bobbie Sue insists she didn't kick her spouse to the curb, and begs for Sophie's help finding the real killer. Digging in, Sophie discovers an assortment of Old Town locals who all had reason to want a piece of Tate. Can she gather together the crumbs the killer left behind in time to prevent a second helping of murder?

Includes delicious recipes and fabulous DIY decorating tips!

Available from Kensington Publishing Corp. in summer 2022.

Chapter 1

Dear Sophie,
My mother-in-law hates my guts. After announcing that I was a deadbeat to everyone within 100 miles, she showed up with a cheesecake. Is it possible to poison cheesecake?
Suspicious in Loafers Station, Indiana

Dear Suspicious,
Happily, I have never tried to poison a cheesecake, but it's my guess that you can poison almost anything. Before you throw it out, remember that giving someone cake is often a form of apology. Invite her to join you. And don't eat any until she does.
Sophie

DAY ONE

I stood under spotlights outside of a closed car dealership waiting for my ex-husband Mars to arrive and feeling like I had been through the wringer. I had spent a long weekend with my parents at their home in Berrysville,

Virginia. On the way back, in the dark of night, my beloved car conked out on I-81. I called for a tow truck and while I was waiting, Mars, who had been staying at my house to dog and cat sit, had texted to find out why I wasn't home yet. After what seemed an eternity of giant trucks barreling by me in the dark, my car had finally been towed to the dealership where Mars had promised to pick me up. I was initially leery when an alpine white BMW rolled up and came to a full stop, the engine idling.

Bernie Frei stepped out and opened the passenger door for me with a playful bow. My hound mix, Daisy, leaped onto the pavement and danced around me in circles, pausing twice for a smooch.

"May we give you a lift?" Bernie asked teasingly in his delightful British accent.

"Thank you, kind sir," I said, playing along. Daisy vaulted into the back seat and I settled on the leather passenger seat, relieved to be on my way home.

Bernie tossed my bags in the back. He slid into the driver's seat and handed me a strawberry milkshake. "I thought you might be hungry or thirsty. I figured this would cover both." Turning onto the road, he asked, "What happened?"

The milkshake was so thick I had to use a spoon. "The shake is perfect, Bernie. Just what I needed. I don't know what happened to the car. The engine started sputtering and slowed. Thankfully, I was able to pull over and it just plain died on me. Thanks for picking me up. I thought Mars was coming. How did you get dragged into this?"

"No problem. I'm happy to pitch in. Mars was going to come but he got a last-minute call, so here I am."

Bernie had been the best man at my wedding to Mars. Born and raised mostly in England, he had met Mars when they wound up as roommates at university. Bernie's mother had married more times than Elizabeth Taylor, dragging him around the world when he was a child. At some point he'd had enough and returned to live with husband number three, who by all accounts was a wonderful father-figure to Bernie, if a bit too outdoorsy and devoted to country life for Bernie's mother's taste.

He now guided the car over backroads to Old Town and we were home in no time. The lights were on in my house, and it had never seemed more welcoming. Bernie insisted on carrying my bags inside.

Mars held a phone to his ear as he opened the kitchen door for us. He had spent the weekend there while I was away.

My Ocicat, Mochie, who had bull's-eyes on both sides of his body and fur that looked like necklaces and bracelets instead of the spots he was supposed to have, mewed like I had been gone forever. I swept him up into my arms. He tilted his head and rubbed it against my chin. All was well again in my world. If there was a second strike of bad luck, it would likely come in the form of the repair bill for my car.

I thanked Bernie profusely, and Mars, too. The two of them left in Bernie's car, which made me smile because they lived, as my grandfather would have said, within spitting distance.

DAY TWO

Tuesday morning loomed early but I was eager to get back to work. I had just finished my breakfast of a soft-boiled egg and toast when the car dealership phoned. It was great news. The part that had failed could be easily replaced for a reasonable amount of money and the car would be fine. The requisite part was being shipped to them as we spoke.

By eleven thirty, I was at Blackwell's Tavern for a business lunch with Mrs. Hollingsworth-Symthe, which she pronounced with a long I and a silent E, and her daughter Dodie Kucharski. I had organized several major charity events for Mrs. Hollingsworth-Symthe and found it difficult to turn her down when she asked me to arrange a very large Fourth of July party overlooking the Potomac River.

Old Town Alexandria, Virginia, where I lived and worked as an event planner, was a hotspot for visitors because we were located across the river from Washington, DC. Old Town was a destination itself, with lovely historic homes, and charming shops and restaurants.

Blackwell's Tavern was an upscale place favored by Mrs. Hollingsworth-Symthe and her friends that had been around for many years. The food was good, but their cheesecake selection was outstanding. I happened to know that they were Bobbie Sue's Cheesecake, the same cheesecake served by many restaurants in the DC area and across the country for that matter. But most restaurants offered only one flavor. Tate Bodoin, the owner of Blackwell's Tavern, happened to be married to Bobbie Sue Bodoin, whose cheesecake-baking business had grown into a small empire. She didn't have a restaurant of her own because she sold directly to restaurants, but it did mean that her husband offered little else on his dessert menu.

Tate, a slightly pudgy man with graying light brown hair, glasses, and a substantial white mustache, stopped by the table to see how our lunch was and to pitch cheesecake for dessert.

To my complete horror, Mrs. Hollingsworth-Symthe declined dessert because she was on a diet, and informed her fortyish-going-on-fifty daughter, Dodie, that she would not be having any cheesecake if she wanted to fit into a certain dress for their big bash. I couldn't exactly pig out on a slice of raspberry chocolate cheesecake in front of them!

I gave Tate an apologetic look. "I'll take four slices of cheesecake to go. You know Nina will want some. Surprise me."

He patted my shoulder in a friendly way. "They don't know what they're missing," he joked before ambling off.

"He's such a gentleman," said Mrs. Hollingsworth-Smythe. Sophie, darling, please be sure that we offer an ample assortment of cheesecake on the dessert table at the fete."

"Mother . . ." prompted Dodie.

"Oh, yes, Dodie. How could I possibly forget? Sophie, dear, I understand that you are friends with the man who runs the Laughing Hound. Please be sure that he receives an invitation. Dodie has her eyes on him. You know, after my first divorce, I went after a working man, too. He was something else. The love of my life!"

"Mother!" Dodie's tone admonished her mother.

"Am I embarrassing you, Dodie? You know I was quite the looker in my day."

"Mother!"

"Yes, well, perhaps enough said about that. But there is something very sensual about men who toil for a living."

Well, well. Bernie would be surprised to hear about this!

Except for the lack of dessert, something *I* never turned down, the meeting had gone well. When I paid the check, I noticed an envelope in my purse. With two potential clients looking on, it wasn't the time to empty my purse and examine the contents. After the requisite goodbyes, I collected my take-out cheesecake and headed straight to my home, which bore a coveted plaque next to the front door that designated it as a historic dwelling.

Mars and I had inherited it from his aunt, who had been

an extraordinary hostess in her day. She had enlarged the dining room and living room to accommodate her parties. Mars liked the house but wasn't particularly sentimental about it, so I had bought him out when we divorced. The mortgage put a mighty kink in my budget, but I loved the old place with the high windows and creaking floors.

After greeting Daisy and Mochie, who dutifully met me at the door, I hung my purse where I always did—on a hook in the coat closet, where I could grab it in an instant. My mother always emptied her purse entirely when she came home. I supposed that made it easier to switch purses to match her outfits, but it seemed like an extra chore to have to locate wallet, car keys, house keys, tissue, comb, and whatever else I needed.

Before I settled down to work, Nina Reid Norwood, my best friend and across the street neighbor, stopped by with her dog, Muppet, an energetic little white floofball whom she had adopted.

Nina flopped into a chair by my fireplace, holding a box in her hands. She was generally energetic and upbeat. But today, she seemed glum.

"Tea and cheesecake?" I asked.

She perked up. "I *need* cheesecake right now. How did you know?"

I grinned and opened the box that I had set on the counter. Each of the four slices of cheesecake looked different. "I think you'd better choose."

Leaving the box in the chair, Nina rose and looked at the selection. "Cherry topping is just boring. What do you suppose this one is?"

I examined the dark crumble on top. "Oreo?"

"I'll have that one." She walked over to the bay window and looked out. "Have you heard of early dementia?" she asked.

I nodded, placing her plate of cheesecake on the table and adding a napkin and fork. "Yes, it's terrible."

"I think there's something seriously wrong with my husband." She turned toward me, her expression grim.

A forensic pathologist, Nina's husband traveled constantly and was rarely home. "Did something happen?"

She retrieved the box and heaved a great sigh. "Last week, a package arrived addressed to him. Naturally, I opened it." She flicked open the box and pulled out a rubber chicken. "He ordered a chicken slingshot."

It was hard not to laugh when she held up the limp rubbery form of a chicken.

"When I asked him about it, he claimed he never ordered it. I stashed it in the closet so I could show him when he came home. Today, this arrived." Nina withdrew a plastic bag, prominently marked *Inflatable Unicorn*.

I stared at it and tried very hard not to laugh. The picture on the bag showed a multicolored unicorn that might be a big hit at a children's party but had no real function that I could see. "Clearly there has been a mistake."

"My husband denies having ordered it. I thought the first one was an error. When the second one arrived, I thought they must be for someone with a similar name. Another person named Norwood, maybe. They came from the same company and we have an account with them, so I called to let them know. The man on the phone was very nice, but insists the shipment was to my husband. But he has no recollection of ordering *any* of these things."

I brought our tea and my cherry cheesecake over to the table and sat down. "I don't think that's a sign of dementia. You know how easily things get mixed up. Unless there's something else . . ." I hoped there wasn't.

The cheesecake brightened Nina's spirits and she was in

a better mood when she left with her chicken and unicorn. But I knew she was still worried. Who wouldn't be?

The rest of the day was spent outlining a schedule for the week-long conference of a research chefs organization, including tours of Washington and a night at the Kennedy Center. Consequently, my purse hung in the closet until Wednesday afternoon, when Nina popped in and asked if I felt like a stroll down to our favorite coffee shop with the dogs.

DAY THREE

Daisy and I were ready for a break. I checked on Mochie, who was lounging in the sunroom, then suited up Daisy in her halter and grabbed my purse off the handy hook. I didn't always take the whole purse. Often, when I walked Daisy, I only tucked a cell phone with cash in my pocket. But for some reason, I took the whole thing, maybe because the turquoise color was so summery and happened to match my sleeveless blouse.

Consequently, it wasn't until I took my wallet out to pay for my caramel latte that I noticed the envelope again. I frowned at it, upset with myself for forgetting about it. I paid for my latte and Daisy's pup cup and joined Nina at a table overlooking the Potomac River.

I pulled out the envelope. It was lilac, the kind that came with a card or stationery, but it wasn't addressed to anyone. It was sealed shut, though. That was odd. I didn't recall placing it *in* my handbag.

"What's that?" asked Nina.

"I have no idea." I ripped it open and slid out a sheet of matching lilac paper. Daisy whined softly and touched my leg with her paw. "Sorry sweetie, I didn't forget you." I held her pup cup in one hand and unfolded the letter with the other.

I read it to Nina in a soft voice, so no one would over-hear.

> *Dear Sophie,*
> *My aunt says you have solutions for all her prob-*
> *lems. I hope you can help me, too. My friend and I*
> *landed great summer jobs. They pay well and the*
> *work is fine. But I think something illegal is going*
> *on there. Can my friend and I get into trouble,*
> *even if we're not involved?*
> *Worried in Old Town*

"Poor kid!" she said. "There's no name?"

I handed her the note and the envelope. "They match," I observed. "The kind of thing you buy to write thank-you notes."

"The violet color would probably indicate a girl," said Nina.

"Could be. Any kid could have this or might have swiped it from a family member. But I'm betting on a girl. Summer jobs. Fourteen and over," I mused.

"It doesn't sound like she knows you," said Nina.

"Good point. She's probably not in college. A college student would have looked me up first and wouldn't have bothered writing to me about a legal matter."

Nina groused, "It's so difficult with printers. If it had been handwritten, we might have been able to deduce something from the handwriting. Where did you get this?"

"It was in my purse. I saw it yesterday when I paid the check at Blackwell's Tavern. But I was with clients, so I didn't want to take it out in front of them. And then I for-got about it until just now."

Nina gasped. "Worried in Old Town must work at Blackwell's Tavern. Who was your server?"

"A man in his thirties." I mashed my eyes shut and tried to remember the name tag on his shirt. "Antonio Hirsch."

"We're seeing Bobbie Sue Bodoin tomorrow night. Maybe we can think of a clever way to ask her."

"There's a good idea," I said sarcastically. "Bobbie Sue, one of your husband's employees thinks something illegal is going on at his restaurant. Could you put us in touch with a server named Antonio Hirsch so we can talk to him about it?"

Connect with  Us

Visit us online at
KensingtonBooks.com
to read more from your favorite authors, see books
by series, view reading group guides, and more.

 Join us on social media

for sneak peeks, chances to win books and prize packs,
and to share your thoughts with other readers.

facebook.com/kensingtonpublishing
twitter.com/kensingtonbooks

Tell us what you think!

To share your thoughts, submit a review,
or sign up for our eNewsletters, please visit:
KensingtonBooks.com/TellUs.